Dedication

Wildflower Redemption is a romance, but romance doesn't happen in a vacuum. Romance leads to love, becomes intermingled with love, can't truly be separated from love. And family has always been the best part of love in my life. So this book is dedicated to my nine incredible grandchildren, who are living reminders of their parents' childhoods yet are their own people: Hermione, Tiari, Athena, Daniel (our Jr.), JC, Gia, Caroline, Ryan, and Neo, my much loved kaleidoscope of kids.

Acknowledgments

I've written since I was six, literally, even receiving my first check for my work as a first grader, and thus decided some time ago that I pretty much knew exactly what I was doing.

There's nothing like a third book to erase all the vanity in a writer's soul. Writing is a journey, and I don't always know where I'm going.

So to my sister Victoria M. Potter, thanks for your technical knowledge and for always being on the other end of a phone or internet connection to advise, console, and correct at a moment's notice. I'm unfair to you, but also extremely grateful. Hope that helps a little.

To Tara Gelsomino, executive editor at Crimson Romance, thanks for the opportunity to tell Aaron and Luz's story. Faith is a precious gift.

To Julie Sturgeon, thanks for tying up loose ends and being the go-to person when I'm not sure what I still need to get done.

And to my development editor Jess Verdi—I'm not sure how to thank you, because your keen eyes and your understanding of what I wanted *Wildflower Redemption* to be makes the book work on every level. Thank you for the hours you spent on a story I very much wanted to tell.

Book 1
Texas Heart & Soul
Series

Wildflower Redemption

Leslie P. García
author of *Unattainable*

CRIMSON ROMANCE

F+W Media, Inc.

This edition published by
Crimson Romance
an imprint of F+W Media, Inc.
10151 Carver Road, Suite 200
Blue Ash, Ohio 45242
www.crimsonromance.com

ISBN 10: 1-4405-7469-3
ISBN 13: 978-1-4405-7469-6
eISBN 10: 1-4405-7470-7
eISBN 13: 978-1-4405-7470-2

Chapter One

Aaron Estes stood at the window, one hand pulling back the drapes to clear his view. Outside, clouds hovered along the horizon, but he doubted it would rain.

Someone from town— Ross something? —had stopped by earlier and offered to do work. The handyman had scoffed at the chance of rain. "Always cloudy," he'd grumbled. "Never rains."

Aaron had shrugged and told the man politely that he didn't need help. And he didn't—at least, not physical help. Spiritual help, maybe, mental health—the kind of health that comes with peace and contentment. The kind of health he'd probably never find again. He closed his eyes and listened for any sound of six-year-old Chloe waking, but heard only silence. Unwelcome memories tried to push in, and he pressed his lids tighter against his face, unwilling to give in again to the pain.

The memories came anyway: the loud, angry words of a marriage shattering. The cheery morning greeting from the one thing he and Stella still shared—a tiny, precious miracle of motion and light.

Chloe's loud kiss and plaintive complaint when her mother tried to leave without kissing Aaron goodbye hovered near the surface. He could still feel Chloe's huge kiss on his cheeks, hear the petulance in her voice when her mother tried to step around them.

"Mommy, you forgot Daddy's kiss." Stella pecked him on the cheek, and Chloe tugged on her mom's blouse.

"Mommy, don't be silly. Mommies kiss daddies on the mouth."

With lips so tight he could feel her anger, Stella stood on tiptoe and touched her mouth to his. Then he watched as Chloe grabbed her mother's hand, delighted that she was playing mom today, not cop. To Chloe, the world was a game, and everyone in it, players.

He closed his eyes, but the burning didn't go away, so he went back to staring blindly outside. There were no daffodils here, as there were in Alabama, but he heard that just miles north spring came in on carpets of bluebonnets and waves of flaming Indian paintbrush. All the locals raved about the Texas wildflowers. They said he should go see them, but he knew he couldn't.

The scene he'd rushed to just over a year ago crowded in: the hysteria, the cop cars with their flashing red and blue lights; the crumpled body of a child, an injured teacher being wheeled toward an ambulance; and an officer who knew Stella pulling him aside. She'd taken a bullet for a kid, the officer told him. Unfaithful, maybe, arrogant often—but nobody doubted Stella Estes's courage.

The tears rolled down his cheeks and he wiped them away with the back of his hand, trying not to remember that there'd been blood on the daffodils the day the world ended.

• • •

Luz Wilkinson tugged on the girth again and nudged Pompom's belly with a knee. "Let it out, girl," she urged. The little pinto sighed heavily and turned around to nose Luz just as the cell phone in her pocket went off. Her horses would have shied at the sudden blast of sound, and the other ponies would have lifted their heads and pricked their ears. Pompom stood there with that complete lack of interest that indicated absolute lack of intelligence.

Frowning over the pony's deficiencies, Luz fished the phone out and hit the button to silence it. She didn't recognize the number. She hoped it wasn't a bill collector, but knew that it probably was.

"Hello?"

"Uh…hi. Is this Eden Acres?"

"Yes." Luz scratched Pompom's ear while she tried to connect a physical image with the deep, masculine voice. She often toyed with visualizing strangers from their phone calls, and almost always was wrong. Silence pricked her into awareness. Perhaps the caller expected someone more enthusiastic, more helpful. Someone who could offer more than one word answers…

"May I help you?" she prodded when he didn't go on.

Another long pause, then came the abrupt questions: "I heard you have therapy horses? And ponies?"

Luz hesitated. Sometimes children from a group foster home came out to ride, and occasionally a counselor who worked with troubled children recommended exposing them to riding. But therapy? She wouldn't go that far.

"We have horses and ponies," she said carefully. "But who told you we have therapy horses?"

"Esmeralda Salinas," the voice said, no longer hesitant.

Luz wrinkled her nose, picturing the elegant redheaded school guidance counselor with her neat suits and perpetual pep. Living in this tiny community, they'd crossed paths several times. They didn't much like each other, but Esmeralda loved horses. That was usually a sterling quality, but this time, Luz's main yardstick for measuring "good folks" didn't hold water, because the counselor struck her as conceited, plastic, and sneaky. Although they avoided each other as much as possible, she boarded the woman's pricey Appaloosa. Undoubtedly Esmeralda would have liked finer stomping grounds for the horse and herself, but no one else boarded horses in this arid, dying community. Very few still owned livestock.

Nevertheless, Luz was surprised that the counselor had referred any male new to town. The director of the children's group home was an elderly woman, and the other referrals were long-time residents, parents in established relationships, but Esmeralda sending a guy her way? He was not single, then, apparently.

"You're Ms. Wilkinson?" Doubt tinged the deep voice. She'd confused the caller. Didn't matter. Confusion was a constant companion these days.

"Yes," she replied. One word again. He could state his business or not. She didn't care.

"Ms. Wilkinson, I need to talk to you about riding lessons for my little girl, Chloe. Or maybe—" Another brief pause, as if he wasn't sure what he wanted. "Maybe even buying a pony. I need advice on what would be best."

He was a client then. She should be happier than she was. She pasted a smile on her face, hoping it would make her voice warmer, more caring. "Great. Advice is what we do best." Quick questions confirmed he knew how to find Eden Acres, and she clicked the phone off and returned it to her pocket. She realized, a little late, that asking the man's name might have been both friendlier and more professional.

"Screw it," she muttered with unusual ire. "Professional never worked for me, anyway. Come on, old lady. Some kid might actually get a pony ride today."

Half an hour later Luz was feeding the menagerie when she heard tires on the gravel drive. She called the motley collection of rescued animals her menagerie, because it took too long to go into the species, circumstances, and problems she dealt with trying to feed and shelter them day to day. Candy, the burro, butted her as she turned away, and the kitten with no name left its feeding dish to run away from some unseen menace, almost tripping her. She wiped her hands on the sides of her jeans and shut the door separating the odd animals from the handful of horses that were both her treasures and bread-earners.

By the time she made it outside, a dark-haired, broad-shouldered man was leaning against an SUV, frowning. He wore long sleeves and a tie, hardly south Texas pony-buying attire. But she wasn't expecting anyone else.

She walked over and held out her hand. "I'm Luz Wilkinson. Welcome to Eden Acres. Are you—?"

"Aaron Estes." He shook her hand briefly, and then cast another look around the premises. Not disapproving, exactly, she thought. It was more a look of disappointment.

"Why don't we go into the office?" she suggested. "It's cooler." And it was well decorated with new paint and shelves of her mother's trophies, recently polished.

They walked into the barn. The half-open stall doors caught his attention. He pointed at one of the horses. "Pretty. Yours?"

"No." She shook her head, and paused to pet the broad blaze of white running down the mare's face. "This is Domatrix. One of my boarders."

"Doma—isn't this Esmeralda's horse?"

"Yes, as a matter of fact." She leaned against the stall door, slanting a glance at him, surprised that Esmeralda had apparently described Domatrix in detail to a man new in town. No wonder Aaron Estes hadn't flinched at the name, even shortened as it seemed to be. Then again…she thought of the tall, regal redhead and the dearth of men in Rose Creek. A man with a daughter likely meant a married man. That would lessen Esmeralda's interest. Wouldn't it? She pushed away from the mare's stall, and he followed the remaining few feet to the office. She waved a hand at the chairs and took her own place behind the small, bare desk.

"So tell me how I can help," she invited.

He looked down for a minute at his hands before looking at her. When he did finally lift his eyes, she could see why Esmeralda had pounced. The man's perfect features and startling green eyes would stop traffic in lots of places, let alone this one-horse, one-eligible-man town.

"My little girl—Chloe—needs a hobby. Something she'll like that's safe."

Luz studied him, perplexed. Somehow the pieces of the big, attractive man across the desk didn't add up. She supposed she was using stereotypes, but he seemed too hesitant and unsure for his own body. Not as if he was uncomfortable in his own skin, maybe, but almost as if he were fearful of something.

She puzzled over the discomfort he seemed to feel, trying to figure out his connection to Esme. He wasn't family; the Rose Creek gossips knew everyone and every relative, no matter how far flung. The counselor had aging parents and a half-brother down in Laredo. A friend? She discarded that. Esmeralda didn't work weekends, and if he were a friend, she would be here. So the relationship had to be professional. Maybe the daughter he'd mentioned was Esmeralda's client?

"'Safe as opposed to bike riding or playing with dolls? Or safe, fun, and a perfect springtime activity—I'm not sure I know what you mean by safe," Luz admitted. "Riding has risks—the same as pretty much everything."

Aaron Estes growled something that sounded profane and hunched forward over the desk, his face tight. "Don't you think I know that?" After a moment, his face muscles eased into smoother lines. His lips twitched, as if they'd known how to smile, but forgotten. "I'm not as weird as I seem. Just a tad nervous and overprotective."

"But you're not in denial," she observed. "That's got to be good." She smiled. "So, tell me about your Chloe."

Pure, absolute love washed across his face. His lips remembered how to smile and he straightened in his chair. "Chloe's my life," he said simply.

Luz returned the smile, but prodded gently for more insight. "How old is she? Does she like horses? Has she ridden before?"

"Six, yes, and no."

Luz blinked, trying to understand the simple, one-word answers. Saw the dimples appear, and then deepen in Aaron Estes' cheeks. She'd always had a weakness for dimples, dammit! Was he one-upping her? "So, is this payback, or do you always keep things so short and simple?"

He actually chuckled. It was a short little rumble of laughter, but a chuckle.

"Payback, definitely. I was nervous enough about calling and you were anything but friendly."

She thought back on her hesitation to answer the phone, how she'd focused on the pinto rather than concentrating on encouraging conversation. He had her pegged, but she didn't care. Wouldn't. She needed customers, but wasn't in the market for relationships of any kind. And professional? She allowed herself a quick mental shrug. She no longer had a profession. She'd been a teacher, and a good one. She'd surrounded herself with kids and poured energy and love into their lives. Then she'd lost it all, including her daughter Lily. Not her daughter, she reminded herself: Brian's daughter, given to her as one more false promise. Now she rescued discarded animals when she could, and was going broke doing it.

So she pounced on something he said. "You were nervous? About asking if we had ponies?" Slight derision might have crept into her words, because he flinched and drew away again.

"Not about ponies." He paused, looking for the right words. "We don't know each other. Esmeralda recommended riding as a form of therapy." He shrugged. "Telling a stranger your kid has problems is hard."

Her cheeks burned with embarrassment. "I owe you an apology—of course it is." She stood up abruptly, annoyed with herself. "Guess it's attack a stranger day—I'm just not sure why. Would you like to look at Rumbles? She would be the pony Chloe would work with first."

"Sure." He got up too, ignoring her apology, and stretched. Outside the office, one of the horses whinnied, and another kicked at the stall. The pungent scents of the stable reminded her it was time to muck stalls—again. Already. Out of the corner of her eyes, she saw his nose wrinkle.

"Do you even like horses?" she asked, curious.

He slanted a glance down at her and shrugged. "Don't know. Haven't been around them. Not really an animal person."

Before Luz could murmur a response, he stopped, turning towards her and holding his hands out in apology. "Not that I don't like them, exactly. I used to travel, and before that—well, I just wasn't raised around them."

"Okay." Luz gave him her own shrug. "So I guess Chloe's mom will be the main go-between here?"

A muscle in his jaw twitched, and the nervous tension he'd shown in the beginning visibly tightened his body. "Chloe's mom," he said through clenched teeth, "is dead."

Chapter Two

Amazing what a few bumps in the road could do to you. Luz slipped into the turquoise blouse and frowned at her image in the mirror. When had she become…like this? She was dour and suspicious of everyone. She'd given in to pain—but she wasn't alone in that. Some drank, some slept around. Some stepped off high bridges. She shuddered. Some threw their kids off high bridges, too. But her husband hadn't done that. No, Brian hadn't taken his life. He'd ruined hers.

The phone rang, startling her. She looked at it blankly for a moment then reached for it, but it quit ringing. A quick glance showed her the caller. Aaron Estes. A tiny part of her wanted to smile. He'd called her twice, preparing himself for Chloe's first visit. Somehow she suspected the little girl would take to riding better than her father took to just the idea.

She grabbed her ball cap and pulled it down over hair that she wished she'd combed more carefully and headed for the door. Not at a jog, exactly, but not dawdling. She wanted to meet Chloe. She hoped she wouldn't be as awkward with the child as she had when Aaron had told her of his wife's death. She'd stared up at him, muttered an incomprehensible word of sympathy, and more or less avoided any further discussion of the situation. How did you talk to a stranger about his wife's death? Or to a child about the loss of a mother?

By the time Luz got down to the stable, Aaron was opening the door of the SUV. A thin, pale little girl scrambled out, looking around with interest. Chloe's green eyes regarded Luz without apprehension.

"Hi, Aaron. Chloe." She smiled at the child. "I've been waiting to meet you. Your dad thought you'd enjoy coming out to meet Rumbles."

"Rumbles?" The pale blond eyebrows went up a little. "What kind of a dumb name is that?" The eyes might be her father's, but the coloring must be her mother's—and the slight air of disdain, too.

"Chloe! That's no way—"

Luz waved off the rebuke. "When you hear her talk to you, you'll understand," she assured the little girl. She gestured at the open door. "Come on. Let's get you ready to ride."

They walked into the shadowy stable together, and Chloe's glance darted from stall to stall. "They're all so pretty!" For the first time, a touch of nervousness flitted across her face. "Big, too, huh?"

"Yeah, but these aren't the ones you'll start on," Luz reassured. "We'll bring out a pony for you. Just wait here a minute." She went into the next to the last stall and emerged leading a caramel-colored Shetland pony. Rumbles' mane and tail fell in thick platinum shimmers, and Luz smiled at Chloe's gasp of delight.

"Pretty girl, isn't she?"

Chloe glanced up at her dad. "She's mine, right?"

He smiled, but shook his head. "Not so fast, friend. You don't even know if you'll like riding."

Chloe might have argued, but the mare's ears pricked with interest and she lifted her head to nicker. The nickering went on and on, a surprisingly deep tone that had given Rumbles her name.

Aaron stared. Chloe giggled. "Horses don't sound like that!" Excited, she rushed forward. The pony threw up her head, and only Luz's quick arm, thrust out as a barrier, and stopped Chloe.

"Hold on, Chloe. You never run up to a horse," she warned.

Chloe's mouth turned down petulantly. "But—"

"Is this the gentlest thing you have?" Aaron asked. "You said—"

Luz breathed out a short puff of exasperation, not unlike Rumbles' muffled snort. *If I could handle a room full of first graders, I can handle one.*

"Chloe, horses—even ponies—are bigger than you. If you scare them, they hurt you. Even when they don't mean to." She patted Rumbles then brushed the pony's long forelock aside.

"She's got a crown on her head!" Chloe crowed, and Luz smiled.

"Isn't it something? Horse people call it a star, but you're right—it's a crown."

"You should have named her Crown, then," Chloe suggested, but without the disdain this time. Suddenly she giggled again. Or even 'Royal Highness'—'cause she's a shorty!"

Luz laughed with her. "That would have been a cool name," she agreed. "But what about 'Princess'? Bet that's your nickname."

A look of dismay darkened Aaron's face, almost as if he knew what Chloe would say.

The child's face turned hard, too hard for someone so young, and disdain became contempt.

"I'm no one's princess," she said. "Mommy said never, ever let anyone call me princess. She hated princesses."

Luz hesitated briefly, but beneath the scorn, she heard a note of pain.

"Why did she hate princesses?" she asked gently, and Chloe shrugged her thin little shoulders.

"They're weak and afraid of everything," she explained, as if any fool would know that. "They're only in fairy tales anyway."

Luz shrugged. "Okay." She held out a hand. "Come meet Rumbles, slowly."

Chloe inched forward, and Luz grinned. "Hold out your hand and let her sniff it." She demonstrated, and Chloe slowly held out her own palm. Rumbles sniffed and brushed it with her velvety muzzle, and Chloe giggled again.

"She's funny," Chloe decided, reaching out slowly to trace the white crown. Rumbles lifted her head and blew softly at the little girl's cheek.

"She thinks you're funny, too," Luz translated. "Let's get her saddled and you can ride her."

While Luz showed her how to lead the pony, Aaron mumbled something about being right back. By the time he came back, Luz was showing her how to check the girth to be sure the saddle was tight.

"We're just about ready, pr—" she assured Chloe, aware of the girl's impatience. She cut off the hated 'princess' that almost slipped out. Her stepdaughter Lily had loved the nickname, had immersed herself in the fairy tale world of princesses and happily ever after, but this was a different girl. Not even a girl she knew well, though kids Chloe's age always captivated her.

A soft thud sounded behind them, and Luz couldn't help gaping at Chloe's father. He had a helmet, elbow pads, and kneepads clutched to his chest. A large bottle of hand sanitizer dangled precariously from under an elbow, and the oversized white box on the sawdust-covered floor was emblazoned with a bright red cross.

No. Accidents could happen, even from a short fall, on deep sand, from a walking pony. She would not laugh at him. But remembering her own wild races across pastures and over fences in the pre-awareness days, she wondered how long he'd stay if he knew how oblivious of such equipment she'd been.

He flushed a little, as if he actually could read her mind, but didn't yield. "Safety first," he told her gravely, but the dimples that came and went appeared briefly.

"You know, it doesn't snow here much," she answered, and he lifted both eyebrows. She waved a hand at the gear. "We can use the time we save putting on snowsuits for all that."

"Look, if she falls, I want her shatterproof. She needs to bounce."

Chloe looked a little concerned. "Me? Bounce?"

"Well, only if you fall really hard from a really high place. And then you'll be really glad I made you wear all this stuff."

He held out the helmet, then the kneepads and elbow pads, watching as she put each item on. When she was suitably padded, he grinned at Luz.

"What do you think? Will she bounce?"

Luz looked the little girl over again. "Sky high," she agreed, making Chloe giggle again. "I'm not sure we can get her on Rumbles before she does, though."

Her dad shrugged. "I'll just lift her up—"

"No." Luz waved him off as he hoisted Chloe into the air, looking like a mini-balloon from the Macy's Thanksgiving Day parade. "I have a rule about the children who ride here. They learn to take care of their own mounts. At least to whatever extent they can. I'll show Chloe how to get on."

"But—"

"Put the kid down and step away from the pony," Luz ordered, and Chloe laughed and squirmed until her father set her back down.

"Good." Luz ignored the anger tightening Aaron's lips, and stood by Rumbles' head. The pony wasn't a biter, but better safe than sorry. Especially, since she'd never been ridden by a Martian before. She beckoned Chloe closer. "Always mount from the left side."

Chloe looked at her skeptically. "Why? What difference does it make?"

Did the girl question everything, darn it? "I read it in a book," Luz answered, trying not to show her irritation. A six-year-old needed answers from her? Answers she either didn't remember or had never learned? "So just do it."

Chloe looked at her dad, then at Luz. "But books aren't always true."

"This book was true." Luz bit back the "dammit!" "It was non-fiction. That means—"

"I know what that means," Chloe sniffed. "They taught us that stuff in Kinder. And I'm in first grade now."

"Look, captains go down with the ship and people mount horses from the left," Luz muttered perversely. Lily had never questioned her wisdom, darn it. Even without words, Chloe managed to express disbelief. And disdain.

"Listen to Ms. Wilkinson," Chloe's father interjected. His tone suggested rather than ordered, but Chloe's shoulders shrugged faintly and she stepped towards the pony's side.

"Today I'll hold the reins," Luz said. "Just turn the stirrup toward you, put your foot in, then hold on to the horn, and swing up."

Chloe looked at the saddle blankly, and then back at her. Then she sighed. "Bikes are easier. Even without the baby wheels."

"You'll get the hang of it," Luz assured her. She reached past to turn the stirrup towards Chloe. "Put your hand here, on the saddle horn, and just swing up."

Chloe put a hand on the horn, but cast a doubtful look at her dad. He looked apprehensive and as unsure as his daughter, but finally nodded. "What she said," he offered by way of assurance. "Swing up."

So Chloe tried to swing, but Rumbles took a sideways step, and Chloe hopped awkwardly along in mid-swing.

"Try again," Luz urged, stopping the pony and reaching out to help Chloe regain her balance.

"I've got you, baby!" Aaron assured, approaching in a rush and reaching out to hoist Chloe.

And hoist he did. Chloe cleared the saddle, rubber padding and all, and plopped off on the other side. Rumbles turned her head to sniff disdainfully.

"You threw me over the pony!" Chloe accused.

"Oh, God! Did I hurt you? Baby, are you all right? I didn't—what hurts?"

"You threw me!" Chloe repeated, walking behind the pony to confront her dad.

Neither Chloe nor Aaron realized that Luz didn't breathe until the six-year-old cleared the pony's rear. Rumbles occasionally kicked.

I'll tell her later, Luz promised herself silently, and pasted a smile back on her face. "Everyone okay?"

"Take me home," Chloe demanded, and her dad fished in his pockets for keys.

"No!"

Chloe, Aaron, and Rumbles turned to look at Luz.

"You always get right back on when you fall off," she explained, not wanting the girl to be traumatized. She'd had enough of that in her young life, apparently.

"Another one of your 'just because' rules?" Aaron muttered, hesitating with the keys dangling out of his clutched fist.

Chloe considered the explanation before shaking her head. "I didn't fall off," she said reasonably. "Dad threw me over the stupid pony."

Her dad looked stricken. "I—I—"

He stopped, and Luz raised an eyebrow. For a six-year-old with no interest in princesses, she had the diva attitude down pat. Part of her wanted to laugh. Another part tugged on the little portion of her that still felt compassion and reminded her that he'd lost a wife. Chloe had lost a mother.

So she stepped between the two.

"Seriously, Chloe, you're not going to wimp out. Try it again. Rumbles won't move."

Chloe looked at the pony, then at Luz, but not at her father.

"And you couldn't just lift me up?"

"Maybe this time," Luz agreed. "Some people never get on their own horses."

She stepped nearer and picked Chloe up. The girl's body was tense, but weightless. Fragile, somehow. Something deep inside pulled at her. She tamped it down.

"Like who?" Chloe demanded. "Who doesn't get on her own horse?"

"Well, of course, a princess never would. They have—"

"Put me down."

"But—"

"I'll get up alone."

Luz smothered her grin against pale hair almost the color of Rumbles' mane and set her down. "Try again, then," she urged.

Chloe obediently put her hand back on the horn and pulled up. Rumbles stood frozen in place, and Chloe settled into the saddle glowing with accomplishment.

"I did it!"

"Sure did!" Luz winked at the little girl. "It's easier when your dad doesn't throw you all the way over, isn't it?"

Chloe giggled, not at all worried by her father's scowl and murmured protest. "Now what?"

Luz unwrapped the long lead she'd been using as a belt and clipped it onto the pony's halter before handing the reins to Chloe.

"Now? We ride!"

Chapter Three

Aaron looked across the small table in the Rose Creek Diner, trying to listen to Esmeralda, but his mind was on other things. The counselor was animated and flirting openly, all silk and sophistication, eyes as green as his own or Chloe's.

Across the table the overly loud clink of silverware on a plate and the sudden silence told him he'd drifted off on her again. What was wrong with him? The redheaded woman had turned every head in the room when she walked in. Esmeralda could have stepped off the runway in her short skirt and high heels, and his libido should have been surging. He frowned, aware of a distinct lack of interest in his eye-stopping dinner partner. He had warned her this wasn't a date, though, so she shouldn't be as annoyed as she seemed.

She didn't seem to realize Chloe was all he had, all he could think about when he left her alone, because he knew, too personally, how quickly life could be snatched away. Everything could become nothing in the time it took for an angry kiss or the slam of a car door or … a bullet.

He brushed at his dark thoughts and focused instead on Chloe as she'd been yesterday, after her third riding lesson. She was alive with excitement and as happy as she'd ever been. Herself again. His lips twitched as he remembered the over-enthusiastic high fives that had Luz cringing away complaining of damaged palm syndrome.

"Well!" Esmeralda's tart retort pulled him back into her presence. "Rejoining me, Aaron?" Under the table, her almost bare foot stroked his ankle. He resisted the urge to jerk away. But she needed to know—

"Relax," she purred, so he obviously hadn't fooled her. She made him uncomfortable. He'd been alone so long, much longer than the year since Stella's death. Alone, really, since their marriage began and the crazy relationship they'd established at college matured. And died. Yet in spite of any sudden surge of desire, he wanted nothing more than to head for the door.

"I told you this was a mistake. Stella—"

"Is dead." Esmeralda didn't say it meanly, just with finality. "It's time to move on."

He shook his head. "Not much more than a year. Not much time at all."

He always felt apprehensive when his feelings for Stella came up, afraid that he'd give too much away. He opened his mouth to lie, but Esmeralda's gasp of surprise saved him.

She was staring in obvious amazement as the waitress led Luz Wilkinson to a booth near the back of the small diner. He stared, too. He'd never seen her in a dress before, would never have expected her to wear something so flowery and feminine. He couldn't pull his gaze away. Her blonde hair shimmered as it tumbled down her back, freed for once from the practical ponytail she always wore. He had the impression that her eyes were bluer than he'd noticed, but he supposed that makeup and the loose hair just made him look longer and more appreciatively at her face—and the rest of her. Where Esmeralda's dress shrieked femme fatale, Luz's dress whispered it. The gauzy material drifted around her, moving enticingly around her as she walked. He couldn't get over this Luz, the one he hadn't met. And he didn't know why seeing her here surprised him; it was the only eatery in town. From the startled glances and belated greetings from other diners, though, clearly Esmeralda and he weren't the only ones taken aback.

Luz settled into the booth, and then she saw them. A slight smile and a nod, and she turned back to the menu.

"Well!" Esmeralda took a sip of wine, then brushed her hair back over her shoulder and straightened in her chair. "Haven't seen her out in a while."

"Why is everyone so shocked? There's nowhere else to go—" Esmeralda shrugged. "She doesn't leave the barn very often."

"Why don't we ask her over? She seems to be alone—"

"You're kidding, right?" Esmeralda's silky voice turned shrill. She apparently heard it, because she immediately lowered her tone and spoke just above a whisper.

"We can't. She's probably waiting for her boyfriend."

Aaron glanced over at her booth. "She's ordering," he pointed out.

Annoyance tightened her face. "Luz doesn't have a regular boyfriend." She seemed to hear the cattiness, and rephrased her words. "That is, her boyfriend lives out of town. He's a trucker, and even when they make plans, sometimes he doesn't show up. Maybe she's ordering for both of them so she can move on to the main course."

Again, her foot touched his as she winked. "Maybe he'll show up before we leave," she purred. "Sort of sad what some women settle for."

Aaron glanced again at Luz's table, and then reluctantly turned his attention to Esmeralda. There was no point in encouraging her obvious dislike for Luz Wilkinson. Who could dislike Luz? Yeah, the woman had too many horses. She was aloof and a little unkind—to him. To his daughter—he caught himself halfway into a headshake.

"What's wrong?" Esmeralda demanded with a quick, red pout.

"Nothing." *Except that my daughter thinks she's the world. And I'm not sure how I feel about that.*

• • •

Luz tore her bread into tiny bits and played with her salad. She'd chosen her usual seat, if you could call a chair you sat in two or three times a year "usual." Too late, she realized that she should

23

probably have chosen the other, turned her back to them, and stared at the wall.

I'm pathetic! She stuffed a forkful of lettuce in her mouth. Esmeralda cast a look at her, then turned back to reach up and touch Aaron's temple, running her fingers into his hair.

There were all these cute little pictures and sayings on the Internet. Things her friends sent her—the ones who still kept in touch, who didn't avoid her like the proverbial leper. Many of her colleagues had turned their backs the minute she had been escorted out of her classroom, accused of child endangerment, harm to a child, and criminal negligence—charges no one took lightly in her profession.

She moistened her lips as the old pain came back, and forced herself to remember the little cartoon. The caption read, "Millions of men and I only want *hers*!" Damn! Four years and she hadn't noticed anyone, been interested in anyone—wanted anyone— until Aaron Estes turned his pained green gaze on her.

Abruptly, she stood up. No point lingering here. Any desire she'd had to avoid the loneliness of her drab little kitchen was gone.

"Something wrong with the food, hon?" Pam bustled up, her face concerned. "Noticed you didn't eat a bite—and I didn't even bring out the real stuff yet!"

"Nah. Just remembered I didn't lock the pasture gate. Don't need any livestock getting out on the road."

"That's for sure! Let me go put it all in a box for you."

She would have refused, but there were all those mouths to feed. Sure, you weren't supposed to feed animals restaurant food, but if you'd paid for it anyway... Besides, keeping food on hand was a struggle. And what kitten, guinea hen, or donkey wouldn't like a bit of potato?

While she waited, Aaron stood up, helped Esmeralda to her feet, and they strolled toward the register.

"Hey, there." Aaron greeted her first, his smile the same, warm smile he greeted her with anytime they met. Esmeralda's thin lips pulled up at the ends and she linked an arm through her man's.

I don't give a darn, Luz thought. She wished she had the nerve to tell the redhead she could just have him. She wasn't in the market, and wouldn't compete for a man anyway. She'd learned that lesson well, and you're only stupid if you don't learn the first time around…

"Hi, Luz. How's it going?"

"Good, Aaron." She took the bag Pam brought back just then, and managed a smile that included all three. "Thanks, Pam. Nice to see you, Esmeralda."

"You, too," the redhead responded coldly, nudging Aaron towards the counter. "Pay and let's go."

"You gonna eat all that, Luz?" Pam asked. "Or are all those spoiled critters gettin' a treat?"

Aaron turned around, pocketing his receipt. "Horses eat leftovers?" he asked curiously.

Pam shot Luz a puzzled glance, but didn't say anything else when Luz frowned at her.

"Of course not." She hoisted the large bag, aware that Pam knew much more about the menagerie than Aaron had figured out. "Midnight snack."

"Better be careful," Esmeralda warned. "Those are the worst kind." Again, she stepped back into Aaron. "If you're talking about food, anyway."

They turned to go, but suddenly Aaron stopped. "Oh, I know! Esme told me you were waiting for your—boyfriend?"

"Aaron!" Esmeralda hissed.

"But—"

"Let's go! Can't you see Luz doesn't want to talk?"

Aaron's mouth opened, but nothing came out. Luz couldn't think of anything to say to him, either, so she watched as the other woman led him out into the night.

"Idiot!" she muttered, as she handed a card to the cashier to pay for her food. So Esmeralda had told him there was a man in her life? Well, hell. At least she'd been lucky enough not to fall for a man as gullible as Aaron Estes. As easily dominated. As…she bit back the word *hot*, and drew a deep breath.

At least she'd been lucky enough not to fall hard for a man like Aaron Estes.

•••

Tears ran down Luz's face as she bent over the pit bull's battered body. Cautiously she reached a gloved hand toward it. The dog lifted her head slightly. Her eyes pleaded for help and shrieked hurt. Gently, Luz patted the broad head.

She wasn't a pit bull person. Here in Rose Creek they weren't as popular as in urban areas, like San Antonio to the north or Laredo to the south. But the mangled animal didn't deserve to die on the side of the road. She pushed the vet's button on her phone.

"Hey, girl." Dr. Ann Cottwell's voice came on immediately, crisp and reassuring. "Let me guess—Candy got herself caught in a neighbor's barbed wire, or a pony got a foot through your floor again?"

Luz frowned. "You know why I took Denim into the house. Mom was so depressed and nothing made her feel better. It wasn't my brightest moment, but it seemed harmless at the time. And it worked! Mom hadn't laughed so much in weeks."

"Your mom was such a good woman," Ann said, sincerely. Then she turned brisk again. "But it cost you a new floor and could have cost you a pony."

"Don't lecture me, Ann. Listen, I need help. There's a dog…"

"Car?"

"No. Mauled by—I'm guessing—another pit bull."

There was silence on the line for a minute. "You probably should stay away from it until I get there, Luz. Pit bulls…"

"Not this one, Ann." Luz knew the vet didn't like the breed. She'd dealt with too many animals that had been savaged by pit bulls. But she wouldn't refuse to help an animal, either.

"I'll be there as fast as I can, then. But be careful."

Luz hung up and reached down to pet the dog's head again. "Hang in there," she encouraged, not at all sure the poor thing had a chance in the world, but hoping it did.

• • •

Three hours later, Luz emerged from her shower still feeling dirty. She'd helped the vet by holding the dog and moving around torn patches of skin to facilitate Ann's work. The dog whimpered, but scarcely moved. Ann had sedated the animal as a precaution, but even she had been impressed at how gentle the badly injured dog seemed. She had gone back to her clinic with the pit bull, promising to try to save her.

"But then you have to take her back or find her a home. I treat 'em, but I won't have 'em at the clinic. I won't risk other animals around them." She'd given Luz a hard look. "Neither should you."

Tires on the gravel outside Luz's house alerted her to a visitor, and she glanced at the clock on the wall, surprised. It was just after three; Aaron had said he'd bring Chloe after she finished her homework—around five, he'd predicted.

She walked out to the door, tiny little darts of excitement spearing her here and there. It was annoying, really: clearly the man belonged to Esmeralda. But she could be glad to see his daughter, couldn't she? Smiling, she pulled open the door and felt all her gladness fade into a frown.

The counselor was sliding out of her bright red sports car. Polished boots, perfectly fitted jeans, and a sweater with a front zipper that appeared more ornamental than functional.

She wanted to go back in and close the door. Esmeralda knew the way to the barn. But with another mouth to feed and more vet bills, Luz needed the board money more than ever.

She forced the smile back and walked out to greet her.

"Hi, Esme." She glanced again at the elegant riding gear. "I'm surprised to see you on a weekday. Easy day at school?"

"Just haven't ridden in a while," the other woman answered, heading toward the barn. "Anyway, I took the day off, so I have time."

"Good. Domatrix misses you."

"It's been a while. But I'm going to make up for lost time."

They reached the barn, and both women smiled at Domatrix's excited greeting. Luz wasn't sure why the horse liked her owner, but there was no doubt she did.

Luz turned to go, but Esmeralda's hand on her arm stopped her. She turned back in surprise.

"Yes?"

"Are you after Aaron, Luz?"

"That's none of your damn business!" She jerked her arm away. "But no, I'm not."

"He's interviewing us, you know."

"Interviewing us? That's your professional opinion?" Luz snorted, and Esmeralda's face contorted.

"He wants a mother for his kid. But *he* needs a wife—a woman, anyway."

Luz shrugged, and turned to go, but Esmeralda continued. "I've never lost a man I wanted, Luz. You have. Just remember that." She pulled open the bottom half of the stall door and led her mare out, pointedly ending their discussion.

Shaking her head, Luz headed towards the other end of the barn to check on the critters before she locked them away.

The kitten with no name scooted up to her as she walked into the barn's temporary shelter area. She didn't exactly know why there were three stray cats, two guinea fowl, a kitten, and a burro here. Theoretically, they were only temporary occupants. The cats had stayed on after her mother's passing. They'd lived their lives as barn cats, disdainful of human confinement, but willing to be fed rather than hunt mice. She didn't mind, and occasionally even managed to pet one or the other if they were intent on their food. Someone had apparently tossed the kitten out along the road, assuming she'd take it in. The guinea fowl—she had no idea where they'd come from with their annoying noise. But you didn't eat guinea fowl, right? At least, not guinea fowl that you knew personally. She smiled, remembering the turkey a farmer had given her mom and dad years ago, a thank you for some help through tough times. And intended as a Thanksgiving entrée, the unimaginatively named Tom had survived seven years, and died a natural death. The guinea fowl would do the same. And as for Candy...

The burro butted her, and she scratched his head. He'd been a victim of circumstances, a novelty for a local family whose children had grown and gone. He would escape from his pasture and wander the streets of Rose Creek. Locals knew him and returned him home, or let him get there himself. Then Candy chased a man down the street, probably intent on stealing the chocolate bar he'd been eating, and Candy's owner decided to put him down.

There'd been an outcry, and someone had suggested that Candy go to "the old Wilkinson place." Everyone had known that Luz's mother wouldn't turn away a critter, even in the last years of her life, and they all insisted Luz carry on the tradition.

Luz had protested, but Candy's owner had shrugged. "You're your momma's daughter," he'd told her. "Anyway, I got no choice. If I can't find him a home, it's a bullet in the head. Can't pay if some fool tourist runs a car into him and sues!"

And so the menagerie had grown. And now, apparently, there'd be a pit bull underfoot, too. Pretty soon they wouldn't fit in their end of the barn, secluded from those occasional guests who dropped by to ride horses.

Luz rotated her head and stretched her arms, feeling the stress again. She had savings. She could go back to teaching if she had to. She could spend her parents' scant insurance money on maintaining the number of animals she had, if she chose to—her parents would approve. She kept the animals semi-contained for safety reasons, mostly. She didn't actively seek new refugees due to her limited space and limited funds. But sometimes, deep down, she wondered if she kept them stashed from her doubts over what kind of a future they represented. Had she given up on herself altogether? She'd been ambitious once. She could remember that. What she couldn't remember anymore was why.

Sighing, Luz pushed the donkey away, picked up the kitten with no name, and stroked it gently. No sense letting it get as wild as its mentors. Not if she wanted to find it a home. But who here in this sparse, mostly agricultural area wanted a kitten? She might as well name it and accept that she had another critter to call her own.

Gently she set it down and headed out to saddle Rumbles and muck stalls. She smiled. Aaron and Chloe no longer made faces if they were treated to the unmistakable smell of manure. One day—soon, maybe—Aaron would grab a shovel and help out. The thought made her laugh out loud. For the first time since she'd found the pit bull lying along her fence line, she felt good.

• • •

Chloe was down to a helmet. Luz stood in the middle of the ring, watching as the little girl trotted Rumbles around. The girl's face glowed, and she never stopped smiling. Aaron leaned on the outside of the fence, and he, too, smiled.

In the middle of all those smiles, though, Luz's own smile suddenly slipped and fell away. "He's interviewing us," Esmeralda had said. Anyone looking at the three of them would see a family—a father and mother watching their daughter ride: their cherished little girl, their princess.

Unexpected tears stung, blurring her vision. The memory of Lily's face, so white and unresponsive, swam before her. Her legs buckled, and she almost fell.

"Luz!" Aaron clambered over the fence and rushed out, his hands reaching out to grasp her arms and steady her. "What happened?"

She pulled one arm loose and drew it across her face, hurriedly brushing away any evidence of tears, of weakness.

"Nothing. I—I just got dizzy. Probably I should have eaten lunch." She looked into worried eyes, and saw concern that surprised her. And warmed her.

"I'm fine," she assured him, seeing that Chloe had ridden up to them and was watching with interest, her little face intent.

"Finished?" Luz asked, reluctantly freeing her other arm.

"No!" Chloe shook her head. "Just came to see what you all were doing." She was quiet for a minute, then said, "I thought you were going to kiss."

Aaron looked stricken. "Well, we weren't. Now, young lady, I think it's time you put your pony away. School tomorrow."

"No!" She turned Rumbles and kicked her. The pony lurched forward, and broke into a gallop. For a precarious moment, Chloe tilted sideways and her tiny foot slipped out of the stirrup. Somehow she righted herself and let out an exuberant whoop.

"Go, girl, go!" she urged, and the little pony raced obligingly around the ring while Aaron's face turned gray and Luz held her breath.

"Can't you stop her?" he hissed after a moment, and she let her own breath out as she nodded.

"Yeah. And I will in a minute. But look at her, Aaron." *Please, don't let her fall.* "She's having so much fun. And she doesn't seem to be having any trouble staying on…"

"She's way too young for this," he muttered, thrusting his hands in his pockets.

Luz slanted a look at him. The apprehension tightening his face was real. He'd said Chloe was all he had after his wife's death, and Luz had lost a child herself. Not to death, but…

Reluctantly she stepped forward.

"Chloe, that's enough. Rumbles hasn't worked this hard in a while. Remember how you stopped her before?"

Chloe pretended not to hear. She cast a brief glance their way then whooped again. "Go, girl! They're coming for us!"

"Chloe! Pull back on the reins and say 'whoa.' Right now!"

For seconds it seemed she'd have to chase them down, or call Rumbles in. But finally Chloe straightened a little, eased the reins back the way she'd been told, and brought the pony to a walk.

"Now turn her in to the middle and ride over here."

Scowling, she did as she was told, choosing to park Rumbles by Luz rather than her dad, whose anxiety was easing but whose mouth turned down in a frown at Chloe's daredevil attitude.

Luz laid a hand on the pony's neck.

"She's awfully hot, Chloe. She's not used to being run so much, and it's almost ninety this afternoon."

Chloe's face fell, and she leaned forward to put her own hand on the damp neck. "She's hurt?"

"Nah. Just tired." She kept waiting for Aaron to say something, but he remained silent, just frowning at both of them. "Go ahead and get off, the way we practiced."

Chloe dismounted gracefully, giggling as Rumbles turned around to nudge her.

"Silly," she scolded, putting both arms around the pony's neck and hugging her.

"Chloe, tomorrow's a school day," her dad reminded her. "Do whatever you need to so we can go."

If Chloe heard the curtness in her father's voice, she paid no attention. She just took the reins and started walking the pony around the ring to cool her down.

"Looks like you need a hug more than that pony did," Luz muttered, moving close enough that Chloe wouldn't hear her. "You couldn't expect her to walk around in circles for the rest of her childhood, Aaron!"

He turned to stare at her, his eyes cold. "How dare you tell me what I can expect for Chloe, dammit!" He spat the words out, in spite of keeping his voice down, too. "You have no idea what I expect for her! You know what I didn't expect? I didn't expect her to see her mother shot dea—"

All the color left his face as he heard what he'd said.

Shot? Luz gaped at him, shocked. Disbelieving, even.

"Walk your own damn pony!" He stormed across the ring, caught Chloe's hand, and urged her toward the gate.

Chloe turned her own green eyes on Luz, seemingly pleading for help, but there was nothing Luz could do but watch them leave.

Chapter Four

The wind was picking up, the way it did during the spring. Texas weather could change four times in a day, which some said was to make up for the lack of normal seasonal change. Rose Creek sat below Austin and San Antonio, not quite far enough down the I-35 corridor to be as arid as the border area, but not really representative of central Texas either. That meant weather more fickle than any other part of Texas, with a cold front likely to blow in by morning, giving way almost immediately to weather that would turn progressively warmer. Occasionally, midnight would set the day's record high.

Luz smiled as she shoved a plate in the microwave. Atlanta hadn't had weather as unpredictable as the weather here, and sometimes she missed its bustle and lights. But that didn't happen very often because here, at least, there was peace.

The timer buzzed, and she pulled out the clumped broccoli and cheese. A far cry from the meals she'd once fixed, when she'd cooked for a man and his daughter. *Oh, Lily.* Pain pierced her. So close to being her daughter. And then…

She shoved her hair back, chasing the memory away. She couldn't go back to that time. It hurt too much.

She cut the packet open and dumped the clotty mess on a plate. She supposed she could feed it to the critters if she didn't finish it. The memory of Candy wrinkling his lips when he bit into mashed potatoes from the diner made her smile. Even the cats had tried the food, but turned up their noses and waited for chow. She'd finish the broccoli rather than share it with any of that unappreciative crowd.

She carried it into the living room and sank down on the couch, nestling into the corner and swinging her feet up. As always when she sat here, her eyes fell on the huge still life on the far wall. Ross Thurmond, a local artist, had painted it for her mother—three saddled horses, standing. Waiting patiently.

She closed her eyes briefly, missing her mom and dad. Again. Still. If it hadn't been for her problems in Atlanta, would they still be here? She couldn't keep believing that and find peace. Or plan for the future. She snatched the remote and turned the TV on, finding an old sitcom but leaving the volume down almost all the way. She shifted a little, finding the perfect spot, completely comfortable. And hungry. She lifted her fork.

And the doorbell rang.

Startled, she dropped the plate, watching it turn upside down on the upholstery.

The doorbell rang again. Ignoring the mess, she crossed the floor and peeked out through the glass inset. Aaron stood there, hands in his pockets, face unreadable.

She jerked the door open.

"Aaron! Come in!"

He nodded, unsmiling, and stepped in.

Luz peered out around the porch, although obviously he hadn't brought the girl. But she asked anyway. "Chloe?"

"I left her with Mrs. Baker. Her teacher's mother babysits sometimes."

"Yes, of course. Mrs. Baker's a wonderful woman. And her daughter's a very good teacher. I've met her several times."

And envied her position, just a little. She pushed the door shut. "I'm surprised you're here. Something to drink?"

"No—or maybe water, if you don't mind."

"Sure." When she came back with the water, she found him cleaning the last of the broccoli and cheese sauce from the couch with a handkerchief.

"Thanks. I spilled it when the bell rang," she explained, handing him the water and taking the handkerchief.

"Probably startled you. You weren't expecting anyone?" He cast a glance at her as he settled into the unspotted corner of the couch.

She smiled slightly. He was handy at cleaning a mess, but obviously unwilling to become part of one. She put her own iced tea on a corner of the table and sat down on the armchair so that she could sort of watch him. *Sort of.* She did not need to suddenly be acutely aware of how attractive his dimples were, or how strong—and annoying—the urge to turn the chair to face him fully had become.

So she focused on thinking back over his question. She never expected anyone at this time of night, not with her mother gone. But Esmeralda clearly didn't mind suggesting otherwise.

"You did startle me, actually," she said, after a moment. "I don't have visitors this late very often."

"Well, I thought maybe—"

Esmeralda. The imaginary boyfriend. She discarded the idea of pretending there was someone. She could be honest without trying to snatch another woman's man, for heaven's sake!

"There's no boyfriend, Aaron. What can I do for you?"

He lifted an eyebrow, and surprise touched his face. "Why would Esme—"

She raised her own eyebrow. Not even Aaron Estes could be that naive, could he?

Realization colored his expression, and he slumped a little. "Didn't see that coming!" Defensively, he said, "I mean, she's a counselor. She gives advice. Why—" He stopped, brushed a hand through his hair, and downed half his bottle of water. Then he took a visible breath.

"Never mind Esme. I—I came to apologize. And to explain—or try to."

The explanation interested her more than any apology. She leaned forward a little. "Okay."

"I behaved like an ass earlier today," he said, twisting a ring on his finger. Not a marriage ring, she didn't think—more a college ring. That surprised her. A grieving widow would wear a wedding ring, wouldn't he?

He couldn't seem to tear his attention away from his ring, or find a starting place. Finally, he looked up, unmasked pain twisting his features. "Chloe saw her mom die," he said. "She could have died herself. A classmate of hers did."

Luz swallowed, and focused on hiding her shock, the grief the death of a child always brought.

He stood up, thrusting his hands in his pockets and pacing across the narrow room. "I usually took Chloe to school, when I wasn't off on business. Stella was a cop. She usually pulled the day shift so she left around the time Chloe did. Chloe loved it when her mom had time to take her, especially in uniform. When her mom took her in street clothes, Chloe usually argued about it. She wanted the uniform."

"I was a first grade teacher," Luz volunteered. "There was a little boy—Tony—whose dad was a cop. It's a big deal to the kids. I can see how Chloe would like her mom to take her."

"Maybe you heard," he said, and came back to the couch, sitting down on the broccoli stain next to her. "About the Alabaster shooting."

She ran names through her mind. There were too many damn shootings, too much gruesome, senseless gore. But yeah, she remembered. Even though her own career had ended four years ago, nothing touched her more than bad news about innocent students.

She laid a hand on his arm. "God, yes," she murmured. "A teacher almost died. A child did, and another was injured." She paused, and swallowed as he had. "And an off-duty police officer—Chloe's mom?"

He nodded and covered her hand with his.

"A gunman opened fire just as she arrived. She didn't even have her weapon with her—usually she would, but that morning she told Chloe she'd go 'just as Mom.' She laughed and said moms didn't need guns, they were tough anyway."

Which explains the princess part. "I remember the news coverage. They said the police officer—Stella—stepped in front of another child. She saved lives. The police were there before anyone else got hit."

"Stella, the hero." His tone grated, and the hand covering hers tightened involuntarily. "The child she saved was Chloe."

He freed his hand and stood up, agitated. She stood too, wondering how to help him. How anyone could help him.

"I understand that I can't protect Chloe from everything," he gritted. "Bike falls, being thrown from a pony." Tears glistened in green eyes gone hard. "Car wrecks. Vicious gossip. Shooters in a peaceful, small-town school. I get it. But sometimes—" He turned away. "Sometimes it's more than I can deal with. Because I already came so damn close!"

She stepped up to him, wrapped her arms around his chest from behind, and hugged him, leaning her face into his back, tears streaming down her own face.

"There's nothing I can say," she whispered. "I wish there was, but—"

Somehow he turned in her viselike grip, and embraced her, resting his chin on the top of her head. "You listened," he said. "I needed you to understand."

Seconds ticked past as they clung together. Abruptly, though, Luz stiffened and pulled away, the unwelcome reminder of Esmeralda thrusting itself between them. She'd been married to another woman's man, and even if this was just honest empathy—no.

"I don't know anything about horses," he said after an awkward pause. "Well, ponies. So I'll trust you with what Chloe can do." A faint, grim smile came and went. "I'll try anyway," he amended.

"Fair enough," Luz agreed, drawing a deep breath. "So no more temper tantrums? If we disagree, you ask me about it privately."

"Makes sense. I guess." He fished in his pocket and pulled out a neatly folded handkerchief. She thought of the broccoli and wondered how many handkerchiefs he carried. And where. "Your face has polka dots."

"Jerk," she muttered, snatching the cloth away and drying her cheeks. Her skin prickled as she scrubbed away the last traces she'd cried. Except, of course, for the round, purplish spots that sprouted when she did cry. Her mother had always teased her about them, saying they were as unique as her fingerprints were. The thought of fingerprints almost brought new tears. She straightened and moved away, suddenly wanting Aaron Estes gone. Too much sadness swam around him, and she had enough of her own.

He sensed the change, apparently, and tried to lighten it. "Didn't mean to offend…I was trying to be comforting."

"By reminding me I look like a Picasso clown?"

He shrugged. "Not a clown. Just…different." He smiled. "Chloe turns bright red when she gets upset. You know you're in trouble if her lips tremble and her fists clench all at the same time."

"You're a good dad," Luz said, and meant it—Overprotective, yes—But clearly his daughter would never feel abandoned or unloved. In her short teaching career, she'd seen kids with so much less.

"Thanks." He smiled, the heaviness suddenly gone. "Bet I'll get better, too—in a decade or two when I can lighten up again."

"Well, I'll do what I can to help." Luz grinned, too. "Like not suggesting a horse for another month or so."

"A—" He bit off the retort and shook his head at her. "Goodnight, Luz!"

"Goodnight."

He started past her toward the door, stopping beside her. "Thanks for letting me talk to you. I really needed to. And Luz?"

"Yes?"

"If you Google the shooting, don't believe everything you find." She gaped at him, trying to be indignant. He leaned forward and kissed her cheek. "See you," he murmured, and went out into the darkness.

For a moment, Luz just stood, feeling the faint warmth of his kiss on her skin. How long since a man had offered even friendship?

"Snap out of it," she ordered herself. "The last thing you want is a man in your life. Brian cured you, remember?" She latched the screen door and went to turn her laptop on.

For several minutes she toyed with doing just what he'd suggested. Human nature demanded information, even tawdry information. She wouldn't be human if she didn't want to know more about Aaron. More about the woman he'd loved.

But information was a thin line from gossip. She'd lost her career to gossip. And she'd lost the daughter she'd had once upon a time, when, unlike Chloe, she herself had believed in fairy tales, princesses, and happily ever after.

Resolutely, she shut the computer down.

• • •

"Ann, you don't think it's too soon?" Luz peered dubiously at the pit bull. The scars that marked the dog's brown-and-white coat were vivid, and she still seemed on the verge of starvation. Plus, Luz thought of the kitten with no name, the guinea fowls, and her newest hard luck case, a crow with an injured wing. The damage a mean dog could do…

She took a deep breath. She'd heard stories from legions of pit bull owners. Not all members of the breed lived chained in yards, prized only if they were vicious and quick to kill.

The dog's tail thudded on the porch. The short white muzzle nudged her hand gently. Luz sighed and patted the dog's head.

"See? She loves you already!" Ann proclaimed cheerfully.

"I'd really rather find a home for her—a good home—somewhere else."

"Post her online. But I doubt you'll find takers. Luz, if you really can't keep her—"

Ann's face was strained, and Luz knew she'd put the dog down if she had to.

"You think she'll be all right—with animals, and the occasional person?" She thought of Chloe suddenly. "With children, specifically?"

"We didn't have problems at the clinic—but you know how hurt and how weak she was."

"Yeah." Luz sighed. "I suppose she wasn't chipped?"

"No. Wish she had been—bet her owner knew a lot about the dogfights that have been leaving carcasses all over. We don't even have pit bulls in Rose Creek, except for Ms. Thompson's mix, and suddenly we've seen four of 'em torn to bits."

"I guess it's a little late to have second thoughts," Luz admitted. "And I suppose I have a dog for the first time in years. I just worry about all those other animals—"

"Which are going to get you in trouble someday." Ann sighed. She held out a bottle of pills. "She's been de-wormed, has her shots; just give her these vitamins to help her pick up."

Luz took the container. "And the bill?"

"She wasn't your dog until just now. Don't think you should pay." Ann bent over and patted the dog, waving off any argument. "I've been calling her Duckie, just so you know."

"Why would you do that?"

Ann straightened, smiled. "She just looks like a Duckie, don't you think? Seriously, Luz, we're out here in the boondocks, but someday even Rose Creek will start regulating animals. I know how you feel—but you can't help 'em all. And you're going to find more and more just mysteriously turn up along your fence line. It's like babies. No one's going to just leave a baby in the middle of nowhere, right? So they find a nice house and leave it on the porch. You're getting a reputation."

"You're exaggerating. And you watch too many *novelas*."

Ann laughed. "Ain't that the truth! But it's what happens when your mother-in-law moves in with you and is addicted to them."

"Bet Ramiro would get you your own TV if you asked," Luz pointed out. "And I get the feeling you kind of like the *novelas* for the same reason a lot of women do."

"Yeah. Forget the fact that they've helped me improve my Spanish, if not my mind. All those bare-chested guys…" She heaved an exaggerated sigh. "I hear *novelas* are actually overtaking American soap operas in some places." She picked up the satchel she carried everywhere and slung it over her shoulder. "Speaking of bare-chested men," she added. "What's up with that green-eyed god everyone's raving about?"

"Aaron? Nothing's up with him, he's never been bare-chested in his life—well, in his life according to me—and who's everyone?"

"Disappointing on the bare chest. You're just not a fast worker. And since almost all of us in this God-forsaken place are married, everyone actually means just Esmeralda, who apparently has more than a professional relationship with him—or wants to."

"Bye, Ann!"

The vet clattered down the stairs, waving vaguely. "Bye, Luz. Get busy."

"Busy doing what?"

Her friend half turned her head. "Deciding what to do about critters. Saving Aaron from Esme—I don't know. Just—"

"I am not calling this poor dog something stupid like Duckie, either!" Luz shouted after her, as the vet swung up into her pickup. Another wave out the open window was her only answer.

"And I'm not keeping Aaron away from Esme, or anyone else," she muttered. The pit bull thumped her tail and leaned against her legs, looking solemnly up at her. Gentle and worn as she was, the dog still looked sturdy enough and toothy enough to tear someone apart if she chose to.

"Wonder if you'll freak him out?" She thought of Aaron and smiled in spite of herself. Esme or no Esme, having him around now and then was…she couldn't find the right word, so she settled on a word she'd always told her first graders to avoid. Nice. Having Aaron around was nice.

Chapter Five

Aaron sat hunched over in the chair, twining and untwining his fingers. He could pull out his phone and catch up on the market. He'd traveled before Stella's death. An investor and advisor with a profitable company, he had benefits and a future. He wasn't hurting for money, either. He could provide for Chloe for years to come, especially here in Nowheresville.

He caught himself up short, knowing he had no reason to bash Rose Creek. Folks here were friendly and, mostly, discreet. If they knew his circumstances, no one talked about them. Except Esmeralda, and with her it was professional, at least to him. He'd picked up on her interest, of course, when she'd suggested they should get together to talk about Chloe, and then tried to turn it into a date. An overnight date, he suspected, remembering how her foot kept finding his under the table. He frowned. Then there was the imaginary boyfriend Esme had conjured up for Luz. What kind of counselor invented men for their female rivals? Once again he considered finding someone else, outside Rose Creek. He'd go as far as he had to for Chloe. And to escape Esmeralda? Her persistence made him nervous. He closed his eyes. Sometimes he didn't recognize himself.

A quick glance at his watch showed Chloe should be popping out of the counselor's office any minute. Last time they'd come, Chloe had emerged wiping tears from her cheeks with her sleeve. He'd bounded to his feet, but a frown and shake of that aristocratic head had stopped him in his tracks.

Esmeralda had said vaguely that Chloe needed her own time and space and he should let her reach out when she was ready. He'd had doubts then about bringing her back, and wondered if he should move to a bigger city. One with more counseling services.

Grief centers. Get over your hero-wife centers. One appointment later, his thoughts were the same.

Christ, does it never end?

He sprang to his feet, agitated, just as Chloe came out. No tears, today, though, just a beaming smile as she ran over and hugged him. *Take that, Counselor.*

Esmeralda smiled. "As you can see, she's doing great. We had a wonderful time, didn't we?"

Pressed close to him, he felt—or sensed—Chloe's momentary hesitation, her apparent indecision. Then, came the green eyes and the smile. "Sure. Esme let me play with her horse collection."

"Esme?" Aaron looked down at Chloe, who fidgeted and didn't meet his eyes.

"Look, Aaron, I'm sorry if you disapprove." Esmeralda came across the room and laid a hand on his arm. "But I asked her to use my first name." She winked at Chloe. "We're besties, right?"

Chloe hesitated, then nodded slightly. "Sure." She looked up at him. "She can be my friend, right?"

Part of him wanted to growl "no!" *Besties? With a six-year-old?* But Esmeralda Salinas was the only counselor in Chloe's life right now. Until he could figure out his next move…

He shoved his hand through his hair, dislodging Esme's hand.

"You can be friends, sure." He took Chloe's hand and nodded curtly at Esme.

"Thanks." He headed toward the door, towing Chloe along. "Let's go home."

Except that they didn't go home. As he buckled Chloe into her booster seat, he suddenly realized he didn't want to go home to an empty wooden structure in the middle of nowhere. He wanted to watch Luz Wilkinson play with his daughter. Make her laugh. Teach her to ride. Safely.

He smiled a little, thinking of Luz's clear amusement at all his efforts to protect Chloe from the dangers of falling off a pony not much higher than the standard issue bike. Or bed.

Chloe patted his cheek, not arguing for once about why she still used what she disdainfully called her baby seat.

"Daddy, you're happy," she noted, almost curiously.

For a second, the words stabbed. Had he been that bad, that careless in pretending for her, in helping her find her own comfort? But just as quickly, the worry fled and he realized that she was right. They were going to Luz's and suddenly, he'd found happiness again.

"You know what," he answered, as he climbed into his own seat and grinned back at her. "You're right! I'm happy."

"Real happy?" she pressed. Leave it to Chloe to never settle for a little of anything.

But his grin just widened. "Totally, absolutely, amazingly happy!" he agreed cheerfully and added the ultimatum they always made into a game. "Take it or leave it!"

She laughed. "I'll take it!"

• • •

Luz stretched her shoulders and rotated her arms. Maybe she should start jogging, something she'd done for so many years before moving back here. Just keeping up the property and caring for the animals seemed to consume all her time and energy, though. Still, she shouldn't be so exhausted. She'd only unloaded a truck bed full of hay, after all. And Ross had helped her. Good thing he did odd jobs and had been willing to pick it up for her, saving her a trip to the feed store almost thirty miles away. She wished he'd let her pay for his favor, though, instead of giving her that smile and telling her he'd do anything for a woman as pretty as her. Folks around Rose Creek helped each other, and she loved that, but Ross had bills to pay, too.

The menagerie had been fed and contained, more or less, in their end of the barn. The pit bull with no name was stretched out on the floor, but looked up and wagged when Luz came in. The dog looked a lot better, just in the brief time she'd been here. The continuing effects of the vet's prescription and regular meals—and affection—were working wonders. Luz bent to pet her. The dog hadn't chosen to be a pit bull. She hadn't chosen to be forced, probably, into a ring with a meaner dog intent on tearing her apart for human amusement and profit.

The sound of a car coming down the drive startled her; she hadn't been expecting anyone. She glanced out and saw Aaron's SUV. Funny, he usually called when they were coming. Friday was usually an off day, because he'd bring Chloe early on Saturdays to spend more time than she could on weekdays.

"Well, here we go," she muttered, not at all sure Aaron would want Chloe around a pit bull. She stepped back out the door to meet them on the porch as they clattered up the stairs. Chloe raced straight to her, wrapped her arms around her waist, and squeezed.

"Dad surprised me," she chortled. "He brought me here instead of taking me home."

Aaron was grinning at his daughter's excitement. "I hope you don't mind being a surprise—and being surprised."

"Flattered," Luz assured, hugging Chloe back briefly. "But are you here to ride? I could turn on the outside lights, but it's a little late—"

"No. I promised her she could ride as much as Rumbles would let her tomorrow." He shifted a little, as if uneasy.

"Actually, I thought maybe you'd let Chloe and me treat you to dinner."

"Dinner? Now that is a surprise, but—"

Chloe headed toward the door. "Too late! Dad has it in the truck! Go get it," she pleaded, softening her tone to relay the order. "I'm starving."

Blissfully unaware that both adults were staring at her, bemused, she reached for the doorknob.

"Well—uhmm, I guess I'd be delighted." Luz shrugged. "Please. Go get it. The girl's starving."

Aaron laughed and headed back toward his vehicle, giving Chloe a gentle spin that sent her toward the kitchen. The pit bull was in the living room. Nobody had come into the house since the dog had come home. And perfectly nice dogs sometimes reacted differently to children than adults…

Luz needn't have worried, at least not about Chloe.

"Oh, the poor little thing! It's been hurt!"

Apparently she'd figured out something about approaching animals from being around the horses. Slowly she held out a hand and made clucking noises. "What's its name? Can I pet it? Is it a boy or a girl?"

"Calm down, calm down. Come here, girl." Slowly she held her hand out and patted the dog's head, and let her sniff Chloe's hand. Chloe patted her gently, but with increasing confidence, and after a moment, the dog leaned into her little legs, making soft, contented snorts.

"She sounds like a pig," Chloe declared. "What's her name?"

"A little help? I'm about to drop—"Aaron came in, a collection of bags, drinks, and utensils clutched precariously in his arms and shelved against his chest. That *damned* chest. With a sideways glance at the girl and dog, Luz plucked the packages away, studiously avoiding his eyes—and any of the bags that were balanced against his chest. If he only knew…

She ruthlessly tamped down a mental count of how long it had been since she'd touched a man's chest.

"What is that?" Aaron plopped the rest of dinner on the coffee table and stared at Chloe and her new friend.

"Isn't she the coolest dog ever? I mean, she's ugly—because she got hurt—but she's—" Chloe stopped. "Luz, you still haven't told me her name!"

"True. That's because she doesn't have a name yet."

"How long have you had a pit bull?" Aaron asked. "Are those scars from a fight?"

Apparently the dog found all the commotion exhausting. She yawned and plopped down on Chloe's feet, making the little girl giggle. "She should be around when it's cold! My feet would stay warm all the time."

"Let's eat and I'll tell you why she doesn't have a name," Luz offered, nodding at the coffee table. "Come on, Chloe, help your dad move dinner to the kitchen. Just slide your feet out carefully."

Aaron's face was implacable. He didn't look angry, exactly. Not even too worried. Maybe he'd be okay around dogs. He'd gotten used to the horses and ponies after all.

She smiled at him. "You surprised me, and I surprised you. That's fair, right?"

"I think so," Chloe called from the kitchen. "Come on! I'm starving."

"The girl's starving," she reminded Aaron. "Let's eat. You can ask about the dog with no name while we're enjoying your surprise."

While Chloe washed up, Aaron opened containers holding fried chicken, wings, sides, and vegetable soup. "We really didn't know what to bring," he explained. "The soup was Chloe's idea. She thought you might be a vegetarian."

"You know. Because you like animals so much," Chloe explained. "Oh, don't worry, though," she went on. She smiled at Luz with that perfect innocence of the very young. "I didn't say a word to Dad about all the secret animals."

Chapter Six

"I can't believe you have a zoo hidden in the barn and I never caught on," Aaron grumbled, casting a glance at his daughter, who took up most of the sofa. She'd fallen asleep after eating and scolding Luz for not having picked a name out for the dog already. She'd been an active conspirator, telling her Dad about the donkey and the weird birds and the cats and the kitten and…

And she'd defended Luz, once she realized she'd slipped up and spoiled the secret. Luz had been touched by how Chloe's face suddenly changed.

"Oops. I told a secret!"

"Your dad could have known," Luz had comforted. "How he never noticed the closed door and the noises is a mystery to me anyway. And they're not really secret."

Now, Aaron sat in the chair across from the couch, while Luz took up the smallest possible space in the corner of the couch, wanting to let Chloe sleep until Aaron went. She didn't mind that he seemed to be in no hurry.

"Not a zoo," she protested. "Let alone a secret collection. Some of them are a nuisance, and if they ran all over and got away, I'd be responsible for them. Besides, Candy sometimes chases after horses when visitors come out to ride. Chloe just found out when you had to go get that expired sticker replaced. She heard them remind me that feeding time had come and gone."

"What did she call them? Your menagerie?"

"A few animals without homes. I couldn't very well let a local legend like Candy be put to death, could I?"

"But what do you do with all those critters? Nowhere to put them…" He straightened a little. "Do you work? I mean—"

"You mean how do I pay bills when I board one horse?"

"I'd intended to pay for Chloe's lessons—"

Luz waved him off. "Good heavens. I had the pony and I have the time." She stood, stretching. "Would you like to sit on the porch or in the kitchen? No point in waking Chloe until you're ready to go."

He cast a glance at Chloe, and motioned towards the door. "Outside might be nice," he decided. They went out, and Luz chose the big wooden rocker. That left Aaron the creaky old porch swing. She didn't want to romanticize the thing, just barely big enough for two. Or maybe just perfectly sized for two. She thought briefly of Ann and her husband sitting there, occasionally forgetting they were visiting and tuning her out...

What had he asked? Oh, yes. About her employment.

"My dad would take animals anyone abandoned or just needed to get rid of. He couldn't ever say no to anyone or anything," she explained. "But he worked in the oil fields a lot, so Mom more or less got the credit—or the blame. After...when he was gone, Mom just kept going."

"So you've always been here, helping her?"

"No." She shook her head and left it at that.

For a moment they were silent, surrounded by the mild air. Winter hadn't ended, technically; spring was a few weeks away, but most of the cold had ended.

"That's right," he said abruptly. "You said you taught first grade. Here?"

Too bad she'd confided that bit of information. Of course if she hadn't, sooner or later someone in Rose Creek would have.

"For a while," she answered, and fell silent again, swinging her foot absently. "But no, not locally. Atlanta."

Out somewhere near the barn, an owl hooted. Luz jerked, startled, and her foot hit the porch with a resounding thud.

"The zookeeper's afraid of an owl?"

Luz stood and stretched. "Terrified, obviously." She smiled. "You may or may not know that in some areas of rural Mexico, *lechusas*— barn owls—are witches who can shape shift. And steal souls, especially of the very young. Are you scared?"

"Of witches? Hell, no. They melt." He stood up, too, and glanced at his watch. "Time for us to go?"

"You don't have to leave. But I need to put stuff up…" He had moved closer, and just for a moment she wanted to sag into him, or trip and fall against him. Just as quickly, she forced the urge away, reminding herself that he was involved. Last time, she hadn't been the other woman, legally. She'd been *the* woman. The wife—of a man involved with another woman. Never again.

She wondered if she'd shown the anger that still bubbled up when she thought of her ex because Aaron moved around her and opened the door, suddenly ready to leave. Maybe he'd seen the pain that knifed through her whenever memories of Brian and his betrayal caught her unprepared. The sadness.

He walked over and looked down at his sleeping girl, and tenderness replaced whatever else his expression might have held.

The sadness cut deeper as she remembered Lily. Brian was gone, not a part of her life. She really hadn't missed him. But losing the little girl he'd called hers…She blinked back tears and went into the kitchen.

There really wasn't much to clean up. She put a couple of the boxes back in a bag and threw out a plate.

"Do you mind if we come early?" Aaron leaned against the doorjamb. "Chloe says Rumbles will forget her if she doesn't ride more."

"Sure, come whenever."

"You okay?"

She blinked. "Why wouldn't I be?" she asked.

He shrugged. "You just seemed…different, all of a sudden. Like part of you just…I don't know. Went off."

"Mood swings. You know, if you don't want to wake Chloe, she could stay. I could throw a blanket over her—"

"Thanks, but even if she wakes up when I move her, she'll conk out in the car."

He waved his hand toward the table when she held the bag out for him. "Keep it. We may need breakfast if Chloe gets her way about what time we should be here."

He bent to pick her up, and surprisingly, while the child shifted a little and murmured something against her dad's shoulder, she didn't wake up.

He started toward the porch, but stopped to look back at Luz.

"You're not old enough to have taught very long," he said, as if the thought had just occurred to him. "And if you didn't live here..." He hesitated. "What I guess I'm asking is—is there someone else? Not Esme's imaginary boyfriend, but—"

"There was. I'm divorced." There, she'd said it, even if she didn't know why he wondered.

He nodded. "The sadness." There was no doubt in his voice. She wondered how much he knew about sadness over a relationship ending as hers had.

His marriage hadn't ended by choice. And though the pain must torture him daily, he'd honored those vows. He'd been faithful. Somehow, she sensed that.

He turned the SUV on from the porch and managed a small nod without dislodging Chloe from her resting place. "Goodnight, Luz."

"Goodnight."

She didn't stand on the porch and watch them leave, too aware of the sudden emptiness around her.

• • •

Something heavy and warm moved on the edge of the mattress behind Luz, bringing her instantly awake. Apprehension bordering on fear gripped her, making her hold her breath and keep still while she figured out options and actions. Rose Creek hadn't had a homicide that she'd heard of. There had been a rape, a few drunken assaults, but no alcohol hung in the air.

Her pistol was in a dresser drawer, across the room. Out of reach.

The dog—where the hell was the dog? Was she cowering in the kitchen—she'd been so abused. Who could blame her?

What if—her breath caught. What if the dog had been killed?

I'll count to three. Then I'll roll out of my bed and get the gun.

Her hand tightened on her quilt as she tensed to roll.

A snort gusted against her head, followed by the rough rasp of a tongue across the exposed skin of her cheek.

She rolled, realizing who the intruder was just as she hit the floor in a tangle of linens. Stupid, ungrateful dog.

"Luz?" called Aaron's voice, worried. And then, from the door, "Luz, is everything okay?"

She exhaled. "Yes. Everything is fine."

"Because I heard this noise—"

She propped herself on an elbow, careful to keep the bedspread and sheet blanket wrapped around her.

"A loud, kind of heavy thud," he continued, humor erasing any of his previous concern. "It's okay, baby. Everything's fine," he called over his shoulder.

Chloe popped into the room. She looked at the dog on the bed and Luz on the floor, and giggled.

"She knocked you off the bed!"

"She didn't, exactly," Luz muttered. "More like kissed me off—" she stopped, seeing Aaron's lips twitch. Last thing she needed was him laughing at her.

"Let me help you up," he offered, holding out a hand.

She glared at him. "I'm not an invalid, Aaron. I can get up."

"Still." He moved his hand closer.

But he didn't know that she'd done her laundry last night after they left. That she'd sat down on the bed in a towel, waiting for the last load to finish, knowing she had other nightclothes, but wanting the leopard print nightgown. And that she had fallen asleep in a towel and never put a thing on. Not a thing, although sometime during the night she'd woken with very little covering her and burrowed under the covers.

The dog had never gotten on her bed before, darn it! Of all the inconvenient—and of all the stubborn, stupid men—

With Chloe still giggling in the doorway, standing up and confronting him stark naked couldn't happen. Typically not her kind of move, anyway, but—she frowned, and tried to put meaning in her words.

"You and Chloe should wait in the kitchen. I'll need to get dressed, anyway."

He pulled his hand back. "Just looked like you could use a little help. Chloe, why don't we go so Luz can get dressed?"

"Sure." She clucked at the dog, and trotted off. After a moment, the pit bull jumped down and followed her.

"Hmmm…I believe you were leaving, too?"

He pulled his hand back slowly. "Yeah. Sure." And then came the dimples, and that quick, killer smile.

"Although I have to wonder why you won't let me help you up. You're practically mummified. Makes me wonder what would happen if I grabbed a corner of something and pulled."

"Curiosity kills a lot of cats. Go away, Aaron!"

He shrugged and went, looking back at her with a wide grin as he locked the door from the inside and pulled it shut after him.

•••

A few minutes later, Luz wandered into the living room to find Aaron studying the oil painting across from the couch, rubbing his hand idly over his chin. Chloe kneeled on the couch, her hands resting against the back of the cushions, looking at the picture too.

"Impressed?" she asked them.

"Didn't notice it last night," Aaron admitted. "But it's okay, if western art's your thing."

"But why did he paint the horses' butts?" Chloe asked plaintively. "You hardly see their heads, and they look all droopy."

"The emperor's not wearing any clothes," Luz whispered.

"Emperor? It's just horses!"

"Just a saying, Chloe. A lot of people say they like paintings when they don't."

Chloe nodded sagely. "They lie?"

"Pretty much," Luz agreed, unable to argue with her logic.

Aaron peered at the signature in the corner. "Who's Ross Thurmond? For some reason the name sounds familiar."

"Ross is a local character. A handyman and an occasional artist. He gave that painting to my Mom—I don't know—six years ago? *Like a Horse Saddled*."

"Oh—that's what he calls it?" Aaron glanced at her, and then back at the nondescript horses in western gear tethered to a rail outside an old barn. The horses stood hipshot, weight more on one hind leg than the other, heads drooping near the ground.

"Yeah. But my mom preferred to call it *Patience*."

"I don't like it," Chloe declared, sliding down the backrest of the couch and managing a turn all at once. "The horses aren't pretty like yours are, Luz." She scrambled off the cushions and grabbed her father's hand impatiently. "Can we go now, Dad? You promised!"

"Luz might want breakfast—"

"I'm good. Besides, we have to feed the menagerie."

"Menagerie means lots of animals that aren't horses," Chloe explained and waved a hand at Luz. "She said."

Aaron nodded somberly. "I'll remember that. Let's go see those secret animals Luz hides from everyone."

Chloe giggled. "She didn't hide them from everyone, silly! You're the only one who didn't know about them."

Luz smiled, but fought off her own laughter. From Aaron's sudden change of expression, he didn't enjoy having secrets kept from him.

"There really aren't many," Luz said. "Just a few derelicts nobody wanted that my mom took care of before—" She bit off the rest, but Chloe slanted her a look.

"Before she died, right?"

Luz kicked herself mentally. The kid was way too perceptive. She glanced at Aaron. He looked pained more than annoyed, but didn't throw any lifeline out.

So Luz just nodded. "Yes."

Surprisingly, Chloe dropped the subject. Luz unlatched the sliding door and pushed it back on its track. Candy brayed a welcome. The guinea fowl flapped around, and one of the barn cats came up, eager for breakfast.

"I don't see the kitten," Chloe complained.

"Maybe if you called her…" Aaron suggested, watching Candy warily as he butted Chloe, who laughed and scratched his ears.

"She'll show up. Come help me with the food." Luz led them back to the feed room and filled one bucket with corn and another with oats. She handed the bucket with corn to Aaron. "You and Chloe can feed the guinea hens. Candy goes a little crazy when he's hungry."

He raised an eyebrow. "So…like…how does one feed a guinea hen, exactly?

"You are so not a farm boy," Luz chided, and he grinned.

"Tell me about it!"

They walked back to deliver the feed to a much-changed menagerie. Candy brayed and stomped, the cats meowed plaintively—they had all appeared, including the kitten who somehow managed to be louder and more plaintive than any of them.

And the guinea hens! Their non-stop, shrill clucking and fussing had Chloe covering her ears and ducking her head dramatically.

Candy got his bucket of oats a few feet away from the other animals. Luz nodded at the corn. "Just take a handful," she counseled, "and—"

"Holy shit, it bit me!" Aaron yelped, half throwing the bucket of grain halfway across the corridor.

"Let it go," Luz finished.

"It bit me!"

"You big baby. Birds don't bite, they peck. Let's see your stupid hand—"

"Luz, you said a bad word," Chloe whispered, appalled, apparently forgetting her own frequent use of the word, and the fact that her father had used real profanity just seconds ago.

Right. That brainwashing we perform on all kids. Be nice. Never say a hurtful word. Stupid is a god-awful word. Memories of a classroom full of first graders shocked that a classic children's book actually used profanity like "stupid" flashed back. She didn't mean to, but she laughed—at Chloe's horrified expression and Aaron's petulant one as he lifted his hand for her inspection.

And reflexively, unthinkingly, Luz lifted his palm and brushed a kiss on the invisible beak wound.

Chloe gaped. Aaron tensed. Stilled. The mesmerizing green eyes sparked.

And the first grade teacher erasing a boo-boo fled, leaving a woman punched in the gut by a desire she hadn't felt in so long. Lower, maybe, than the gut, but punched, definitely. She dropped his hand and took a step back. He did, too.

"Well," he said.

The word reverberated deep inside her, added to the impact of that lower punch, and melted her legs. Just a little.

So she managed an indifferent shrug. "All better now," she told Chloe with a wink. "And look—the guinea hens are eating even after he threw the feed bucket at them!"

Chloe laughed. "Hey, he threw me over Rumbles, and now I can ride. And he threw the bucket at the guinea chickens and they get to eat it all at once. Maybe throwing is like good luck when he does it!"

Aaron groaned, but Luz laughed too, and went over to retrieve the bucket.

"You, young lady," Aaron told his daughter, "are way too rude and way too smart."

"Oh, well." She shrugged at her dad. "Can I ride now?"

"Ask Luz."

"Sure." She hooked her arm through the pail, and caught Chloe's hand. Better not to even look back at the little girl's dad. Not until she forgot how lust felt. And remembered betrayal, and how illicit relationships destroyed lives. The man had a woman. She wouldn't be part of that picture.

Chapter Seven

Saturdays were good days, Aaron thought a few hours later, as he watched his daughter jog around the arena, radiant. He'd wanted to see her like this, and her happiness eased the pain that cut into his soul at odd moments. He glanced at Luz, who was trotting around the ring leading a little boy on a spotted pony. Pompom, had she said?

That kid's face was alight, too, and his parents were sitting on chairs under the barn awning, sporting expressions that probably echoed his own. Kids should always be this happy. Maybe there was something to that old saw about small town, country living.

He massaged his neck and realized that he had burned in addition to stiffening up from leaning on the fence too long.

Stella would have loved seeing Chloe like this, although she would have called out to her girl to boot the pony into a flat-out run, dismissing any dangers and sucking in the excitement. She'd lived that way, and it had cost her—her parents had disowned her when she'd gone into law enforcement, not long after he'd married her. They'd told her never to go home, and had never even acknowledged Chloe's birth. He didn't think they disapproved of him, though, so much as Stella.

His hero wife. The dregs were so bitter. For a moment his fingers dug into the fence rail, and then he forced himself to relax. He turned his gaze to Luz, still trotting that splashy pony around. He wasn't sure why she'd told him she'd never let Chloe ride such a pitiful excuse for a Shetland pony. It looked fine to him. Looked really good, trotting around the ring…Realization hit him that Luz wouldn't appreciate that last assessment, because it had nothing to do with ponies.

And what kind of a bastard was he, to think about how Luz looked from behind when his daughter was right there beside her, restored to innocent childhood? But the brief touch of her lips on his palm—that shouldn't have made him think of slow dancing. Long walks. Wild nights…

"Luz, we've gone over our time," the other dad called, and Luz immediately slowed the pony and led her over to the gate.

"Thanks, Miss Wilkinson," the little boy chimed, and Luz helped him down and hugged him briefly.

"You're welcome, Timothy."

"I should pay for an extra hour," said Timothy's mother, opening her purse.

"Don't worry about it," Luz protested. "I charge by approximate times, and Pompom needed exercise."

Moments later, she waved a final time at the departing car and walked over to the fence. Aaron knew she'd felt something she hadn't expected when she'd put her lips to his palm so impulsively. She'd probably heard his own overreaction in his one word response.

But nothing showed in her face.

He pushed off the fence, straightening and stretching. The midday sun, already hot, hammered into him like a welcome massage. He could get used to being a country boy. Get used to the farm life. Except…he glanced around. Except this wasn't a farm. And it wasn't a ranch. He wasn't sure what Luz would call it, but it wasn't exactly what he'd planned on when a chance encounter with a nice clerk at the gas station had him settling in for a while. He smiled at the memory, thinking of how meticulously he used to plan his life. Then he'd pulled into Rose Creek and stopped at the gas station for a bathroom break and snacks for Chloe. He supposed he'd looked like hell, because the elderly woman behind the counter clucked over him.

"Where y'all going?" she'd asked as she bagged the purchases.

He'd shrugged. "No idea," he admitted. "Just going." He'd forced a smile.

"Well, maybe you need to stop and figger it out," she'd advised. "Look, my husband and I have a house we need to rent. Take a few days, get that girl settled in somewhere 'til you make up your mind." She'd handed him the bag, and as they'd walked toward the door, he heard her murmur, "God bless them, they just look lost."

He had looked down at Chloe, squeezed her hand gently, and turned back to the counter. He'd planned on the anonymity of a big city like Dallas, but he'd walked back to the counter and given the woman a weary smile.

"Could you tell me about the house?"

She had, and they had become Rose Creek's newest residents just after Christmas.

He glanced at Luz and wondered if something more than an old lady's kindness had stopped his headlong flight away from everything. Something buzzed near his ear, and he swatted the air, feeling a tinge of soreness from his sunburned neck and realized if he'd been out in the sun too long, so had his girl.

"Chloe, time to give that poor old pony a break," he called.

She frowned, but obediently slowed Rumbles, then rode her over to the fence and slid off.

"Aren't you supposed to use the thingee there on the side and step off?" he teased.

She sniffed. "It's a stirrup, Daddy. And I'm too tall to do it that way. Sliding is faster."

"So is falling, but it doesn't look as good in a show ring," Luz interjected, grinning at Chloe. "Hungry yet?"

Chloe gave a half shake of her head, then turned it into a nod. "Sort of. But I don't want to stop for lunch. Then it'll only be a little while 'til I have to go home."

"Maybe you should just move in with Luz," Aaron suggested.

Chloe's face lit up. "Really? You'd let me?" she squealed. "You, too?"

He shook his head. "Not room for me on that short little couch of hers. You'll have to come by yourself."

Chloe shrugged, but her eyes twinkled, and she clearly knew he was kidding. "What do you think, Miss Luz? Ready to have your own little girl?"

To his amazement, all signs of laughter fled, and Luz stiffened and visibly drew back.

"No!" she said. "No, I am not ready to have a daughter!" She snatched Rumbles' reins and turned toward the barn. "I'll cool her. You two go to the house and wash up, if you want to."

• • •

Idiot! Ass! Nothing she could call herself seemed hard enough. She stumbled slightly over a rock she knew had always been there, seeing only Aaron's shock and Chloe's hurt. How could she have gone off on an innocent joke, a game Aaron and Chloe were playing, thinking she'd join in?

They didn't, couldn't understand. Lily's little face rose in her mind, brown eyes serious, or smiling. Tiny hands clutching. First steps, temper tantrums, and huge hugs. Dainty kisses. They didn't know she'd had a daughter—and that child, another woman's, like Chloe—had been torn from her life. Or that Lily had been at the center of the storm that had driven Luz from Atlanta, and brought her here, killing her father with the worry and hastening her mother's death.

She liked Chloe. A lot. She also liked the troubled man who doted on her. Too much. But if she ever had a child…she blinked back tears. A child was unlikely, but if she did have one it would be the product of her own body. Someone she could never lose.

She tied Rumbles to a ring and pulled off her saddle. The pony was hardy and not too hot, so she did something she rarely did and just left her there, standing patiently, while she jogged to the house. She couldn't explain about Lily, but she could say something. She could let Chloe know it wasn't about her.

She was relieved to see the SUV was still there as she reached the house, but perplexed to see a second, beat up vehicle parked next to it. She recognized the pickup—Ross Thurmond—but couldn't imagine why he was here. She hadn't ordered anything or asked for a delivery—surely he didn't just want to visit?

She walked through the kitchen, surprised that the pit bull stood by the door to the living room, sticking her head into the room and growling—something she hadn't done before.

And when Luz walked through the door, the dog pressed itself into her leg and moved with her, either seeking to give or get protection.

Ross was sitting in her father's old recliner, and Aaron was on the couch. Chloe, like the dog, seemed apprehensive; she was pressed into her father's side for shelter, too.

"Ross, what a surprise!" No lie there, and she didn't have to face Aaron and Chloe quite as quickly with a guest sitting there in his dust-cloaked, drab clothes.

"Have you met Aaron Estes and his daughter Chloe?" she asked, walking over as he stood and offering him her hand.

With the unnamed dog still shadowing her and rumbling low and deep in her throat, Luz fought an urge to stiffen and push away when he unexpectedly leaned over and brushed her cheek. The greeting was pretty much universal here in Rose Creek, but she barely knew Ross, and for some reason, the polite peck made her skin prickle.

She stepped away, quickly. "Sit down, Ross, please. What can I do for you? Some water or tea?"

"Nah. Just came by to say hello. Used to visit your mom all the time, and felt bad I hadn't been very neighborly since…" His eyes fell on his painting, and he hesitated. "Since you've been out here all alone."

"Thanks, but I'm not all alone," Luz assured him. "And you've been a godsend when I haven't been able to pick up feed—"

"Not much to brag about, though. This Aaron fellow did introduce himself," Ross confirmed. "Brings his daughter here to ride?"

From a distance, Luz suddenly remembered a snatch of a conversation she'd overheard when she'd visited, not long after her move to Atlanta. More an argument, really, between two people who never disagreed over anything.

"Bastard's a pervert," her father had grumbled.

"Joe Allen Wilkinson, Jr.!" Her mother's sweet voice had blistered her father. "Don't you use that language to me or I'll whip *your* ass! The man's an artist without a family and nobody to take him to heart. There's nothing perverted about him!"

"He's sweet on you, a married woman!"

Her mother's indignation turned into a peal of laughter. "You're jealous! I swear, Joe! When would another man look at me? And if I thought he was, wouldn't I tell him just where to go?"

Lord, I miss them both. She hesitated, not wanting to confirm or deny Ross's statement.

"We're in and out," Aaron said from the couch, then stood and gave Ross a wink and a smile.

Ross flushed, apparently taking Aaron's words as a declaration of interest.

"Well, that's fine, then," he said after a moment. "Being alone ain't what the good Lord intended for no one." He plucked a cap from the armchair and pulled it over his uncombed gray hair. "Told your mom that," he added. "After your dad passed. She mightn't have pined so much…"

Luz swallowed. "Mom wasn't alone, Ross. I moved back from Atlanta right away." *And mind your own business.* She didn't say it, though, convincing herself she shouldn't overreact.

"Oh, I know." Ross cast her a smile, but under the bill of the cap, his eyes seemed dark and hard. "But you were a married woman, Luz. You know how it is. Women are meant to have men, and men—well, we men need our women. Can't be news to a big city woman like you."

Aaron moved over to Luz and draped an arm casually around her shoulder.

"Don't worry, Ross. You're right." He smiled down at her. "And we're working on it. In fact, Chloe and I thought we'd take you to the diner tonight, Luz. May be a little too late to go to San Antonio like we'd talked about, though."

She knew what he was doing, and playing along wasn't too hard given the weird turn this encounter with Ross Thurmond had taken. "Sure." She gave him a quick smile and looked across at Ross.

"Was there anything else?"

"No. Just wanted to say hello." He nodded at her and held out his hand, forcing Aaron to remove his arm from her shoulder. "Nice meeting you, Aaron. You, too, Chloe." He nodded again and walked out, and Luz and the dog both sagged with relief.

"Well!" Aaron rubbed a hand through his hair and scooped Chloe up into a bear hug as she bounced into his arms. "That was a little strange."

"Yes."

"You really should consider locks on your door. When Chloe and I walked in, he was sitting there staring at a picture."

"You mean his painting?"

Aaron shook his head slowly. "No. I mean that picture." He pointed toward the mantel, toward her mother's gold-framed engagement portrait.

Chills made her shiver. Could her father have been right?

Shaking herself free of the questions and the niggling uneasiness, she shrugged. "Nothing to worry about. Guess I could get the lock fixed, but it's the odd door in Rose Creek that's locked."

Aaron didn't say anything, just stared at the wall for a moment, then leaned over and kissed the top of his daughter's head. "Chloe, do us a favor."

She turned expectant eyes up. "Yes?"

"The dog needs food, water, and a name. Could you do all that?"

Chloe sniffed. "Of course. I know where Luz keeps the food and water." She frowned a little. "But a name—"

"Well, Luz has been kind of busy teaching kids like you to ride," he pointed out. "And I'm tired of saying things like 'Here, dog. Nice dog.'" He winked at her. "So write down your top fifteen choices, and we'll ask Luz to choose one."

"Awesome!" Chloe turned to the kitchen, clapping her hand on her leg. "Come on, girl! Let's get you dinner and a name."

"She won't be long, and she's all ears, but—" He shrugged again. "We need to talk, Luz."

"About?" Luz bit her bottom lip, and curled her fingers into her legs. "Look, what I said at the corral—I wouldn't hurt Chloe for the world. And you were joking, but—"

"But you're not ready for a daughter. And mine would come with baggage?"

"No, dammit! No!" She wanted to kick him. To scream in frustration. To do anything except talk about the little girl she had lost. She inhaled slightly and steadied herself. He couldn't understand. She'd never explained.

He reached out suddenly and cupped her cheek in his hand. The touch burned, but with a deep, soothing heat. She saw compassion in his eyes.

"The divorce." He didn't question, and she couldn't argue with finality. "I'm sorry."

She just stood there, soaking in the comfort. Relishing a touch that demanded nothing.

"What happened?" he asked, after long moments, and the comfort shattered and fell away. Then he shrugged and drew his hand back, and answered himself. "He cheated, right?"

In the worst possible way. She wasn't thinking of Brian's sexual betrayal, though. No, he'd cheated her into believing she'd be Lily's mother forever. What had he said? Our daughter will never call anyone else "Mom"? She shook herself out of her plummeting thoughts and stepped away from Aaron, avoiding his eyes.

"I bet Chloe's finished her list," she said.

On cue, Chloe popped into the room, waving a notepad, her face glowing.

"Got some good ones?"

"Yes! Look!" She thrust the list out at Luz instead of her dad, and Luz scanned it then handed it to Aaron with a grin but no comment.

He read it with raised eyebrows before handing it back to Luz.

"Goddess?" he asked. "Jellybean?"

"She needs to feel pretty," Chloe explained sincerely. "Goddesses and jellybeans are pretty."

"Where did you even hear the word goddess?" he probed, and Chloe sniffed in disdain.

"You don't remember anything!" she sniffed. "Mom used to say I'd be her goddess of good luck when she'd let me give her numbers for that game she played."

Aaron looked like she'd punched him in the gut. Color drained from his face and his lips tightened and thinned. "I'd forgotten," he muttered.

Luz glanced at the list again. "Princess?"

Chloe immediately focused on her, and Aaron looked visibly relieved.

"Thought you hated princesses, Chloe?"

"Well, the name isn't for me," she snorted. "It's for a dog."

"Good point." She looked at the nameless dog, curled in her corner asleep. "So, I think you should choose one." She winked at Chloe. "After all, I haven't even been able to name one little old kitten!"

Chloe gave an exaggerated sigh. "How can a kitten be old?" She shook her head. "I think you should name her Princess."

Lily's nickname. Luz shook the momentary hesitation off and even smiled. Maybe it was a good thing, Chloe being a little more accepting to what was, for many girls her age, a shared vision of make-believe and possibility. Besides, the kid was right—the pit bull wasn't a pretty girl. A royal title couldn't hurt her doggy self-esteem.

Aaron looked surprised at the choice, but not annoyed.

"Well, then! We have a name and a dinner date!" he declared.

Luz thought about arguing. She didn't want a dinner date with the man whose touch still warmed her shoulder. And then there was Esmeralda.

"Don't think I'm up for dinner," she told them. Chloe's face fell. Aaron frowned.

"But a few minutes ago—"

"If you mean when Ross was here, I thought—" She bit back the rest of her statement. She'd been going to say that he'd been trying to make the other man leave. That she'd just been playing along. But what kind of conversation was that in front of a kid? Kids learned all about manipulation and adult gamesmanship too soon. And she could hardly say anything about Chloe's counselor in front of her. She tapped her toe on the floor, cornered and not happy.

Then she remembered their impromptu dinner, and Chloe slumbering peacefully on her couch, dead to the world, or any conversations adults might hold. Conversations, for example, about how another woman's man would never hold any interest for her. At all.

"Would you invite me to your place for dinner?"

Luz asked Chloe, though, not her father. Chloe wouldn't say no, and her father wouldn't override her. Ha! The negotiating skills that endeared her to her former students without compromising her own agenda had finally resurfaced!

"Uh—sure." He hardly even hesitated. "Not sure what we have to feed you, but—"

"Dad, we have tons of stuff—"

"I'll bring dinner."

They all spoke at once, stopped at the same time, and broke into laughter.

"All that being said, shall we go?" Aaron asked.

"You two run along. I'll wrap things up and take a shower. I did run kids around on ponies all day in the heat."

"But—"

"Now, would I leave you without food? Seriously, go so we won't all die of hunger! Just tell me if there's anything you hate?"

"Chinese food!" Chloe's face twisted. "Horrible stuff!"

"Anything but Chinese," Aaron agreed. "I like it, but someone here doesn't care for it."

Luz shrugged off Chloe's drama, and smiled at her. "Scram, kid. It's my turn to surprise y'all."

Aaron looked like he wanted to try one more time to get her to go with them, but she shook him off and walked with them to the door.

Aaron settled Chloe in the middle seat in her booster, and walked around to open his own door. Suddenly he stopped and leaned across the hood. "Don't you need my address?" he called.

She laughed. "Aaron Estes, this is Rose Creek! I knew your address the day you rented that place from the Thompsons! Go home!"

Inside, she checked that the newly named Princess had food and water. The dog seemed fine, and she could go out the kitchen door if she needed to. Then Luz called the diner, which featured barbecue every Saturday night. She placed her order, throwing in a couple of their hot dogs just in case Chloe felt about barbecue the way she apparently felt about Chinese food.

Humming, she went to take a shower. It wasn't until she was in the stall, letting the hot water pound the day's activity away that she remembered Aaron and Chloe walking in to find Ross Thurmond sitting in her living room. Staring at her mother's picture.

Chapter Eight

Chloe and Aaron liked barbecue. Watching them eat amused her. They truly must have been starving, from the amount both put away. She ate a respectable amount herself, but the idea was not to stuff herself and be unable to think coherently. She hoped that Chloe would decide on an early night, but the six-year-old dragged her into her bedroom to show off her collection of stuffed animals and action figures.

Luz supposed the action figures fit right into the hate-princesses attitude Chloe professed, even if the dainty peach walls and prim white furniture didn't. These were women from games and movies, apparently, warrior women with fashion doll figures but alarming weapons and sleek, tight-fitting, and strange outfits. She fingered one of the two or three she recognized. Catwoman. She and Lily had looked at one, once, in a toy store, when the little girl was five. Lily, however, had returned the hard plastic figurine to its place and asked for a baby doll instead.

They went back to the living room, where Chloe plopped down on the floor and began coloring a book full of animal pictures.

Aaron smiled and patted the couch. "Come sit a spell," he offered.

"You do not say things like that," Luz noted, arching an eyebrow at him. "You're just not Texan—not southern—enough."

"I resent that," he protested, stretching. She didn't think he was doing it on purpose, muscles stretching against taut fabric like that, but her throat went a little dry anyway. She sat down, not at the farthest end, and decided to watch Chloe color—a much safer pastime than watching Aaron do anything. *Four years. Has it really been four years?*

She shifted a little, uncomfortable with the sheer, physical need slowly simmering through her, making it difficult to think of anything but his profile. The lips, tilting up slightly at the corners. And the muscles, stretching again as he leaned forward to retrieve the remote and change the channel.

She thought she'd stifled her sigh until he turned his curious eyes on her. "You okay?"

She managed a smile. "Fine. Just…achy."

"You put in a full day," he said easily, and abruptly lifted his arm to cover a yawn. "Guess we all did."

Chloe rolled over and sat up. "Not me," she declared. "I'm not even a teeny tiny bit tired." Almost before she finished speaking, though, she yawned and dropped back to the floor.

"Time for bed," Aaron announced firmly, standing and smiling at Luz. "She doesn't know her own limits, sometimes."

Luz wanted to side with Chloe, if for no other reason than to put off being alone with the little girl's father for a little while longer. But Chloe looked tired, and Luz needed…she needed to talk to Aaron Estes. All those other needs clamoring for her attention—she'd beaten them back before. She could ignore those dimples and muscles and that occasional sideways smile and focus on the problem: he was Esmeralda Salinas's man.

So instead of defending Chloe's pout and mumbled protest, she just smiled. "There'll be other days, Chloe. Good night."

Chloe heaved an exaggerated sigh and pushed herself up. For a moment, Luz thought she might come over for a goodnight kiss, the way Lily always had. Pain bit into her, and she felt guilty but relieved when Chloe murmured "good night" and left.

"I'll be back in a minute or two. You don't have to go yet, right?"

"No, I'll stay, Aaron. For a few minutes."

He followed his daughter out of the room, and Luz stood and walked around the room, massaging the base of her neck. She hadn't done anything unusually hard today, so it was annoying that her whole body ached. Or burned.

As she turned to go back and sit down, she bumped the end table she hadn't even noticed, and glanced down. School papers covered the surface: a math worksheet, a journal entry with a sticker, a letter announcing a school-wide rally for the upcoming statewide assessments—signed by the school counselor. Esmeralda Salinas.

The burning went away. The aching eased. She'd never suspected the existence of the other woman, when she'd been a naive wife clinging to her social-climbing husband and loving his little girl as if she'd been her own. She wouldn't walk into a relationship with a man who was spoken for. Grimly, she decided against sitting at all, picked up her bag, and drew out the keys. Then she propped herself against the counter that separated the kitchen and dining areas, and waited.

Aaron came through the door almost immediately, humming a snatch of a lullaby he must have been singing to his daughter.

"That 'I'm not tired girl' is down and out," he announced, then noticed her pose and purse and stopped, lifting his eyebrows.

"I thought you were planning on staying a while."

She shrugged. "It's time for me to go."

He didn't say anything, just stood there, watching her, then walked toward her. She watched him come, wondering exactly what he thought he was doing.

But he didn't really do anything, just stopped inches away from her.

"I got the distinct impression when you came here you wanted to talk," he said after a minute, slowly, as if giving her a chance to deny it. "That you were waiting for Chloe to leave the room."

Busted.

Almost as if he heard her thought, or saw the admission in her face, he reached out, brushed a strand of hair off her cheek, then caught the strap of her bag and slid it off her shoulder.

"So, stay? A little longer?" He waved a hand at the kitchen table then nodded towards the living room and couch. "Dessert and something to drink, or we can go sit on the couch."

Or they could just stand here while she told him once and for all to quit asking her to dinner. Quit including her in Chloe's plans as if she were more family than friend. *Quit making me want you.*

Maybe just standing here wasn't a good idea. Her legs might buckle and leave her sprawled on the floor. He'd reach down to help her up, the way he had when she'd fallen out of her bed. Naked.

He leaned in and peered at her face. For a minute, his breath brushed her cheek. Then he drew back and grinned. The dimples flashed.

"Private fantasies, Luz? I'm open to suggestions."

She pushed past him, going back to the living room, knowing he'd follow her. Then she turned to confront him. "You need to quit, Aaron!"

Genuine confusion flickered across his face. "Quit? Quit what?"

"Asking me to dinner. Flirting."

"Why?"

"Because I won't let Esme worry about my intentions, that's why! I think the world of Chloe and I like you just fine, but it's—it's business, okay?"

Aaron just stared at her for a moment. Then he laughed. Laughed!

"Just what is so funny?" she sputtered indignantly.

"Business, Luz? You won't even let me pay for Chloe's riding, and you bring me food, and you claim I was flirting, and suddenly—we have a business relationship?" He chuckled again, his eyes sparkling with his amusement.

"Quit giggling!" she muttered.

"So, first I flirt and now I giggle—" He shook his head. "Just cruel, Luz. Give a man a little credit!"

Luz glared at him a minute longer, then shrugged. "Okay. I've said what I needed to, anyway."

"No. You really didn't say anything. Not anything that made sense." He reached out and caught her hand. "Look, come sit down. You might be able to run around rings and feed animals and people all day, but I get worn out just watching."

She frowned, but he didn't notice, so she sat down and watched as he disappeared into the kitchen, clinking around for a minute or two, and then came back with two bowls of ice cream.

"Here."

"Aaron—"

"Add it to my bill when you run the totals for this business relationship," he teased, and waved at her with a spoon of ice cream. "Eat your ice cream."

Luz didn't argue; the chocolate almond mound in the bowl, already melting around the edges, looked heavenly. She finished before he did, and went to rinse her bowl out. She stood for a moment at the sink, staring out into the darkness. She couldn't remember the last time she'd had actual human companionship this late, and loneliness seldom bothered her. But sharing ice cream with Aaron didn't bother her much, either. Annoyed at herself, she stalked back to the couch. Aaron finished and set his bowl aside, then locked his hands behind his head.

"So, you were saying?"

"Aaron, Esmeralda—"

"Is Chloe's counselor, Luz. That's all."

"No. You date. We ran into each other."

When Luz didn't sit back down, he stood, too, bringing him closer. She wished he'd stayed there, farther away.

"That wasn't a date, exactly." He held up a hand. "She invited me to dinner to talk about Chloe, and—she said—to find out if there were any behaviors she needed to deal with." He rubbed a hand across his neck and flexed his shoulders. "She didn't exactly follow through on that end." He hesitated. "Luz, from what little I know about you, I know your marriage ended because some ass of a man cheated on you. I've got no reason to lie to you—I'm not that big a jerk. Esme might have decided to turn it into a date, but she and I aren't involved." He paused, as if thinking back to their encounter at the diner, and grinned a little. "In fact, I asked her if you could join us. She didn't much like that idea!"

Luz laughed. "That I believe! But it doesn't matter, Aaron. She's decided that you're hers. And I learned the hard way—I don't fight over men." He started to say something, but she held up a hand, stopping him. "Aaron, even if you don't think you're interested in Esme—I just don't need the hassle of someone coming after me out of jealousy or—or whatever. Chloe can ride. You can come over when she does. But other than that—"

"But what if that's not enough, Luz?" Aaron reached out again, this time catching both her hands, his eyes intent. "What if we want more?"

For a crazy moment, she wanted to close the distance to him, press her lips to his, and let him know that she did want more. But then the sound of the clock ticking loudly penetrated. In her bedroom, Chloe coughed softly, and Aaron tilted his head, listening.

Luz gently pulled away. "I'll go as far as friends," she said. "But that's all." She retrieved her purse and headed for the door, then paused, as one of Esmeralda's barbs came back to her. "Esme says you're interviewing the two of us," she told him.

"Interviewing you?" He sounded puzzled. "For?"

"The position of Chloe's mother."

He didn't say anything for a minute. Then he moved toward the door and opened it. "If I were, would you be interested?" he asked.

She hadn't expected the blunt question, and when she said nothing, he shrugged and watched her walk through the door. "Just for the record—seems to me that would be an honor, not an insult. Goodnight, Luz."

She almost turned to tell him she wouldn't be insulted, but the door closed. Slowly she walked down the steps to her old truck. Alone, and noticing it.

• • •

Luz straightened up and leaned on the shovel for a moment. Her hands were full of blisters, and she could only be thankful her mother and father had decent soil, not as rocky or hard as it could have been. Wetness trickled down her cheek, and she swiped a hand over it. Sweat; the tears had come and gone quickly, stolen away by burning anger.

The mound of dirt in front of her covered the savaged remains of a dog that had been discarded along her fence line. The dog clearly had been killed in a fight, and she'd bet money it hadn't been a street fight, but one of those clandestine monstrosities held in some secretive place, in front of a crowd of drunk, cheering bastards. She couldn't think of a stronger word, or one that could express her contempt.

She threw the shovel aside. She'd called the sheriff's office when she'd seen the dog's lifeless body near her mailbox. A deputy had come out, made notes, and said he suspected someone from San Antonio or its outskirts was merely using isolated patches of road to dispose of evidence. He'd been polite, but dismissive. He didn't think it was happening here, and he'd keep an eye out, but he doubted she'd have a problem again.

She fished in her pocket remembering she actually had tucked a handkerchief in this morning and dried her face more thoroughly, ignoring the salt sting of her perspiration on her palms, then picked up the shovel and headed back to the barn. She'd turned the ponies out, since no one came on weekdays to ride anyway, and Rumbles nickered her unique greeting.

"Do you miss Chloe, girl?" she asked. She couldn't help wondering what had happened. Surely Aaron wasn't so thin-skinned that he'd decided not to let her come again, could he? But Chloe hadn't been out all week, and Aaron hadn't called.

Hadn't she told him she didn't want a relationship? Maybe Esmeralda had cornered him. She toyed with buying feed a day or two before she needed it, because if there were gossip, she'd hear it within minutes of going anywhere in town. She cast that idea aside as she put up the shovel, and leaned down to run gentle fingers over the kitten with no name.

Her phone went off, sending the kitten fleeing in a frantic escape, and she laughed and fished it out, clicking it on and checking the number.

"Hello, Eden Acres."

There was a long pause before a voice spoke. "Hi, baby. How have you been?"

Brian? The phone fell into the straw on the barn floor.

"Baby? Luz?"

Her heart slamming her chest, she reached down, picked up the phone, disconnected the call, and blocked the number.

•••

"So, you think there's dog fighting around here?" Ann leaned against the counter, considering Luz's concerns. She smiled at a departing customer who was holding her Chihuahua close as she left. The little dog climbed up on its owner's shoulder and barked a final time at Luz. The one dog in town, Luz decided, that actively disliked her.

"I think so," she answered, turning back to face her friend. "First someone left Princess for dead. Then that poor dog this morning. It wasn't even a pit bull! Must not have had a chance in the world. And there were others, but not as near my property. That worries me, too, Ann," she admitted. "Why are they suddenly along my fence line where I have to find them, when before they just turned up randomly?"

"And you called the sheriff?"

"The deputy came. Doesn't think it's local."

Ann tapped a pencil on the countertop, glanced out at the empty parking lot, and sighed. "Looks like I don't have anyone trying to beat the clock. Wanna get the blinds, Luz?" She put a folder away. "You know, I think the deputy's probably right, because in this town—I don't think even something as sick as dog fights could stay secret."

"I guess. What happened to Teri?"

"Poor kid was stressing out over a test this afternoon. I told her to stay home and study."

"Think she'll hang on and make it?"

"She'd better!" Ann grinned. "I'll need help one of these days."

Luz nodded agreement. "You could have used it yesterday, I imagine."

"Ram's talking babies again," she admitted. "He's always busy and so am I, but…"

"But?"

"I want kids, Luz. Job, craziness, I don't care."

"You'll be a great mom, Ann." Luz paused a minute, smiling at the image of a baby Dr. Ann. "Bet your first born is a girl and she's doctoring as soon as she walks."

"Lord help us," Ann retorted, but smiling. "Changing the subject—have you thought any more about finding out what you'd have to do to start a formal shelter? Folks already just discard animals on your place. If you're really not going back to teaching—"

"Haven't checked into it yet, but I will."

"Well, I have a proposition. Since you board horses and all."

"A proposition?"

"Let me set up a holding pen with a stall on your property. I have trouble when I need to remove a horse from a property—can't really treat them here in the back. I'll pay rent, and you'll have a little more income. Win win."

"Except that I'd have to deal with sick, mistreated animals, which is a bummer."

"You already do," Ann pointed out. "No sympathy from me, but if you don't want to—"

"Tell me what you need and be sure we don't need building permits."

"Knew you'd help me!" Ann came around the counter and gave Luz an enthusiastic hug. "Now, since Aaron's back—"

"Back?"

"Where have you been? You didn't know he'd gone back to Alabaster?"

"No."

Ann shook her head. "Nose in your own business—what kind of a freak are you?" She laughed. "Not sure you belong in Rose Creek, woman. You're not nosy enough."

"So, he and Chloe weren't here—"

"He left Chloe with Mrs. Baker. Didn't want to interrupt her schooling, Mrs. Baker told me. I know she'll be happy he's back."

"Yes, she'll be delighted," Luz said as she pocketed the receipt Ann had given her and pulled the door open.

"You're probably happy, too, huh?"

"Bye, Ann!"

She heard her friend laugh as the lock clicked behind her and she frowned. The vet could be downright annoying when she tried. But more than annoyance, she realized, she felt relief that Aaron apparently hadn't been avoiding her after all. And Chloe might come to ride, maybe even in a couple of hours. Smiling, she hurried to the truck to finish her chores and get back home.

• • •

Aaron looked around the living room critically, thinking how Spartan the decor was. The trip to Alabaster had been painful, but he'd signed the papers, and the house he and Stella had owned was gone. Not the memories, though. He shouldn't have expected them to be.

He glanced at his watch. "Almost ready, Chloe?"

His daughter popped out of her room in her boots, jeans, and the sweater he'd brought her. "Ready!" she answered, and before he could ask she said, "Yes, my homework is done."

He smiled and handed her a baseball cap. "You look so grown up."

"I'm still only six," she pointed out, and grabbed his hand to tug him impatiently toward the door. "Be seven soon, though. I'm getting old already, right?"

She had no clue about his turmoil, the doubts he still had about whether Rose Creek was a vibrant enough environment to raise a child in. The lack of adornment in this house could be fixed. Or he could look for a different house. And he supposed the trappings weren't all that important in the long run.

A beautiful house hadn't kept his marriage alive—or Stella, or an innocent five-year-old.

"Daddy, what's wrong?" Chloe had stopped to peer into his face, and her own happiness seemed to fade in front of him. That he wouldn't allow.

He laughed and scooped her up, then sprinted toward the SUV. "Nothing's wrong!" he said in her ear. "I'm just old and slow."

She hugged him fiercely. "Don't ever be old and slow," she pleaded.

He kissed her head and loaded her into the car, regretting his comeback. He only hoped she'd see him grow old and slow. Breathing a prayer as he went around to get into his own seat, he knew old and slow had become a luxury in their lives.

Chapter Nine

Might as well be in high school. Luz propped herself against the barn wall and waited while Chloe saddled Rumbles, but her eyes never left Aaron, standing across the corridor kidding Chloe about being too tall to ride a pony any longer.

"Guess we'll just have to go home," he told her, heaving a pretend sigh.

And while father and daughter joked, Luz just kept thinking, over and over, that Aaron looked good.

She kicked the sand with the toe of a boot. The man hadn't been here in what, five days? She hadn't really expected him to look any different, had she?

Aaron stepped up to tug on the girth, then gave Chloe a thumbs up and nodded. "Guess you can go on out," he told her. "But if you race off—"

Chloe sniffed. "Everyone knows you have to warm your horse up first."

"That sorry thing's a horse?" he teased, and they both laughed when Rumbles snorted.

"Better quit talking bad about her," Chloe warned, and then led her toward the door, leaving Aaron and Luz alone.

Luz's smile slipped. She wasn't ready to face this man alone.

He smiled and closed the distance between them. "I'm surprised to hear myself say it, but I'm glad to be back in Rose Creek."

"I'm surprised to hear you say it, too," she admitted. "Thought you might be planning on taking Chloe back home."

"There is no back home. Not anymore." Strain tightened his face, but he wiped it away with a hand. "You look good, Luz. Chloe and I missed you."

She shrugged. "Can't say I did. I didn't even know you'd gone until you were back."

"I had to leave quickly to tie up some business there. I'm not really sure why I didn't call you, except that it was late when I found out—"

"And you were angry at me because I asked if you were interviewing," she interjected, not wanting to leave it unresolved.

"Angry is too strong a word." He thought for a moment before finishing. "Hurt. Hurt is a better word." He paused briefly, considering. "You were wrong, though. When—if—I have a real relationship again, yes, that woman would have to be able to love Chloe. But I'm not interviewing. And if I were…"

He reached out and grasped her shoulders, easing her to him. "I'd be interviewing for a lover, not a mother for my daughter." His lips brushed hers.

Her breath caught, and she reached up to clasp his face, leaning toward him, into him. He urged her closer, his desire raging as fiercely as hers, his breath growing as ragged as hers as the kiss deepened.

"Uh—oh!"

The voice behind them ended in an embarrassed cough, and Luz turned to find Ross Thurmond standing in the corridor, holding his ball cap in one hand and a bag in the other.

Aaron turned too, but unlike Luz, he didn't turn beet red and flounder for words.

"What the hell are you doing here, Thurmond? This is private property."

"For your information, *Estes*, Miss Luz and her momma always had an open house here for folks with business, and I got business. Not funny business, either." Thurmond leered, and Aaron's hand curled into a fist.

Luz stepped away from both men, not really wanting to be the subject of a schoolyard fight between two apparently stupid men, neither of whom had a claim on her.

"What brought you here, Ross?"

He held up the bag. "Dr. Ann sent you some samples from a feed company she had no use for. I was coming out this way anyway, and she asked me to drop it off." He surrendered the bag to her and glowered at Aaron. "I never expected…well, you know."

"Come to the house and let me give you a glass of tea and gas money," Luz offered, ignoring the "well, you know."

"No need making Ross walk up to the house," Aaron protested, reaching for his wallet. "Let me give you the gas money. Anyway, Luz and I need to get outside with Chloe."

Ross seldom took the money Luz offered, but although he looked furious, he reached over and took the twenty Aaron held out.

Luz gasped unintentionally as she noticed Ross's hand. "What in the world bit you?"

Ross glanced emotionlessly at his hand. "Dog," he said shortly. "Over at Crawford's ranch—don't know why he thinks those big dogs are good for anything."

Luz barely knew the Crawfords, but remembered that Ann claimed to have fallen in love with the bull mastiffs that protected their flock of angora goats from coyotes—and apparently from Ross Thurmond.

"Didn't know y'all were…busy, or I would have honked," Ross added, shuffling his feet.

Luz managed a smile. "Thanks for bringing this out. I'll call Ann and let her know I got them. If you're sure you don't want something to drink—"

Aaron's forced smile turned down at the corners.

Luz wanted to smack them both. Why was Ross acting like he was jealous? He had no interest in her, and she wouldn't allow herself to dwell on what his feelings toward her mother had been.

And Aaron—yes, he'd kissed her. Caught her close, so close that she could still feel the hard wall of his body, so close that her skin still burned and remembering made her breath catch, keeping her from speaking. Yes, he'd kissed her, and she'd wanted so much more. The thought flooded her with new longing. But if Ross hadn't walked in at just that moment, Chloe might have. Cheeks burning, Luz turned away from them both. How stupid could one woman be? How could she have risked Chloe being the one to interrupt?

"Dr. Ann wanted me to tell you something else," Ross said.

Reluctantly, she stopped and looked over her shoulder. "Yes, Ross?"

"Said to tell you Hermie Clark bought a horse."

The words were innocent enough that Aaron looked puzzled. He hadn't been around the last time the warped loner bought a horse. She thought of Chloe, and of her father's fears for her, and breathed a prayer that Ross wouldn't say anything else.

"Thanks for letting me know," she answered dismissively, and the handyman tugged at his hat in a gesture more routine than respectful.

"Be seein' y'all."

"Uh huh." She made herself walk out the barn door with him, and watched until he climbed in his truck and drove away.

"What the hell just happened?" Aaron came up beside her, after glancing to where Rumbles and Chloe were trotting over the logs in the arena that probably looked like real jumps to the child and pony.

Frustrated and a little bewildered, she buried both hands in her hair and massaged her scalp, sending her hair into absolute disarray. She'd done that occasionally when she taught, as a stress reliever, and because first graders howled with amusement when she warned them she might pull her hair out if they didn't settle down.

"Need help?" he asked softly, and pushed her hands away to rub his own through her hair, his fingers easing away tensions—and igniting sparks all over again.

She stepped away. "I'm fine. Anyway, Chloe—"

"Has no idea we're here." He sighed, though, and dropped his hands, trailing them down the sides of her neck and moving away. "Let's go lean on the fence and watch my girl ride."

She followed without comment, smiling a little at how naturally he hoisted a foot to the bottom rail and stretched his arms along the top, moving them until he found the perfect position.

He might have the makings of a country boy after all.

"What's funny?" he asked.

She mimicked his position on the rail and just grinned again. "Nothing."

From the ring, Chloe waved, and they waved back.

"So…"

Aaron's tone made her teeth clench.

"Yes?"

"Does Ann tell you every time someone in Rose Creek buys a horse, or was that some weird kind of code or—"

She blew out her breath and wondered if she sounded like one of the horses. The idea amused her, and she laughed.

"You're just strange," he muttered, without condemnation. "So what's the joke?"

"Don't worry. I'm making fun of myself." Her laughter faded, though, as she realized they were standing like Ross Thurmond's horses, one foot up, butts stuck out…she didn't want to think about Ross Thurmond. She also didn't want to tell Aaron why Ann had sent her word about Hermie Clark. He'd probably snatch Chloe from the pony and head out of town.

Then again, she really didn't want to lie to the man. She thought of Brian's unexpected attempt to contact her, and of flinging her phone away in contempt and loathing. His lies had destroyed her life. She wouldn't do that to someone else.

"It's a long, ugly story, and it probably doesn't mean anything," she explained reluctantly, moving away from the fence and lowering her voice to be sure Chloe couldn't hear. "And Hermie Clark's just someone I ran into when I first moved back here."

"Ran into?" Aaron looked serious and, she thought, apprehensive. Maybe her tone had conveyed something of the anger and horror she still felt when she thought about Hermie Clark. "As in a car accident, or…?"

She shook her head and drew in a deep breath, turning to face him squarely. "Things were difficult for me. I decided to go out riding to clear my head and I got sort of lost."

"Sort of? Lost in this one street town?" His apprehension seemed to be turning into full-blown confusion. Or skepticism.

"Yes, in this town. There are a lot of little side roads leading onto, through, and around ranches and pieces of property, Aaron. Even those flat pastures you see have some arroyos, stands of trees, and outbuildings on deer leases. I didn't want to ride along the highway, and I got lost—but I didn't know I was lost."

"So—what happened? You ran into this Hermie person?"

She still had trouble when she thought about the scene she'd stumbled across. She'd met Ann that day, as a matter of fact.

"I came up on a fence line—sagging, obviously not well cared for. There was a rundown house and an old livestock pen." Her fingers knotted against her legs. "He was there—Hermie Clark."

Images flashed back. The horse on the ground was screaming in agony and fear. Dying. Dr. Ann Cottwell, stoic, unflappable, collapsed against the fence in tears, beating her fist on the ground. And Hermie Clark holding a chain saw and whip and laughing like the maniac he was.

"He butchered a horse—cut it up with a chain saw." She blinked frantically, trying to stop the tears that always threatened when she remembered. "While it was still alive." A few tears escaped and she brushed them away. "My horse panicked and threw me—he ran home, and thankfully got there safely. Ann was there—I met her that day. She drove me home."

Aaron looked away, at Chloe who had gotten off Rumbles and was braiding her mane. Then he looked up at the sky, which was going dark, and, finally, back at her. "And now he has another horse? Didn't anyone do anything?"

"He got a few days for slugging Ann when she tried to stop him. Animal cruelty penalties were nothing back then. He argued that he couldn't feed himself and he'd bought it for meat. He got a slap on the wrist. Ann found out later he'd done it before, in Laredo."

"Lord!" He swallowed hard, apparently visualizing the scene in his own mind. "And you think he'd do it again?"

"We don't have a TV station here, but he'd called the photographer at the local paper and told her she should be there. She was in San Antonio and called Ann, who came out to try and stop him. But there's no doubt he did it to attract attention."

"Sick bastard," Aaron muttered.

"Ann almost lost her husband over it. He was furious she'd risked her life stepping in, and he left her for a while. He loves her, and I guess that was why he freaked out and then why he didn't want her out of his sight when he decided to quit being a jerk."

"You know, a lot of men would prefer their wives not endanger themselves that way if they don't have to and can't stop what's happening any way."

She started to defend Ann, but remembered abruptly that this man's wife had risked her life daily. And died defending others. Did he resent her courage? Maybe he hadn't really accepted her work?

"I didn't mean to offend you or insult Ann's husband," Luz said. "That's when Ann and I got to know each other, and I just know she was pretty torn up over what happened and feeling that her husband wasn't there for her."

He nodded. "I can see why she might be," he agreed, then pulled out his cell phone and glanced at the time.

"Chloe!" he called, "We're going to have to go. Start saying goodbye to your friend!"

Luz smiled as Chloe made a face and buried her face in the pony's neck, hugging her as if they'd be parted forever.

"Ann and Ram want a baby," she announced, without conscious thought.

Oops.

"Although I'm not sure I should have said that."

He laughed. "You're becoming a true Rose Creek resident again. Don't worry—I won't tell, and I knew anyway."

"You knew?" That surprised her.

"Sure. Ram has come by the house a couple of times—when Ann has something come up unexpectedly or is watching her *novela*, we visit. He knows Chloe and mentioned they really want children."

Luz smiled. "They'd be such good parents. They love each other."

"Yeah." He said it absently, though, already turning to Chloe as she came out of the ring, her well-groomed little pony in tow.

"Why do we always have to go?" She pouted. She looked up at Luz. "Couldn't we have a sleepover?"

"Well—"

"Dad can sleep on your couch." She had it all worked out. "I have a sleeping bag. I can bring it, and Princess and I can sleep in Rumbles' stall."

A sleepover? Luz and Aaron exchanged glances, but Luz waited for him to shoot the idea down.

"Well…" he said.

"That means we can, right?" Chloe dropped Rumbles' reins and threw her arms around her father. "Thank you!"

"Chloe, I didn't say we could—"

"You always say yes right after you say 'weelll'!"

Aaron freed himself and knelt down to Chloe's height. "Not always, young lady! And anyway, tomorrow's a school day. It's only Thursday."

"You don't ever read my teacher's notes. Tomorrow there's no school because all the teachers have to go to some kind of service—"

"In-service?" Luz asked helpfully. "A training, right?"

"Yeah, for some tests or something. But the kids don't have to go."

"How convenient," Aaron murmured, but his eyes twinkled as he stood up again. "So, Luz…how do you feel about a sleepover?"

Chapter Ten

How did she feel? Her mouth went dry. Heat curled through her. Her legs turned liquid.

"A sleepover?" she eventually managed to repeat. "Here?"

"Well, we can't have it at home," Chloe pointed out matter-of-factly. "Then I couldn't sleep in Rumbles' stall. And Luz might not like sleeping on our couch. Or—Dad!" Her voice was full of excitement. "You have a sleeping bag, right? If Luz has one, you and Luz can sleep in the stall with me! We can have a real slumber party!"

The kid isn't helping. Luz waited for Aaron to explain why you didn't hold sleepovers in pony's stalls. Maybe especially why the two of them were not spending the night anywhere near each other. Sleeping bags were confining, but probably not nearly hard enough to escape.

"Chloe, you really can't ask me," Aaron said. "You have to ask Luz. It's her house, after all."

Four green eyes waited expectantly. She was trapped. And they knew it, darn them both!

"Sure," she said, eventually. "But you can't sleep in Rumbles' stall. You'll have to share the living room floor with your dad—unless he wants to give you the couch."

"Okay," Chloe agreed, with only a little reluctance. "But where will you sleep?"

She directed her smile at Chloe, but her words at Aaron. "In my room." *With the door locked.*

"Well, then." Aaron looked pleased, not uncomfortable. Then again, he'd only been alone for a year. And he'd loved the wife who'd died a hero. She shuffled, the aching need surging through her making her uncomfortable. She'd been divorced for four years—but she'd been alone almost since she vowed to love and honor Brian for a lifetime. Funny how empty words could be.

"Luz, if you'd rather not—"

Was the man psychic? Or had her smile slipped into her more habitual frown? She forced the lips to turn up again, not wanting to hurt Chloe.

"Tonight's as good as any for a sleepover." And that, at least, was true.

"Let's go get sleeping stuff. Anything special you need in the way of food?"

"Aaron, I could cook—"

"Nonsense. We're not inviting ourselves over *and* making you work. Pizza?"

Chloe hopped up and down. "Pizza! Pizza!"

Luz laughed. "I'd been going to ask for Chinese, but I guess that would be cruel."

"Yes, it would be! As bad as Cruella de Vil. As bad as a wicked stepmother—" Chloe was already halfway to the door, citing examples of horrible people as she went, unaware that behind her, her father and Luz were exchanging looks of dismay and discomfort.

Luz waved him after her. "Go get your gear," she admonished. "I'm going to do a final check for scorpions and poisonous spiders."

Chloe and Aaron stopped at the door and spun around.

"Scorpions?"

"Dad, she's teasing," Chloe told him, after seeing Luz's smile. "Right?"

"Right." Luz didn't mention that there really were scorpions throughout the state, and that occasionally she'd found one in the yard—and once in the kitchen. But the exterminators had been out a week or two ago, and maybe the unwelcome critters wouldn't put in an appearance any time soon.

She did look around the living room anyway, and even the kitchen. Princess snorted and nosed her for attention. A sleepover! Grown-ups didn't have innocent sleepovers. But with Chloe there, luckily, she should be able to stay in her room and think pure thoughts. *Right*. Well, the part about staying in her room, at least, would be easy. Out of sight, out of mind.

She thought back to Aaron's unexpected kiss in the barn. He'd sure seemed interested in something more than a platonic friendship. But he'd lost his wife so recently. Did he just want sex? Just a quick roll in the hay? She laughed out loud, startling Princess.

Aaron Estes might be getting better around livestock and other critters, but she couldn't see him enjoying doing anything much with hay poking and pricking him. She glanced at her watch and decided she probably had ten or fifteen minutes. She could shower in a hurry, eat with them, and excuse herself in short order.

Minutes later, with the comforting pounding of the water on hard and hot, she heard Princess bark suddenly and unexpectedly. The dog almost never barked; the only time she'd even growled was when…

Her heart thudded hard.

When Ross Thurmond had invited himself in.

And— dammit! —she'd still forgotten to put a new lock on the door! Suddenly, she felt alone and insecure, a feeling she hadn't had since the first days of her divorce in Atlanta. The feeling of helplessness she'd suddenly developed there had been part of why she'd come home. There had always been safety here.

With a silent prayer that Princess was barking at dust bunnies or a deer wandering into the flowerbeds, she finished showering in record time, and dressed just as quickly. Appearance be hanged, she thought, as she made a trip around the small house, checking windows and peering outside.

Princess trusted her to defend them apparently, lying down as soon as Luz came into the kitchen. Nothing seemed to be amiss, and the security light outside lit most of the path to the barn and much of the yard. She decided nothing could be gained by going outside, especially since if she decided to, she'd probably take her mother's pistol as a precaution.

Aaron was okay with his daughter riding now, and he even had forgiven the secret animals, as far as she knew. But seeing her running around in the dark with a pistol might make him nervous all over again. Smiling a little, she took a frozen pie out of the freezer to thaw for dessert and hummed as she tossed a salad.

Half an hour later, she decided they'd changed their minds—or that Aaron had. Maybe he'd reconsidered the wisdom of them being in the same house, late at night, once Chloe fell asleep. Frowning, she plopped down on the couch, across from the painting.

Like a Horse Saddled. Patience. She'd always liked it well enough, and thought her mom had cherished it. But now, doubt stirred. Even given the fact that Ross didn't paint professionally, western art would sell in tourist towns, maybe even San Antonio. So he could have made a tidy sum for the painting, and while she couldn't say that he didn't have money, he drove one of the oldest trucks in town and almost always dressed in the same, faded work clothes. He must have had no family, because if he had had anyone, she would have known. Everyone knew everyone here.

Why had he given her mother anything, let alone something that might be worth a fair chunk of money? Her mother and father had married in their teens; there'd been no others clouding the picture, so he couldn't have considered her a love interest.

Could he?

The sound of tires crunching up the gravel drive broke her train of thought, and Princess lifted her head, listened, and flopped over to sleep. Clearly Chloe and Aaron were back.

The door burst open and Chloe clattered in with an armload of stuff, which she dropped in the middle of the room, almost tripping her dad.

"I can't believe we're doing something fun!" she crowed. "Besides riding Rumbles," she amended, and ran across the room to hug Luz impulsively.

Aaron frowned. "Something fun," he muttered. "Movies, museums, malls—all the 'm' words, and I'm no fun?"

Chloe released Luz and ran to give him a hug. "You're the best," she assured him. "If you let me stay home from school, just think of all the fun stuff we could do!"

Aaron made two more trips to the SUV before he announced that they were ready to eat. And she'd thought he'd overdone the first day of riding?

He caught her amused glance at the huge pile of belongings taking up a good portion of the living room and grinned.

"Just the essentials," he said. "Besides—Chloe packed most of it."

"Can we eat in here by the television? The kitchen isn't as fun."

"Eating isn't supposed to be fun," Aaron protested. "It's something we do because—"

"Because if we don't, we die," Chloe explained matter-of-factly, as she put three paper plates on the coffee table. Which kind do you want?" she asked Chloe.

"Whichever you think is the ickiest. That way, you'll have enough."

Chloe laughed. "I can't eat that much! And Dad didn't get the icky ones with onion and green pepper." She slanted a look toward the grown-ups. "Do you wish he had, Luz?"

"Nah, pepperoni and sausage are fine. Besides—I made salad."

Chloe looked less than thrilled, but didn't say anything, concentrating on choosing the biggest slices and piling them on her dad's plate.

Suddenly she stopped short, dropping the last piece of pizza she'd chosen. "Oh, no!"

"What? What's wrong?"

While Aaron moved toward his daughter, Luz checked covertly for any rogue scorpions or spiders. But she didn't see any.

"I forgot to wash my hands!"

"That's it?" Luz asked in disbelief.

"Germs! I gave you all germs!"

"Bet we'll live," Aaron retorted.

Chloe was already rushing to the kitchen to wash her hands, but Luz saw the apprehension come and go in Aaron's eyes, and heard his soft curse.

"Will I ever quit being afraid of those damn words?" he asked. She knew the ones he meant. Life. Death. Live. Die. The prospect of an evening together changed from torture to the idea that at the very least, she could comfort. Be a buffer between this fragmented family and the world that had hurt them so.

And if Chloe's hug and her teasing reminded Luz of Lily, and of all that she had lost herself, well…she'd been dealing with her pain longer than they had. She put her hand on his arm and squeezed. "She didn't seem to notice. Maybe they'll just be words again if you can let them."

"Yeah." He covered her hand with his. "Thanks."

Chloe came in then, shaking her hands dry.

"I had towels and paper towels in the kitchen," Luz said.

"Sorry. I was in a hurry. Anyway, drying your hands in the air is better."

"Where did you hear that?" Luz asked, not wanting to avoid conversations with the child, but hoping it wasn't something her mother told her.

"Well, it has to be," she said. "Otherwise, why would they have those air dryers in the restrooms everywhere? Well, not at school, but everywhere good." She dropped to the floor and began eating.

"Floors are more fun," Luz said.

Chloe giggled as Luz got down to coffee table level.

"Floors are more fun?" Aaron asked, managing to maneuver his legs into a space under the table without bumping anything or sending pizza flying. At first Luz thought he was humoring Chloe, but then he added, "That explains a lot. But I still wonder why you wouldn't let me help you off the floor that day." He shifted, and his leg pressed hers intimately.

Maybe he didn't need a buffer at all. But she certainly did.

•••

"Luz, are you awake?"

Luz propped herself up and peered into the relative darkness. She'd left the bathroom light on, and it provided a slight glow to keep Chloe from falling over anything if she needed to get up during the night. Aaron was also half-sitting and looking her way.

Things hadn't gone as planned. Chloe insisted that in a sleepover, everyone had to sleep in the same room. At least she hadn't demanded that everyone sleep in the same bed. The three or four feet that separated the three of them from each other was already too close. Knowing how near Aaron was, hearing him breathe and move in the night had been slow torture, and sleep hadn't come.

"Midnight snack?" he whispered, managing to clamber to his feet without stepping on Chloe or hitting his shins on the table, which they'd moved to one side.

He leaned over, and even in the dark, she could see the quick gleam of his teeth as he smiled and reached his hand out to her.

This time, though, knowing she was fully clothed, she let him help her up, and they tiptoed to the kitchen like teenagers escaping watchful parents.

The irony wasn't lost on Luz. "We're hiding from a six-year-old! I feel silly and a little embarrassed!"

He chuckled. "Me, too."

"So I guess you got a lot of practice sneaking away from your parents to see some girl?" she asked lightly, pulling out the salad and left over pizza. "You did want food?" she asked, remembering how much the three of them had eaten while they watched videos and played games that Chloe invented as they went.

"Not really," he admitted, and stretched a little, then rubbed an arm. "I'm getting old, or else that bag is. I don't remember floors being that hard."

"Right?" She bit back a comment about the part of her that felt bruised. He might decide to be helpful and massage her hip. "So, no answer on sneaking out of the house?"

Some of the humor faded from his face, and he seemed to be thinking back. Finally he shook his head. "Not really," he answered. "I didn't live with my parents, and my aunt hadn't ever married. She didn't pay much attention to what I did or didn't do."

That surprised her. He clearly doted on his daughter; and in her experience, here in Rose Creek, at school in Atlanta—everywhere—parents who loved their children like that had been loved by their own parents.

They settled into chairs and she poked at the salad she'd served herself. "You lost your parents?"

His laugh grated. "No. They just had—have—other priorities. They traveled my entire life. Foreign service, low-level diplomats. Then they emigrated to Europe. They've lived in England, France, and Germany. They work for a travel company now."

"But they didn't take you with them?"

"No. I spent a few weeks a year with them when I was young. Occasionally they'd come stateside. But they love each other, and they're happy." He swallowed a piece of pepperoni he'd picked off the pizza. "And my aunt loved me. But she treated me more or less like a grown-up all my life. I never had to sneak anywhere—I just told her hello and goodbye when we crossed paths."

They sat in silence for a bit, not really eating, but not talking. Luz glanced at the clock on the stove. Almost three, which surprised her. She hadn't noticed the time flying by. Eventually, though, when he said nothing else, she had to ask.

"Aaron, what about Chloe? They've met her?"

He pushed his plate aside and stood up, pushing his hands into the pockets of his shorts. "No."

"I'm sorry I asked. I—"

He forced a smile. "I'm not angry that you asked. Anyone would. Chloe has."

"But—"

"They've called. They sent us a present when she was born. They bought some beautiful baby clothes. And they sent her some savings bonds. But they said they didn't know when they'd get home. I haven't seen them since we buried my aunt four years ago."

There really weren't any words, so Luz just sat silently. How much pain did one family deserve? First, the empty childhood, the unloving parents—now grandparents—and then the loss of the woman who loved him. Chloe's loss of her mother. She drew in her breath and bit into her lip to keep from showing her anger for him. And her hurt.

"You know what makes it even worse?" he asked.

She didn't want to hear that it could be worse. But if he'd been hesitant to talk before, now he seemed to need to. He gripped one of his hands with the other, as if trying to keep them from forming fists, from pounding the walls enclosing them.

"Stella's parents disowned her when we married. It used to make me crazy, thinking she had to choose between them and me. But somewhere along the road, I decided they'd given up on her before she and I even started dating."

Luz thought of her parents, the memories so warm and her confidence in their love so absolute that they still seemed to be with her at times. She thought of Lily, and how sharp her pain over losing her still was. How did parents shove a child away, and why? She moved a little, not wanting to say the wrong thing. "That's so hard for me to understand," she admitted finally, and gave him a small grin. "I mean, as disagreeable as you are, I wouldn't disown anyone over you."

He chuckled, a forced laugh acknowledging her efforts to be supportive. "You probably would if you knew me better." The momentary levity fled. "I found out after we were married that she'd gotten into some fairly embarrassing situations her first year at college, before I met her. Her folks have money and smoothed some things over, but…" He paused again. "It wasn't criminal, but there were behaviors that just shocked her parents and their friends. They're very conservative, and—well, I think when she married me and announced she was going into law enforcement, they just glommed on to that as an excuse to cut her off. They've never met Chloe and said they never would. Even after her death, they didn't come for the funeral. Not to see their little girl buried. Not even to meet my baby girl who looks…looks so much like her mom."

His voice was raw with emotion, and she thought she saw moisture in his eyes before he turned away.

She wanted to get up, to go to him and wrap her arms around him. But she wasn't sure that she should. He'd think she couldn't understand, that she'd never had a baby, never suffered the pain and the fury of having someone hurt a child who meant everything.

He didn't know she'd had a child, if not a baby. Her mother and father had known Lily the day after Brian had married her. They'd bragged about their granddaughter and carried her photo with them and loved her with everything in them. How could he believe the depth of her compassion, the unwelcome memories that sprang to her own mind? Maybe—maybe now she could talk to him about Lily. Make him understand why she wasn't ready to be a mother of any child that wasn't truly her own—

She stood slowly and pushed her chair under the table with a knee, a reflex action from her years of being sure the classroom traffic lanes were clear. Her mother had claimed that if she saw a chair out of place during her own wedding, she'd stop and push it in before she walked down the aisle.

Behind them, there was a flurry of motion, followed by Princess's low growl. Then the dog lunged for the door, barking as she had earlier. She was out the door before either of them could react, running in the direction of the road, her barking frenzied and full of fury.

Luz headed after her.

Aaron caught her before she got to the door.

"Where are you going?" he demanded. "It's late and it's dark—"

"And something's wrong!" she snapped. "Stay here with Chloe! I'm just checking for anything that might have set the dog off." She bit back "again."

As she rushed outside, she couldn't help wishing she'd had the dog on a leash—and her mother's pistol in her hand.

She went around the side of the house, tripping once on a rock hidden in the shadow the house cast since the security light was on the other side. In the front yard, she stopped and peered out toward the road, where she could make out the shape of a dark car moving slowly along the fence line.

"What's going on?" Aaron said from close by. "And don't tell me to stay with Chloe, dammit! She's asleep, and I'm not some panicked little kid afraid of the dark, even if it's stupid to be out here—"

Tires screeched and taillights glowed as the car suddenly accelerated and sped away.

Not Ross Thurmond's truck. The thought surprised her. Worried her. How had his brief, strange, visits here unnerved her like this? And then sudden suspicion hit her. Hard.

"God, no." She thought she hadn't spoken, but Aaron's hand on her arm and the alarm in his face told her she had.

"God, no, what?"

She thought of Chloe in bed asleep. Of Princess—where? At least she hadn't heard yelping. But the pit bull hadn't come back, either. Would Aaron leave when she told him? She really didn't consider him a coward. He'd obviously gone through a lot without cracking. He just couldn't bear to lose his precious daughter. She understood that.

"What, Luz?"

She covered her face with her hands, and breathed a silent prayer that she was wrong. "I think," she told him slowly, "that tomorrow we'll find another dead dog."

Chapter Eleven

The sheriff himself came out, huddling with the deputy who had come before, and talking briefly to Ann before coming over to talk to them.

"We don't know what to think," he admitted, shoving his hat up a little. "Doesn't make sense that they'd choose this site every time. There were those other cases, and they were all scattered. There's lots of highway with no one at all alongside. Folks go to bed early, don't watch 'cause there's never anything to see. This really bothers me, that suddenly they're all here."

"What you're saying, Sheriff, is that this is deliberate?" Luz tried to keep her voice from shaking with the rage gripping her. "That someone has decided not to dump live animals here for me to shelter, but these–these–"

She couldn't go on. The tortured body of the pit bull had shocked all of them. To his credit, after telling Chloe to stay in the house and finish her breakfast, Aaron never left the gruesome scene, hadn't left her alone. In fact, he'd even dug a hole to bury the animal. Luz knew how hard she'd worked, and wondered if his hands were more blistered than hers had been.

Damn whoever it was! She couldn't believe the inhumanity of people sometimes. But for someone in Rose Creek to be participating in this butchery left her speechless.

The sheriff looked around. "I don't know why anyone would do this to you, Luz," he said. "Maybe someone's just too stupid or lazy to look further down the road?"

"No." Ann had joined them, and she frowned at the sheriff. "Everyone knew she'd take in any living thing that needed a home. Someone's mocking her, leaving these…carcasses here. And I know you don't think so, but these dogs aren't being brought in from

San Antonio or even Hondo or Devine." She rattled off the names of towns in the general vicinity, discarding them all. "Someone here in Rose Creek, or maybe right outside it, is holding dog fights here, and not even hiding it, to send some sick message to Luz."

"Sure," the sheriff agreed. "Although if I was you—I'd let Doc Ann take the body and dispose of it. Maybe someone knows that you and Luz go to all the trouble of burying them."

Luz shivered, chilled by the thought. Had someone watched her bury the other dog? Seen her tears as she shoveled the dirt over the mutilated body? Who in the world would want her to suffer? Briefly she thought of Brian's unexpected call, but dismissed it. He was in Atlanta, and he'd been cruel in totally different ways. The ambitious son of an important Georgia political dynasty wouldn't be caught dead around dogfights. Brian Chambers hadn't wanted her enough to be faithful, or to fight Lily's mom for his own daughter. He wouldn't stalk her now.

Who, then? She could only think of Ross Thurmond. He'd been bitten by a dog. What if it hadn't happened the way he'd said? She could check his story. But he didn't make much more sense than Brian. What possible motive could he have for wanting to hurt her? She'd spent much of her adult life away from Rose Creek. He'd been friendly and polite, at least until Aaron moved into town. She closed her eyes and wished she'd gotten some sleep.

"Who are you looking at, Sheriff?" Aaron demanded, anger and lack of sleep hardening his voice and surprising all of them. "Seems to me it's pretty obvious."

"What the hell are you talking about, Estes?" The sheriff shoved his hands into his pockets and rocked on his heels, and the deputy, who had turned toward the patrol car, stopped and listened.

"Clark! Hermie Clark!" Aaron almost spat the words out. "What kind of a sick creep is he? Ann sent word to Luz about him buying a horse, so obviously she thinks he's a danger—"

"No." The sheriff, deputy, and Ann all spoke at once.

"Look, Estes," the sheriff explained, "you're new here, and I guess someone as crazy as old Hermie seems logical, but he isn't. He can't drive, and doesn't own a car, and I doubt there's a soul around he can call a friend. 'Sides, he only has these…fits…every so often. Always horses, far as anyone knows, and he always calls news media first."

"The sheriff's right," Ann agreed. "Don't know if it's true, but I've heard he's scared of dogs—no one's ever seen him with a living thing out there, except—" She and Luz exchanged glances and she swallowed before she finished. "Horses. The first one, and the one he just bought."

Aaron looked off into the distance, before sighing and turning his attention back to the small group. "Thurmond, then," he suggested. "Ross Thurmond."

"Now you're just crazy," the deputy scoffed. "Ross does what he can to help anyone and never complains about all the folks who ignore him or make little of him. Man doesn't have a soul to call family, but the whole town calls him a friend."

No one argued with the deputy, but no one agreed with him either.

"Can I bury the dog now?" Aaron asked. "I need to get back to my girl." He glanced at the house.

"Sure, you go on," the sheriff urged. "Take care, now."

Aaron nodded curtly and went to shovel dirt back into the nearby grave.

Luz watched him, wishing she could replay the happy hours of the sleepover and avoid the whole sordid ordeal they faced now. No point in putting off the rest of the day, though. She opened her eyes and thanked the sheriff and deputy.

"Come have coffee," she told Ann, who looked like she didn't want to stay, but nodded and followed her.

"We can't talk, though," Luz reminded her. "Chloe—"

"I know," Ann interrupted. "I'm not a dummy."

"Never said you were," Luz retorted, as they clattered up onto the porch.

"Guess I need to start practicing tact, anyhow," Ann said, behind her.

Ann's words didn't register until Luz opened the screen door. She let it swing shut with a soft bang, and whirled around.

"You're—"

"Yes! Yes!" Tears of joy were rolling down Ann's always-emotionless face. With an answering "yes!" Luz clasped her in a huge hug.

Suddenly, the day looked just fine.

Chapter Twelve

Ann's news did make the morning brighter. Teasing her about what a fast worker she was and hearing her excitement eased the pain and anxiety over who was targeting her property and why.

After Ann left, vowing not to let anything get to her and to not overexert herself, Luz and Chloe headed down to the stable to feed the animals and get Chloe where she wanted to be—in her pony's saddle.

Aaron stayed behind to shower away the dirt, sweat, and lack of sleep his overnight stay had generated. Not thinking about him in her shower was easy enough, because she'd seen the tightness and concern in his face. And who could blame him? What was happening wasn't normal. But could it actually be dangerous? When she ran over the list of people in Rose Creek again, she couldn't think of anyone capable of doing what was being done. No one. Could it be an outsider, then?

She couldn't bite back a loud sigh as she watched Chloe feeding the guinea hens.

The little girl turned curious eyes on her. "Luz, what's wrong? I know something's wrong. Dad only makes up stuff for me to do when he's worried about me seeing something bad."

"I think all grown-ups do that around kids," Luz acknowledged, not wanting to provide details. She didn't know what Aaron would want her to say. Better to wait for him. Still, she gave Chloe a smile, and then walked over to add a comforting hug before going back to be sure Candy hadn't driven the cats off to nose their food, although he seldom ate the cat chow.

Her hesitation to tell Chloe anything else irked her. She had an early childhood degree. She had minored in child psychology, but had decided not to pursue a counseling degree. After just a few years in the classroom, she didn't think she could handle the issues counselors dealt with. But for the moment, she could distract the little girl until her dad came.

"Chloe, do you think you can brush Pompom and Rumbles? That would help me a lot."

Chloe's face lit up. "Sure. Even Esmeralda's horse if you want," she offered.

"No, not yet. If one of the big guys stepped on you they'd squish you," she teased.

Chloe laughed and hurried off to begin her chore. "I'll do Pompom first. Since Rumbles is kind of mine, it would be rude if I did her first."

"Very true."

Luz picked up a comb, brush, and hoof pick and went over to bring the Appaloosa out of her stall. The mare was a beauty, with blood bay forequarters that almost matched her owner's hair. Her white blanket was spattered with bay and black spots, and she had black stockings to go with her black mane and tail. Probably the best horse in town, in terms of bloodlines, conformation, and looks. But her name!

"You're looking grim," Aaron murmured, coming up behind her. She started, dropping the comb, and he bent to pick it up. Startled or just annoyed, Domatrix lifted a hoof and aimed it in Aaron's direction.

Without thinking, Luz grabbed his shirt by the collar and jerked him back and toward her, out of the hoof's reach.

Aaron wound up on his backside, glaring up at her until he noticed Domatrix calmly planting her hoof back on the barn floor.

"Oh." He frowned. "Dangerous around here, isn't it? I'm not sure what's worse—her wanting to kick me or you saving me. You almost took my head off!"

"Better me than her," Luz retorted, smiling wickedly and holding her hand out. "Let me help you up, city boy."

Aaron carefully scooted a few inches away from the mare's hooves. Then he caught Luz's hand. "I don't think so!" With a quick pull, he toppled Luz into the sand with him.

Behind them, Chloe burst out laughing. "Like the wrestling! Pin him, Luz!" she crowed, leaving the pony she'd finished grooming to edge closer.

"Whose side are you on?" Aaron grunted at Chloe as Luz elbowed him without meaning to, trying to move farther away from the appaloosa, but collapsed back in a heap when she couldn't stop laughing.

"Better watch out," she taunted. "Bet I could take you."

His eyebrows lifted slightly. Laughter faded from his face.

Her breath caught in her throat.

Unaware of the heat building between them, Chloe clapped her hands. "Come on! I'll referee—"

Luz fished for an answer.

"Well! I thought it was strange no one looked out the door to see who was here," Esmeralda said from a few feet away. "But I see you all were too busy—what, body slamming each other?"

Contempt and insinuation hardened her words, and Luz stiffened. Beside her, Aaron sat up straighter and looked at Esmeralda without embarrassment or welcome.

"Good morning, Esmeralda." He stood, then held out a hand to Luz as if nothing were unusual about sprawling in the sand with his daughter's…what?

She didn't know what she was to Aaron, and though he belittled her apprehensions, the counselor's demeanor and sarcasm clearly said she expected to be Aaron's woman and didn't think much of Luz's attempts.

Her face colored more by anger than embarrassment, she let Aaron pull her up, but when she would have stepped away, his hand still holding hers kept her from doing so.

"Luz and Daddy were wrestling," Chloe offered helpfully.

God bless innocence. Because I don't think that's what we were doing.

"Luz was winning," Chloe added.

Esmeralda gave the girl a false smile and stepped over to pet her mare's neck. Domatrix turned and nuzzled her shoulder. Esmeralda ignored the greeting, and looked back at Luz. "How nice for you," she muttered.

"I assume the tack room is open?" she asked.

"I never lock it," Luz answered, irritated a little by the question. Was the woman trying to get her away from Aaron? And hadn't she promised not to get into this kind of situation, trying to thwart someone else's interest in a man?

"Do you know why I named her Domatrix?" Esmeralda directed the question at Aaron.

"No, and—"

Her hand slid caressingly over the glossy neck. "She says who rides her or doesn't," she almost purred. "Completely controls who rides her." She untied the horse and moved her toward the tack room, but looked back to give Aaron a wink. "Maybe you should try her sometime. I'd let you."

"Well!" Luz freed her hand and moved away, and Aaron made no move to stop her. "Think I'd better finish some stuff. And then I need to go out and see if I can find anyone who's seen Princess. I keep hoping she'll just come home."

Aaron's face had turned hard and he looked irritated more than interested in the counselor's invitation. Weren't men generally flattered by that kind of attention? Maybe she'd been wrong about not competing with Esmeralda, Luz realized. She'd thought that Aaron wasn't ready to move on, but when she'd seen him with Esmeralda, she'd changed her mind. A kissed palm and a kiss or two later, she'd given herself permission to hope. To reach out to the only man who'd interested her since her disastrous marriage and divorce.

But she'd been wrong. She should follow her own rules. She hadn't wanted to compete against Esmeralda, because through looks, persistence, and the ability to play on her horse's name, the woman would win.

Luz raked a hand through her hair. No. Esmeralda wouldn't win, either. Because Aaron Estes already had a woman he loved heart and soul. Clearly, he wasn't over his dead wife.

• • •

Aaron cursed under his breath and fought not to fling his cell phone against the far wall.

Chloe was in her room, but she might pop into the living room any minute, wanting help with her homework or just not to be alone.

She'd complained bitterly when he'd told her that they wouldn't go out to visit Luz this afternoon, claiming that he didn't love her. Always the drama queen, she'd thrown in that Rumbles would forget her and maybe even die of a broken heart. And who would help Luz look for Princess again? Luz might die of a broken heart, too. Chloe never gave in without a fight.

Unbidden, the thought came to him that she truly was her mother's child. Never giving an inch. Always taking more than she needed. Never getting enough.

The bitterness threatened to overwhelm him. The call, the worry over a little girl's need to exaggerate—he couldn't let Stella reach out from her grave and control him.

After Esme's clear invitation, Luz had withdrawn, busying herself with chores, some, he suspected, which wouldn't have been done if she hadn't needed to rebuild those walls she wanted around her. She said she wouldn't fight for him. In a macho-man kind of way, he resented that. He wanted to be worth fighting for. He snorted derisively at his own conceit. Worth fighting for?

Stella certainly hadn't thought so. And Luz hadn't indicated she'd like to be the woman in his life. There had been a couple of stolen kisses—hell, not even necessarily lip to lip—that was just play, right? Play sometimes turned to really fun play…

Desire threatened to slug him, so he forced himself not to think of Luz and games two lonely adults could play.

Instead, he stood up and looked around the room. He'd bought a new end table and lamp, and at Chloe's insistence, a framed oil painting of a horse's head hung on the wall. The half-hearted attempt to dress the house up for his daughter couldn't change the loneliness he felt. Or ease the pain.

And now, the detective had called from Alabaster. Could he answer just a few more questions? The investigation was wrapping up, but only he might have the information that they still needed to close the case. He supposed he could refuse to go. He really had no information. He didn't know why they just didn't close the case; the man who'd taken Stella's life died when the next officer arrived on the scene and took him down.

He jerked a hand violently through his hair, and then massaged his temples with his fingertips. Nothing helped ease the tension.

He had to go, though. When the investigation after the shooting revealed that Stella had been targeted, and the other victims were innocent bystanders, the rumors and the accusations had become unbearable. That was why he'd taken Chloe and fled the little town she'd always called home. How could he bear to have Chloe grow up among the whispers and the rising hatred aimed at Stella by those who were finding out what really happened? There were insinuations that he must have known something, and those seared his soul. But he could deal with everything except Chloe being hurt worse than she already had been. So he would go one last time, and try to lay ghosts to rest.

He didn't want to keep leaving Chloe, though. When he'd been traveling around in pursuit of the fortune he thought Stella wanted, leaving had been easy. "Dammit," he muttered, and walked over to retrieve his phone, hoping it still worked.

He had no choice but to call Mrs. Baker and see if she'd keep Chloe one last time. He'd make it clear to anyone in Alabaster that it was just this once. And while he was away, he'd think seriously about Luz, and just where she might fit in his damaged life.

Chapter Thirteen

Luz stared at the wall, frowning. The day that had started with such expectation had turned ugly in a hurry. Aaron and Chloe hadn't stayed long after Esmeralda turned up with her leering remarks and clear expectation of prying Aaron away.

Princess was still missing, and although Luz hadn't wanted a pit bull and didn't need a dog underfoot, she worried about her and wanted her back. She hadn't taken pictures. She should have. Ann had the dog's information in her office, but no picture. It didn't seem like posters without a picture were likely to attract attention.

And now, this. She slowly put the cell phone back on the arm of the sofa. Chloe's teacher, Joannie Baker, had called in a panic. Her mom had fallen and injured a hip. Thankfully, the hip hadn't broken, but they were admitting Mrs. Baker to the hospital to run tests and try to discover why she had suddenly had a dizzy spell that led to her injury.

Luz remembered her own mother's decline, the pain of watching an active, vibrant woman lose her shine and health, and breathed a prayer for Mrs. Baker.

She could help Joannie Baker. She didn't want to, but for heaven's sake, she'd been a first-grade teacher for five years. She could manage part of a week, even with the differences she was sure she'd encounter between Rose Creek's tiny elementary school and the large, affluent school back in Atlanta.

Chloe would be there. She didn't know how she felt about that. Chloe was bright and she sparkled, remarkably happy for the tragedy she'd suffered in her young life. Luz loved—she liked the girl a lot. But be a teacher in her class? She stood up abruptly, angry with herself.

Chloe wasn't her daughter.

She closed her eyes and drew a deep breath. She should never have had Lily in her own classroom. Lily had been an opportunity to ruin her life, in the guise of an innocent, loving little girl. And she'd stepped into the trap without the faintest concern. When Lily's mother had come into her life, she should have insisted that the principal move the child to another teacher. After all, teachers never taught their own children. But Lily's mother insisted that she wanted her daughter with Atlanta's teacher of the year.

"What conflict?" Brian's ex had demanded. "I'm her mother."

A chill shook her, and she rubbed her arms, trying to recapture some warmth. Where on earth had her brain been back then? A woman Brian had sworn would never want Lily back, a woman who had been in jail for drug use, then in rehab, stepped into her life, and she thought she could handle the situation?

Luz snorted, a sound half bitter laugh and half hysterical sob. Sometimes she'd wished that her parents hadn't loved her so absolutely, that she hadn't believed Brian's empty promises of love held the same truth as her parents' unconditional faith and support. Maybe she would have seen her world crashing down in time to avoid at least the loss of her career. She could never have saved Lily, because once Brian wound up back in his ex's bed, she had no legal claim on the child of her heart.

She knew soon after Lily entered her class that she'd been set up. Lily's mother wanted to hurt her, to destroy her, even though she'd already taken Brian back.

One morning, Lily had come into class looking sleepy and Luz thought she must have come down with a cold. She went on with the morning activities, watching Lily with growing worry. Once she had groups in their centers and noticed Lily had dozed off, she filled out a nurse's pass and went over to wake her little girl up.

She couldn't. Lily's skin wasn't feverish; she felt clammy and looked pale. Fighting a wave of panic, she'd called the nurse, who said she'd call 911, and seconds later, the principal and nurse were in her room. The nurse lifted Lily and carried her out of the room, while the principal made reassuring remarks and called a paraprofessional to keep the class so Luz could go to the nurse's office to wait for the paramedics and be with Lily.

By the time the ambulance came, Lily's mother was there, accusing Luz of trying to injure Lily out of anger over losing Brian.

Luz had never walked into another classroom, because due to the severity of the charges, she was immediately placed on administrative leave and barred from being alone with children. *Damn you, Brian.* Suddenly she wished she'd taken his call, if only to tell him to go to hell. She forced herself to take several deep breaths and work on pushing all the hurt back into the past where it belonged. He'd destroyed her once, but she was remaking herself into someone who wouldn't be hurt again. Maybe then she'd pick up the phone and call him.

Grimly, she headed to the kitchen. She'd eat and get an early night's sleep. Monday would come too soon, and there was a lot she needed to do before walking into a classroom again.

* * *

Even on Sunday, Dr. Ann Cottwell could turn out the volunteers. Luz stood aside as laughing men shook hands with each other. A couple stood apart, gulping the water and lemonade she'd brought out to help in the process.

Surprisingly, that process seemed complete. Two stalls, each with a tiny but separate paddock area, sat neatly tucked into one corner of her mom's land. A larger corral backed up against the hospital stall, and a little utility building had been adapted to house a cabinet for medical supplies and an area for small amounts of feed.

"We should probably invest in a bathroom," Ann noted, "seeing as how pretty soon I'm going to be living in them." Her husband looped an arm around her shoulder and squeezed.

"What do you think?" Ram asked Luz. "It's your land—"

"But it would keep me out of your house—"

"Like that's a selling point?" Luz laughed. "Seriously, if you all want to invest in one, go for it. What would you need?"

"You might need to get us a building permit, I can ask tomorrow."

"Okay, but don't count on me for anything until after four," Luz warned.

"Going into San Antonio?"

"I wish. Mrs. Baker's going to be in the hospital part of the week and Joannie asked me to sub."

Ann smiled. "Good for you! Just wait—you'll want your job back in no time!"

"No," Luz said slowly. "I don't think so. Sometimes, even if you loved something once, you can come to resent it just as much."

"Or someone?" Ann asked. She didn't know Brian, but Luz had told her the whole story.

Luz shrugged. "We both know that's true." She forced a smile. "Wish me luck."

"I don't think you'll need it," Ann retorted. "You act like you've been a bum for a lifetime, not just a few months."

Bum. The word bit into her soul. She'd been hardworking and ambitious. Still could be, if she wanted to. But she didn't want to. She was living off the money her parents' insurance provided, and her only needs, really, were for the animals and utility bills. She could afford a little more time off...unless she never did go back to doing anything. Could she spend her life in this limbo, not wanting more, content to trot children around on ponies and salvage animals discarded by uncaring owners? She thought briefly of the menagerie. Of Princess, gone missing and facing unknown danger again. She could find out what she'd need and do the paperwork. She could open a shelter. She'd need income, but she could seek donations. Improve her boarding facilities. Hire Aaron to manage her finances.

Her thoughts were distracted by Aaron's SUV turning unexpectedly into her drive. *How the devil did I conjure him up?*

Ann grinned and elbowed her. "Ooohh! Sunday company!"

"Wonder what he wants," Luz muttered, annoyed at Ann, Aaron, and the whole damn world.

"Well…"

"Shut up!" Luz flipped a hand in Ann's direction in farewell and headed back toward the house, not hurrying. He'd taken off because Esmeralda had embarrassed him? If she were generous, she might suppose he'd been shielding Chloe from the other woman's sly innuendo. But regardless of the reason he'd gone so quickly, he'd reinforced what she'd known all along—the man was taken. And she didn't need another fight over a man who'd wind up in another woman's bed. Not ever again.

Aaron was sitting on the porch step when she reached the house, twisting his hands slowly. She'd never seen that before, and wondered if he was apprehensive about something or if his fingers itched. Maybe he'd gotten chigger bites in the hay.

"Where's Chloe?" she asked, not even greeting him, and seeing surprise flicker across his face.

"Hi, Luz. Sorry to just drop by—"

She plopped down on the porch beside him. "Don't be. Don't know what bit me. Let's start over. Hello, Aaron. What a nice surprise." She knew the humor she was attempting probably came out tinged with sarcasm, but couldn't stop anyway. "Where is your beautiful daughter Chloe on this lovely Sunday?"

"She's right here," Chloe announced, sticking her head out the door. "I'm fixing a surprise in the kitchen."

Luz stood. "Oh, well let me help—"

"No! You'll ruin everything!" The screen door closed, followed by the door.

"My daughter locked us out."

Luz started to remind him that the door didn't lock, but she'd planned on getting it fixed and hadn't. It was one more piece of proof that she really didn't have a shred of motivation left. She sat back down beside him.

"Just so you know, I set her up." He shifted on the porch so he could lean against the post holding up the stair railing. On her side, she did the same.

"Why?"

He looked distinctly uncomfortable now. "Luz, I have a huge favor to ask." Again the brief massage of his fingers, and she wondered if he always did that and she'd just never seen him this way.

"I have to go back to Alabaster again. Two, maybe three days. Hell, if I'm lucky, I might be able to wrap it up in a day—but I haven't been lucky recently."

"And?"

"Last time I left, Mrs. Baker sat with Chloe. She's a wonderful woman but—"

"She's in the hospital for tests."

He seemed surprised. "You know?"

"This is Rose Creek. Of course I know." She drew air into her lungs to force out the admission. "Besides, her daughter Joannie couldn't find another sub, so I agreed to go."

"Wow." He fell silent for a moment, then straightened and stretched. "Everything either just got easier or harder."

Luz narrowed her eyes and frowned. "How can my subbing for a couple of days make anything different for anyone except Joannie Baker?"

"Luz, I came to ask if you'd keep Chloe until I got back." He shrugged, extending his arms. "There's no one else I know or trust, and I can't take her."

Luz gaped a little. "Me, keep Chloe? But—"

"I understand if you don't want to. But I had to ask." He started to stand, his expression one of disappointment. Or hurt.

She could understand that. She'd been wounded soul-deep whenever she thought someone had slighted Lily. Quickly, she caught his arm, keeping him there on the porch.

"Of course I can, Aaron. It'll make my scheduling a little iffy the first day—getting two of us ready to get there on time when I haven't been going anywhere that early in the day—but if the two of you don't mind—" She shrugged. "I'd be glad of the company."

He smiled, and all her warning mechanisms failed in the onslaught of his heat and light. Impulsively, he leaned across and pulled her forward, hugging her.

"You saved my life and my sanity!" he murmured, and she laughed.

"Keeping a sweet little girl for a couple of days? Sort of sounds like an exaggeration, but you're welcome." For the briefest of moments she lingered in his embrace, then gently scooted back and stood up.

"Chloe might have redecorated the kitchen by now. Can we go in yet?"

He stood, still smiling, but not quite as broadly. Worry seeped back into his expression. She could see it in the fading smile, the slight tightening of lips.

She understood that, too, though. She'd left Lily with Brian once, when she'd gotten to go to an out-of-state training in Philadelphia. Lily should have been safe with her own father. Still, she'd worried. And her worries had proved unfounded, as far as Lily's physical safety. The child had been fine. Only Luz's life had fallen apart not long after.

"If you're not sure—" They said it together, gaped at each other, and cracked up like kids.

"Grown-ups!" Chloe chided behind them. "Come in. You're ruining the surprise."

Aaron shrugged. "We've been ordered in by Grumpy Troll."

Chloe stuck a tongue out. "Don't call me that! I hate grumpy trolls!" Then she grabbed Luz's hand and tugged, excited again. "Hurry, Luz! It's just for you!"

She practically dragged Luz into the kitchen and waved at the table. Mounds of whipped cream and fresh strawberries buried a sliced pound cake, arranged artistically enough to appear in any cooking magazine. She'd even brought a couple of mint leaves along, and garnished the top with a few sprigs.

"Wow!" Luz reached out and hugged her. "Incredible, Chloe! I can't believe you did all this yourself."

"Well, Dad bought the stuff," Chloe admitted, then plopped into the nearest chair. "Let's hurry and eat so we can bring the stuff in!"

"Stuff?" Luz looked at Chloe, then glared at Aaron. "Stuff, as in—" She stopped short of accusing Aaron of assuming she'd be available. Chloe wasn't to blame for having a father who apparently expected everything and everyone to simply fall in place with a smile—or a hug. She flushed, anger curling slowly through her. She'd relished the hug, not as a reward for babysitting a girl she was fond of anyway, but as a brief, intimate moment between them. Had that been as calculated as bringing his daughter's clothes with him?

Chloe dug into her own dessert, and Luz reluctantly began eating her own mound of fruit and cake, reminding herself over and over that Aaron, not Chloe, was the villain here.

Something of her agitation must have puffed out between the bites of whipped topping, though, because Aaron straightened in his chair and looked at her, clearly puzzled, and Chloe wolfed down her own food and pushed her chair back with a clatter.

"Dad, can I go get the stuff?" she asked, her impatience transparent. "You all aren't ever going to finish!"

He considered that for a second, and then fished his keys from his pocket. "Be careful on the stairs, and shut the doors in and out." He clicked the lock to open the doors, and Chloe bolted from the kitchen.

He wouldn't have shocked her as much if he'd reached out and hit her. He'd sent Chloe out alone? To carry in who knew how many suitcases? She shoved her own chair back, but was dumbstruck to hear Chloe's feet clattering back up the porch steps and into the living room.

"You look—shocked by something," Aaron muttered. "What in the name of—"

Chloe popped into the room, beaming. Carrying a large, but not huge, box full of model horses and ponies.

"Neat, huh?" she asked, arranging them around and between the plates of dessert. "I've named them all, too." She sniffed. "You can't even think of a name for one little kitten!"

"Chloe, that sounds pretty rude."

She shrugged. "I'm just saying." Then she grinned at Luz. "Sorry. You'll think of a good name sometime."

Luz picked up one of the models and examined it, but Aaron continued watching her, frowning. Suddenly his eyebrows shot up and he pointed at her. "I know what pis—what set you off!"

Luz glared at him, but he continued anyway.

"You thought she went to get clothes! You assumed I had assumed—"

"Dad, I'm going to need clothes—"

"Chloe, Luz and I are talking—"

"No, you're all mad and so is she!" Chloe's cheer evaporated, replaced by the hard expression she'd worn so often when she first started riding.

"Chloe—"

She turned on her father in a fury, her face red with emotion. "You ruin everything! You started fighting with Mom and now that I have Luz, you're fighting with her, too! I don't want Luz gone—" She stopped, choking on anger and pain, and hurled one of the horses against the wall. "Stupid horse!" Then she fled the room, her footsteps pounding across the porch.

Aaron lurched to his feet, and Luz, too, jumped up. He headed after his daughter, but Luz looked out the kitchen window, and as she expected, saw Chloe heading toward the barn. Ann's truck had been moved from the construction site to the barn, so she and Ram were probably taking a break or visiting the animals.

She punched Ann's number.

"Hey, what did y'all do to Chloe?" Ann's voice asked immediately.

"Long story. Can you watch her? Her father and I need to have a discussion."

"Um, sure. I don't know how you talk to a crying kid."

"Practice." Luz ended the call and headed out the back door, heading Aaron off as her rounded the corner of the house.

"Chloe—"

"Is with Ann. She's fine."

"But—"

"Aaron, I don't mind keeping Chloe while you're gone. But we need to talk first."

For a minute, she thought he'd refuse, that he'd just barrel past her and race on to the barn.

Then he drew a deep breath and nodded. "We can take a few minutes." He headed back, slanting a sideways glance at Luz. "So how on earth did you cut me off like that?"

She snorted. "I outrun horses regularly when they don't want to go where they should. No city boy's beating me!"

They went in through the kitchen door, and Luz went over to fish water bottles out of the refrigerator.

Aaron took his without comment, and setting it aside, watched Luz drain hers.

"At least I wore you out," he murmured.

"Please! Walking out of the kitchen? Don't forget I spent the morning helping Ann and the gang move lumber and dig post holes!"

"I can't leave Chloe with Ann too long," Aaron said, after a moment, finally opening his bottle and drinking. Then he recapped the bottle and pushed it away with a sigh.

"First graders—children—throw tantrums sometimes," Luz pointed out gently. "And really, we weren't even arguing—were we?"

He shrugged, then pushed himself up from the table and paced around the small kitchen, stopping to look out the window.

Finally, he turned around. "It's hard, Luz. I don't want to baby her too much—to cripple her. The counselor we saw in Alabaster said we couldn't dwell on the past, but that I needed to know she wouldn't just magically put everything behind her, either."

He hesitated, and the muscles in one cheek flexed. "We had fought," he admitted softly. "The day before..." His voice trailed off, but she knew what he meant.

She stood and moved closer, wishing she could wipe Chloe's pain away—and his. "Aaron, no marriage is perfect. People disagree. But—"

He closed the distance between them and hugged her gently. "Thanks, Luz. You're a good friend."

The heat of his body pressed against her burned, but he was already loosening his hold, moving back. Putting distance between them. She bit back a sigh. *Patience*. She'd been alone since her divorce. He'd lost his wife less than two years ago. Maybe when he came back...

"I should go," he said. "Thanks for everything. I'll pack clothes for Chloe—and Luz, I want to leave emergency money—"

"Aaron, I'm not a babysitter. There's not going to be an emergency. And if you think you can't trust me to take care of Chloe, then we need to make other plans."

"But—it's just—I'd do it no matter who I left her with."

Luz shook her head firmly. "No. Keep your money. Have a safe trip. Now, let's go get your daughter."

"Luz, there's something I want you to know."

"What?"

"When I get back home, I have to call Esme. She needs to know. Maybe she'll want to see Chloe tomorrow."

The words bit into her, but she masked her annoyance carefully. "Over a temper tantrum? A misunderstood reaction to our conversation? Aaron—"

"Chloe has to come first, Luz." He sighed. "I just wanted you to understand why I was calling Esmeralda."

She stiffened, and brushed her hair away from her face. "You don't have to tell me anything about Esmeralda or anyone else, Aaron. I thought I told you before—you're not worth fighting for. No man is."

She walked to the back door, and paused to look back at him. "I'm going to see if Ann needs anything. If Esmeralda lets you bring Chloe, please have her here at a reasonable time." She went out and closed the door behind her, wishing the fury bubbling through her could take away the frustration of losing again. Because she had no doubt that sooner or later, the sexiest woman in Rose Creek would get her man.

Chapter Fourteen

She hadn't lost it. Luz discreetly slipped her heels off and wiggled her feet, massaging one with the other before sliding her shoes back on. Then she finished the water on her desk and glanced at the clock on the far side of the room. The kids would be coming back from P. E. in a few minutes, and then she'd send them on home.

They'd been a bright group, quick with answers and reasonably well behaved. She'd fed off their energy, chuckled inwardly at how predictable some of the behaviors were—the tattling, the feuds over small things, and the perpetual attempts to get away with minor infractions.

She'd been careful not to favor Chloe over the others, and Chloe, obviously well schooled by her father, never once called her by her first name instead of Ms. Wilkinson.

Esmeralda had come by, professional and courteous, and called Chloe out for a few minutes, and Luz hated the pinprick of resentment that wouldn't go away. She wasn't Chloe's mother. She tried to credit Aaron's reasoning, tried to believe that if her daughter had gone through what Chloe had, she'd overreact sometimes, too. She just couldn't make herself believe that Aaron needed to call Esmeralda over a temper tantrum.

"Luz, dear," the principal said from the door. "I know your students are almost back, but you have a visitor."

Mrs. Carter's voice vibrated with excitement or pleasure; Luz really didn't know the woman well. She pushed her feet into her shoes a little more firmly and stood, all color draining from her face as Brian stepped into the room.

"Brian! What the hell are you doing here?"

Mrs. Carter's face blanched. "You weren't expecting him? I thought…"

"He's my ex-husband, Mrs. Carter!"

"Yes, but he said you all might be getting back together. Oh, dear, I am so sorry!" Voices outside grew louder—the first graders coming back from the gym.

"You leave at once!" the principal spat at Brian. "I should have you escorted out by the security guard. Lying to get into a school—"

"Luz—"

She ignored him, stepping out into the hall. "Come on in, Miranda," she greeted the first child in line. "How was P. E., everyone?"

"Let's go, Mr. Chambers," Mrs. Carter repeated. "Right now."

Luz focused on the students, but after a minute, she heard footsteps leaving.

Thank God!

"Was that your husband?" one of the girls asked, and several of the students giggled, but most seemed to assume that it was.

"No, just some man I used to know."

"Oh, a friend."

"A friend came to see you—"

"Take your homework folders and sit down, please." She passed out the folders, recognizing most of the names, not answering any further questions.

Chloe took her folder without comment and went to sit down, quiet and unhappy. Luz wondered if she missed her dad already. He'd always traveled, though, apparently, so that seemed unlikely. Maybe she was just tired after the chaotic weekend they'd spent with sleepovers and disappearing dogs…and wrestling matches. Heck, she missed Aaron already herself.

• • •

Aaron leaned back into the softness of the couch and stretched an arm out along the back, looking at the remote lying on the coffee table in front of him. He thought about turning on the television, but decided not to. Instead, he'd grab a couple of hours of sleep, eat, and head back to Texas. Back home.

Maybe now that the Alabaster chapter seemed over, he'd be able to have a home again, to make a home for Chloe. The detective he'd spoken to most often had said their questions were all answered. No one thought now that he must have known that his wife not only cheated, but that she was the main player in a sex club. The ugliness haunted him. She'd been killed by a man who'd become infatuated with her, who decided he would no longer share her with anyone—not even the fool of a husband who didn't know he existed. The detective had shaken his hand and thanked him for all his cooperation. Then, with mild embarrassment, the man told him how sorry he was that the story turned so sordid, that the media found the story of Stella the dominatrix more engrossing than the story of the hero wife shot dead protecting school children.

Aaron was so tired. He glanced at his watch. He'd drink one glass of Scotch, nap, and then get up and go home. Chloe would love him coming home sooner than expected. He got up and poured a drink, then walked over to look out the window. Would Luz be as happy as his daughter to see him?

His phone rang, and he pulled it out and glanced at the screen. Esmeralda Salinas. His chest tightened, and he sat the drink down on the windowsill with a shaking hand as he accepted the call.

"Esmeralda, what's wrong? Is Chloe?"

"Calm down," the counselor said crisply into the phone. "I just wanted to let you know I did speak to her at school."

"How was she?"

"Fine. A little upset, but nothing major."

Relief surged through him, although he wondered why she'd called him to tell him that Chloe was fine. Maybe Luz had been right and he shouldn't have mentioned the incident at all.

"You know Luz is subbing, right?" She held a slight pause, not for an answer, but to build suspense. "I have to say, I was a little surprised about Mrs. Carter being okay with that."

"Why?" he asked.

"Well, you know, after she was charged with negligence in Atlanta and all. A lot of schools wouldn't hire her, I imagine."

"What?"

"You didn't know? Aaron, I assumed she would have mentioned—after all, that's why she's not teaching."

He couldn't think, couldn't get the questions out, so he just waited, afraid what he would find out about Luz next.

She continued after a moment. "Of course, they did clear her—well, her husband was very well-connected. Still, I have to admit they cleared her, so I guess Mrs. Carter went with that."

Again, silence, and then the knockout punch.

"It was just so strange. The little girl who almost died was her husband's. Apparently, Luz didn't want to give up the little girl when she found out her husband was cheating on her again. And then for the little girl to be drugged in class…well, I guess the kids at school are safe. She's not involved with anyone, there, right? But can you believe—her ex husband dropped by the school today. Just out of nowhere. No one at school could quit talking about why he'd suddenly just show up there."

He slumped against the wall, anger and fear pounding through him, making him unable to support himself for a minute. Again. Luz had a hidden life, full of secrets and lies, and he'd turned Chloe over to her to keep.

She'd never told him about being charged with hurting a child, never told him her teaching career had ended with a criminal investigation instead of a parent's illness. Stella hadn't told him about her damned bondage games, either. Not the same secrets, but the same exact betrayal.

He picked his drink up and gulped it down. Then he stuffed his cell phone into his pocket and decided he'd stuff everything in his suitcase and leave immediately. Go home and pick up Chloe, and to hell with Luz. And Esmeralda. Even Rose Creek.

Then he stopped and made himself take a breath. He pulled his phone out again. Esmeralda said reluctantly that Luz had been cleared. He could check on that with a few clicks on his tablet.

He glanced at the time. School was almost out for the day. He couldn't wait. His first priority was Chloe—she couldn't go home with Luz. Not until he checked into Esmeralda's information. And anyway, if Luz's ex-husband were there, would he have his daughter with him? Aaron needed to think, but couldn't. With clumsy fingers he dialed the school's number and asked to speak to the principal.

Mrs. Carter came on the line, calm and pleasant as always, and he asked her to send Chloe home with the counselor, assuring her that everything was fine, but that a personal problem made the switch necessary. She seemed hesitant, but said that she'd let both women know.

He hung up, went to the bathroom, served himself another bourbon, then sat down at the desk and turned on the tablet. His home screen showed an impending storm moving in, and he frowned. Maybe he should wait to check out the information Esme gave him and beat the cold front that would be sweeping east from Texas, making traffic a bigger headache than usual. He checked a sports score he didn't care about, the headlines and markets, and then he realized he couldn't bring himself to find out that Luz wasn't who he believed she was. He couldn't bring himself to find her a woman capable of injuring a child out of vengeance. Even if she'd been cleared, maybe…cursing at himself, he typed in her name and then added "Atlanta teacher."

The stories popped up at once. "Atlanta Teacher Accused of Drugging Stepdaughter." "Atlanta Teacher of the Year Placed on Leave."

Reading through the reports chilled him. The little girl, Lily, had almost died of an overdose of a migraine medication. Luz carried her prescription for the medicine in her purse, and while she insisted the purse had been locked in the closet, Lily's mother forged ahead with accusations that Luz had threatened Lily when Brian asked her for a divorce.

Anger directed at Luz faded as he followed the legal tangle through almost four years, and disgust at the people involved overwhelmed him. Rich-boy Brian apparently simply slunk away, not defending his wife, nor supporting his ex's claims, simply vanishing from much of the media coverage.

Ultimately, though, Aaron loathed himself far more than the cheating ex-husband or the vicious, drug-addled woman or the fair-weather friends and colleagues who seemed not to support Luz until after the case ended in her acquittal.

He'd blown it. Just flat blown it to freaking hell. Furious at himself, Aaron grabbed the plastic bottle of tea beside him and hurled it across the room, watching it bounce off the wall.

Something akin to common sense pushed into his consciousness and he fought to control the fury scorching him from the inside out.

He looked at the clock—almost six-thirty. If he called Chloe, could he bear to hear her anger? Her hurt? But even when he'd traveled constantly, he'd called her every day. He couldn't take the easy road and not call.

Chloe wouldn't answer the phone. Esmeralda would.

He wanted to grab the bottle of bourbon and empty it. He'd already drunk more than he had since his aunt's death, though, and he wanted to make the long drive back from Alabaster early. Try to get there soon enough to retrieve his daughter from Esmeralda's manipulative hands. He jumped to his feet and walked around the room, kicking the couch once before reminding himself that he didn't need to get himself arrested for throwing a temper tantrum.

He couldn't blame Chloe's temper on Stella alone, it seemed.

God, he hated being used. He'd let Stella use him, and the result had been to come within inches of losing his little girl. The counselor had used him, and he'd just rolled over and let her. Fallen for her tricks again.

He could hear the smugness now; the same cattiness the counselor had used to insult Luz's taste in men—and the imaginary boyfriend. Why hadn't he heard it when she first called? What did it say that he'd been so quick to believe Luz might pose a threat to Chloe? He tried to remind himself that Brian had turned up in her life again, but knew he was grasping at very flimsy straws. Suddenly, he had new understanding of why Luz struggled to believe that Esmeralda meant nothing to him. A carefully constructed piece of gossip and he'd been swamped with jealousy. But he hadn't realized his own doubts until they'd completely destroyed every step forward he thought he'd taken by reaching out to Luz. By trusting her with Chloe. Luz wouldn't forgive him. He searched for a lie, a reason why he'd had Chloe removed from her care. Nothing came to mind, and he wouldn't use it if it did. She deserved better than what he'd given her, dammit, even if he'd been too stupid to see that in time. He walked back over and sank down on the couch.

"Atlanta Teacher Cleared of Wrongdoing." The story still on the screen taunted him.

The picture under the headline was Luz, flanked by her parents—he knew them from the pictures at her house. She had her mother's smile and there were tears in her eyes as the three walked down court stairs surrounded by a press of people. Those were happy tears, though. Was she crying now, crying for Chloe? Over his betrayal?

He almost wished remorse hadn't hit him so quickly and so hard. Maybe he should have waited until he drove back to look up the news stories. Then he wouldn't feel so worthless. How could he have listened to Esmeralda's carefully chosen words and been such an ass?

He drew in a deep breath, feeling pain go clear through. Then he reached for the phone to call his daughter, but as he dialed the number, he didn't see Chloe's stricken face, but Luz's.

• • •

Mrs. Carter reappeared at the door, her face full of worry. "Miss Wilkinson," she said formally, "may I speak to you outside please?"

Luz followed her into the hall, surprised by the principal's sudden change of tone. The woman sounded somber, not supportive as she had when she'd booted Brian out of the room. A chill shivered down her spine. Not again. The thought was insane, she'd done nothing wrong. But she hadn't done anything wrong before, either, and she'd spent years and a small fortune proving it.

"I've had a call from Chloe's father," she whispered.

Luz's heart thudded. Had something happened to him? The stab of fear she felt surprised her—he shouldn't mean that much to her.

"He's fine, but..." Surprisingly, Mrs. Carter fidgeted and colored slightly, obviously uncomfortable with what was coming.

"Ms. Salinas will be taking Chloe home with her and keeping her until he returns. She's been counseling Chloe, you know, and well—he just wanted me to let you know."

The shock of seeing Brian was nothing compared to the dagger thrust into her by Mrs. Carter's words. She clenched her hands into fists, dug her nails into her palms, and waited for the roar of blood through her head to subside and the dizziness to stop.

Again. Dammit, again.

But why? He couldn't have changed his mind after he talked to her last night. The three of them ate ice cream while Aaron presented lists of rules and phone numbers, and joked about being over protective. He'd left Chloe at her house around eight and everything was fine.

She forced herself to remain impassive, an employee listening to her boss give orders. Tried to force herself not to remember Chloe's shy goodnight kiss, and how she'd gone to the bedroom door three times to lean on the doorjamb and smile in at the little girl sleeping in her own old room.

Last night she'd relished the feeling of having a child staying over again. Last night, Aaron had trusted her with that child, and she'd relished the feeling of him trusting her that much, too. But all that warmth, the feelings of renewed purpose—that had been last night, apparently. What had happened today?

For a minute, she tried to find an excuse, a reason. Some new problem turned up in Alabaster, and he'd wanted to be sure Chloe would be okay, psychologically. But that didn't make sense. She pushed the futile effort aside. Better simply not to think.

"Ms. Wilkinson—Luz—are you okay?" Concern replaced the hardness in the principal's face.

Luz smiled and nodded. "Of course, Mrs. Carter. Thanks for letting me know."

She stood in the hall and watched the woman walk away, discarding every flimsy excuse she'd tried to conjure up. No. I will not cling to false hopes. I will not believe lies and truth are all the same—I did that before. And I lost Lily.

The first graders were lifting their chairs up on top of their desks. The unholy racket slowly penetrated, and she turned back to them with a huge fake smile. "Time to go, I guess? You all are a wonderful class."

Someone— Miranda? —asked if she'd be back tomorrow. She said she would, but the circumstances of being hit with such dire news brought back unwelcome memories of Atlanta. She'd been escorted out of her room without explanation, after the paramedics had taken Lily away. Only later had the significance of what had happened been driven home.

She nodded anyway. "Yes, unless Ms. Baker's mom is well enough that Ms. Baker can be here." Another forced smile. "I know she must miss all of you."

She led the procession down the hall to the gym, and turned them over to the security personnel who released them. Chloe walked with the line, but ran up to her, green eyes joyful. "We can go now, right, Lu—Ms. Wilkinson?"

She took Chloe's hand and gave it a gentle squeeze. "Let's walk back to the room."

On the way, Chloe babbled excitedly, but when Luz didn't respond, she seemed to realize something was wrong. When Luz opened the door for her, Chloe barely walked into the room before she spun around to ask questions.

"Luz, what's wrong? You aren't saying anything! I know I'm not supposed to talk in the hall, but—"

"Ssssh." Luz drew a chair over to her desk. "Sit with me."

Chloe sank into the chair, and worry darkening her eyes. Luz's eyes stung, but she blinked once and drew a deep breath. Chloe would be upset enough.

"Your dad called Mrs. Carter." She hesitated, but couldn't think of any way to explain, so she just said it. "Ms. Salinas is taking you home instead of me. I guess she'll go pick up everything after school."

"What—no. No!" Chloe pounded the chair with her small, clenched hand. "You said I could stay! Why don't you want—"

Tears streamed down her face, and she choked on sobs.

"Sweetheart, I want you to stay. But for some reason, your father thought that Ms. Salinas would have a better place for you." Helpless in the face of Chloe's tears, she tried to think of something to offer the girl. Nothing came. "Maybe he was afraid we'd stay up all night visiting or riding."

Chloe jumped up. "I'm not going! Call my dad! I want to talk to my dad!"

"Your dad will talk to you tonight, Chloe." Esmeralda stepped into the room. For a brief moment, Luz could swear she looked embarrassed. Sorry. For what?

But she knew, didn't she? Any chance of pretending this wasn't what it looked like fled. Esmeralda Salinas had convinced Aaron that she was the better woman to leave Chloe with—the better woman, period.

"Chloe, let's take you home. Mr. Thompson is letting me into your house to pick up enough for just tonight—your dad will be home tomorrow. And he'll call in a bit to say hello to you."

She nodded at Luz. "Good afternoon, Ms. Wilkinson."

"Luz, I don't want to go."

Luz walked over and wiped her hands across the girl's cheeks, drying her tears, then reached for the tissue box on the edge of her desk. "Here."

After Chloe took a handful of tissue, Luz wrapped her arms around Chloe's shoulders and hugged her. "Talk to you later," she murmured, and drew away.

"Come on, Chloe. Let's go get your stuff and some food," the counselor said, and escorted her out of the room.

Luz closed the door and sank into the swivel chair behind the desk. She propped her elbows on the desk and covered her face. But she'd be damned if she cried.

Emotional and physical exhaustion threatened to overwhelm her, and unwilling to risk falling asleep and cause more speculation—undoubtedly everyone at the school at least knew about Brian's visit—she straightened and fished in the drawer for her purse.

Behind her, someone tapped on the door. Half afraid to turn and find Brian again, she almost gasped when Ross Thurmond stepped into the room, tipping his ball cap.

"Hi, Lu—Ms. Wilkinson." He gave her his mirthless smile. "I heard you were teaching today for Ms. Baker. Bet you're glad to be back with little ones, after leaving your job to care for your momma and all."

She stood, managing her own joyless smile, relieved that he didn't know how her teaching career had ended. Did Esmeralda? She shook off her vague unease.

"I'm surprised to see you here," she admitted.

"Oh, I work for the school off and on. They got their own, of course, but you know how it is—some things can't wait for the maintenance guys from the main office to come. The big kids busted some faucets clean off the sinks, and they needed help pronto. Already fixed them."

"Great." She took a tentative step toward the door, but the handyman moved with her.

The school district employed him. There were cameras in the hall, and she'd known him, sort of, for years. She forced herself not to sidle a little farther away.

"Miss Luz, can I talk to you? You know, 'fore we get to the front and all those custodians and everyone listens in."

"Well—"

He stopped, and she watched as he pulled the worn cap off completely.

"Just wanted to say, I figgered out that my showing up at your place, like when I went into your house and all—well, I just always did that when your mom was there. She'd have been hurt if I'd waited for her to ask me in. Your dad, too, but of course he was gone sooner." He paused, worrying the hat. "Sorry. Don't mean to make you feel bad. Just wanted you to know—I didn't mean nothin'. Just what I was used to."

She reached out and touched his arm. "Thanks, Ross. Living in a big city kind of changes our habits, I guess." She felt relieved, in a way, that he'd stopped her. She'd let memories and Aaron's apprehensions blind her to a man everyone in town thought eccentric but honest.

"Well, good afternoon. Be seein' you around," Ross finished, and ambled off toward the exit.

People in the office called goodbye as she signed out and left. Luckily, no one asked her about Brian. Or Aaron. But she realized as she got into the truck, she didn't want to go home. She'd have to—the animals needed feeding—but she couldn't face the unexpected feeling of aloneness just yet. So she headed to Ann's office, glad it was just a couple of blocks away.

Ann didn't have anyone in the waiting room, and her assistant Teri looked up from a textbook and smiled.

"Hi, Luz. You look dressed up today!"

"Subbed at the elementary school. How's your semester going?"

"Good." She smiled. "I might even finish sometime."

"Is Ann—"

"Come on back," Ann called from her office.

The vet looked pale and irritated, but she immediately focused a sharp gaze on Luz.

"What's wrong?" she demanded.

"Hit me if I cry?"

"That bad?" Ann wiped a hand across her forehead and gulped air. "Okay. You hit me if I puke."

"Morning sickness?"

"Yeah, but mine lasts twenty-four hours a day."

"Like your job." Luz hoisted herself onto the stool that she knew Ann once preferred, and tried to pretend nothing was wrong.

Ann shifted in her chair and reached for the glass of water on her desk. "Used to be this time of day Ram and I would have a beer," she grumbled. "Now I'll be drinking this crap 'til the baby comes."

"That 'crap' is called water," Luz reminded her. "You've been on my case since you met me because I don't drink enough."

"Yeah, whatever. So what's up? Missing Aaron already?"

"Aaron!" She practically spat his name out.

"I see," Ann muttered. "Come on over to the house, Luz." I can drink crap and hate you while you guzzle wine."

"Almost wish I could." Luz sighed. "But I'm not a bum anymore, remember?" She looked around the tiny space and slid off the stool. "Let's go."

Chapter Fifteen

Luz wasn't sure how she got through the next day. Chloe came, silent and withdrawn, answering politely but robotically. Then there was the chaos of fire drills and lockdowns, and lunch in the room because of a state test, but she could cope automatically with the regular craziness. She couldn't deal with seeing Esmeralda up and down the halls, or the thought that when the final bell rang, she'd go home again. Alone.

But this time, at least, she knew it was coming. And there wouldn't be another time. Chloe wasn't to blame in any of this, and if her father wanted to drop her off again to ride, that would be fine. But there wouldn't be any more dinners. Or hugs.

Or sleepovers. Even if they were nothing more than sleepovers to please a little girl who'd lost a lot.

On her way out, Mrs. Carter stopped her. "Luz, Joannie's coming back tomorrow. Her mother's doing fine now."

"I'm so glad," Luz replied sincerely. "Her class misses her."

"Thanks for stepping in—I'd have been in a bind without you."

"No problem."

The principal seemed reluctant to let her escape though, walking with her to the door after she signed out.

"I'm real sorry about letting your ex-husband in. He just sounded so lonely, like he really thought y'all were getting back together—"

"It doesn't matter."

"Well, if I ever need a teacher—" She cocked her head, considering. "Would you consider teaching again? Here?"

Would you fire Esmeralda Salinas for me? She shook her head gently. "I don't think so, Mrs. Carter. I just don't think it's my calling anymore."

"Well, keep us in mind if you change your mind," Mrs. Carter insisted, and Luz nodded and stepped out, surprised to find that wind was beginning to sweep in from the north and dust eddied around the parking lot.

She hadn't watched the weather last night. She'd stayed late visiting Ann and her husband, gone home to feed the animals, and fallen asleep.

Tonight she doubted she'd be so lucky. She didn't have to wake up at the break of dawn. She'd probably be up late tonight, making sure the animals were secure, and taking all of Chloe's things out of her room, where'd she stored them, and putting them by the door.

On the short drive home, the weather worsened. Clouds started moving in, and rain started to pelt the windshield as the temperature plummeted.

She thought briefly of Chloe, hoping the weather wouldn't scare her. Then she set her anger aside for a moment and breathed a prayer for the little girl's father, who would be driving into the oncoming front.

You can wish someone safe travel without forgiving him, right?

She changed while the wind and rain ratcheted up their clamor, knowing she still had to go out and tend to the menagerie and the horses and ponies. On her way through the kitchen, she glanced again at the corner Princess had preferred, praying that the dog had been adopted, and afraid that she hadn't.

Grimly, she went out into the storm.

Chapter Sixteen

Luz huddled in a corner of the couch wrapped in a blanket, balancing a laptop on her lap while she tried to determine what state government she could contact to find out about starting an animal shelter. The time in the corner of her screen glared at her—almost two A.M.

But then again—she wasn't subbing and didn't have to get up at some ridiculous hour. The rattling off the window meant ice pellets, not rain. Again she thought of Chloe, and worried about Aaron.

A glare of lights pierced the window suddenly, making her blink and drop the laptop. Luckily it fell over her knees on the couch side; she could ill afford it hitting the floor. By the time she got untangled from the blanket and padded warily to the door, she heard footsteps and a muttered curse on the porch. It was Aaron, probably slipping on the slick wood.

She pulled the door open just as he reached for it, and he almost fell headfirst into the room. It would have served him right, but she didn't say so; she just stood staring at him, wishing she were more angry than relieved.

"Finally got here," he said, by way of greeting. He looked exhausted, and she didn't have to ask to figure out the drive had been torture.

"When I left Alabaster, the weather was sunny and warm," he added. "Then I hit Texas."

She pushed the door shut and forced any sympathy out of her voice. "Why are you here? It can't be to pick up Chloe."

The barb stung; she saw it in his eyes, in the shoulders that sagged a little more.

To his credit, though, he didn't answer the taunt, just closed his eyes briefly and breathed deeply.

"You have to know why I'm here, Luz," he answered after a minute. "I was an ass—again. You don't have to listen at this time of day, but I didn't want to wake Chloe up and take her home, because there might not be school today. And I needed to talk to you before I talked to anyone else."

He brushed at his hair, and she was surprised to note a slight tremor, as if he just had no strength left.

"Sit down, Aaron," she invited stiffly, but he rolled his shoulders, stretched his arms, and shook his head.

"I've been sitting for hours. But—I'll be right back." He headed down the hall. He probably hadn't stopped except when he had to. That could be uncomfortable—she remembered drives back from Atlanta when Brian had been waiting impatiently at one end and her parents at the other.

She should give him something hot to drink. She didn't keep coffee or tea, since she didn't drink either. She could boil a bottle of water…there was a certain vengeful pleasure in the idea of giving him a scalding cup of nothing. Instead, she filled a mug with milk and emptied most of a bottle of chocolate syrup in it, nuked it, and added a handful of mini marshmallows and a cinnamon stick. There! Not gourmet, but he didn't deserve that.

She set the cup down on the coffee table near where he usually sat and moved over to slouch into the armchair as he came back into the room.

His hair glinted with beads of water, so even though his face was dry she knew he must have splashed water on his face. Trying to stay awake, she supposed, for whatever he'd come here to say.

After walking around aimlessly for a moment, he sat down and lifted the cup, looking at it skeptically. "What is this?"

"Improvised hot chocolate. Take it or leave it!"

He looked like she'd slugged him. "I'll take it," he said. "Did Chloe tell you about our game?"

"What?"

"I guess not. It doesn't matter. Chloe and I always ask each other that when we're bargaining over something." He took a tentative sip, and marshmallow-chocolate froth painted a mustache above his lip.

I'm angry. I'm furious. I wish I could kiss the chocolate away.

He gave her the slightest of smiles, and then turned serious again.

"You know why I came," he repeated. "Too little too late and all that, but I cannot believe what I did to you. I can't understand why I listened to Esme and hurt you and Chloe and—" He shrugged. "There's really nothing to tell you, because 'sorry' isn't worth squat when you do something as stupid as I did."

She felt her anger and fury slipping away at the same time she realized his coming here first to apologize made her want to wrap her arms around him and forgive him. She bit her lip hard, unwilling to be a doormat again. Brian had walked all over her with his excuses, apologies and easy lies. *Never again.*

"So just shut up," she snapped, standing. "If you've said what you came to say—"

"I looked the story up," he said dully. "I knew maybe an hour after I called the principal that I should never have gone off like I did."

He fell silent, and she turned his words over.

"What did she say?"

He smothered a yawn, but didn't answer. "Does it matter? My behavior's what we're talking about."

"You're defending her?" All the anger was back. She stormed up to him, bent over to be eye level. "That I cannot believe! That…"

"Calm down. I'm not defending her, but she really doesn't have anything to do with me being an ass. Yes, she told me you'd been accused of negligent injury to a child—your husband's child with the woman he jilted to marry you." He fished the cinnamon stick out of the chocolate and drained the mug. The mustache grew.

She picked up the cup. "I'm going to rinse this." She stalked out of the room, frustrated with her own spinelessness.

He admitted he'd been a jerk, that apologizing wasn't enough, that he'd let Esme lead him around by the—whatever.

And all she could think about was how worn out he looked. How attractive chocolate mustaches were on clean-shaven men.

Well, okay. He wasn't clean-shaven; obviously he hadn't even shaved before he jumped in his car at some ungodly hour this morning. But the scruffiness only heightened his attractiveness.

She heard him come into the kitchen, and turned from the sink, surprised.

"I only read the part where you were acquitted, Luz. I'd already assumed that. You're not capable of hurting a kid, no matter what."

"Have you eaten?"

"No, but I'm more tired than hungry." He yawned, unable to stop it, and she wound up doing the same.

"I want to pick Chloe up before school. Mind if I crash on the couch?"

"No."

"No, you don't mind, or no I can't?" In spite of his weariness, he smiled slightly.

"You can sleep on the couch, on the floor, wherever. Think I'll call it a night, too."

She went to her room, closed the door, and changed out of her warm-ups into another of her long, silky nightgowns. She had one pair of flannel pajamas somewhere, but she never wore them. Besides…she pushed thoughts of walking through the living room in her gown out of her head. She wasn't sure she should forgive him. He had been the worst kind of jerk.

She wondered if he'd wiped the mustache away.

Frowning at her own insistent hungers, she wrapped herself in her thickest plush robe and picked up a pillow and blanket from the store in the closet.

Halfway to the door, she stopped and loosened the belt, letting the robe fall open. Just a little. She walked back into the room, holding her breath, hoping—

He'd stretched out on the couch and was sound asleep, an arm shielding his eyes from the light.

The mustache was gone. Grinning wryly, she flicked the blanket over him and balanced the pillow on the armrest behind him. He'd find it if he got uncomfortable enough.

She tiptoed out of the room, turning off the light, and laughing at herself over her pitiful attempt at seduction.

• • •

Smoke crept through the door she'd left partially open to light the hall—something she'd have done for Chloe. Why had she done it for Aaron? She lay still a moment, half uncovered, sniffing again.

Yes, something smelled like it was burning. Her heart jerked, and she sat straight up. Cold air washed over her, reminding her she'd worn her nightgown, not her flannel pajamas. She might as well have slept naked.

The house was burning and she was worried over Aaron's lack of interest?

Flinging on her robe, she raced to the kitchen.

Aaron stood there, rumpled and groggy, waving a hand through the smoke still curling around the stove. "Oh, sorry," he greeted her. "Just the biscuits. The bacon and eggs are fine."

"You got up this early to fix bacon?"

"Always get up early—well, now. Chloe doesn't like school food much."

"Ah, yes. School food." Luz joined him in fanning. "How burned are the biscuits?"

"Way past 'nicely browned'." The dimples flashed. "But just short of incinerated."

In spite of the early morning hour, her lack of sleep, and the unresolved issues dividing them, Luz smiled back. "I'm not a breakfast person, anyway. Although…" She inched closer to the stove, and peeked at the bacon and eggs. "I could try really hard."

He laughed. "Don't torture yourself, though. If you're not hungry—"

He started to put back one of the two plates he'd pulled out of the cabinet, but she swatted at his arm and pulled the plate toward her.

Caught off balance by her tug, he stepped forward, his arm caught between them, pressing into her chest.

She gasped. Involuntarily, her arms slipped around him, keeping his arm trapped, urging him closer, opening her hands to caress the warm skin beneath his thin shirt.

But she jerked away when the plate she'd taken from him shattered on the floor behind him.

He jumped a little, too, and then looked from the burned biscuits in the sink to the mess on the floor. And laughed.

I could love this man. She didn't laugh, just grinned and bent down to pick up the broken pieces of porcelain.

"I'd offer to help, but we'd probably bump heads and wind up on the floor."

He didn't seem at all interested in picking where they'd left off, in spite of the momentary vision she had of winding up on the floor. Once again she reached the same conclusion she'd come to so many times—Aaron wasn't a man she could have. Esme had undoubtedly lost any chance with him when she'd spirited Chloe away, but Aaron wasn't free. Clearly, he was a man married to his wife's ghost.

• • •

Aaron left while it was still dark, determined to pick Chloe up and take her home. With temperatures hovering around freezing and the weather predicted to worsen, school had been canceled. Luz wished he wouldn't go, but of course he had to get out while he could.

She tried not to think about what Esme would say to defend herself, or how hurt and upset Chloe might be.

Reluctantly, as day broke, she bundled up and headed out to feed the menagerie and see how the barn had held up under the wind. The clouds were low and barren, but for the moment, dry. Although she usually didn't feel the cold, today she couldn't shake the feeling that winter had finally settled in to stay.

She made short work of the chores in the barn, relieved that not a piece of tin or a board had come undone. The kitten meowed plaintively, but when she picked it up thinking she'd take it to the house, no name clawed her and jumped down, racing for her usual hiding spot behind the partition.

Luz trudged back toward the house, going around it too, to make sure that nothing seemed damaged.

A car honking startled her, and she turned in surprise to see Ann's pickup parked up by the road.

"Stupid woman," she muttered. "Oughta be inside keeping my goddaughter warm!"

She jogged toward the road, seeing Ann open the door and walk towards her, holding a hand up to stop her. "What—"

Ann didn't bother with a greeting. "Had a call from someone—I don't know who. Sent me out to check on a dog 'hit by a car'."

Dread settled like lead in Luz's stomach. She thought she knew where this was going. "Princess?" She brushed past Ann even as she asked, and covered her gasp of shock with a hand, fighting back her nausea.

Behind her Ann said, "No," but she'd already seen that it wasn't the pit bull. At least, not that pit bull. This was a large brindle, ripped apart with sickening violence.

"Why? Why me?" Luz moaned, turning away from the lifeless body.

Ann shook her head. "I don't know. This time whoever it is called me, so in a way, I have to wonder if I'm being included in this sick game. What have we done to anyone, Luz?" She looked again at the carcass. "I'm taking pictures and taking it into town. I'm going to dump it onto the sheriff's desk, or whoever's there. They have to do more than they're doing!"

Luz hugged Ann. "Go home. You shouldn't be driving. You shouldn't get this upset—"

"I'm fine. But I want to know who called. Didn't sound like he was from around here."

"You can't know everyone's voice in Rose Creek."

"Hmph! In this town? On one hand, almost." She looked at Luz, assessing her face. "I heard your ex—I heard Brian went looking for you at school. I suppose you'd say it couldn't be him? How sick was he? Is he stalking you?"

Luz watched as the vet pulled her phone out of her pocket and snapped several pictures of the dog and its location, positioned almost exactly as the other had been.

"No. He's not stalking me. He tried to call, but I have no idea why he turned up, and I'm sure he's gone again. Not to defend Brian—but I've told you about his family. His father's grooming him for political office. No way he'd kill a dog. Someone would have seen him and asked me about it."

"And he wouldn't have paid to have it done? Maybe he's trying to drive you from Rose Creek. Maybe he wants you back."

"No, he wouldn't have paid, and he can't believe I'm stupid enough to go back to a man who dumped the same woman twice and used me when he wasn't using her."

"Which leaves us with nothing!"

"No, not nothing." Luz took her arm and led her to the truck. "You are the mother-to-be of a precious little girl—"

"Or boy."

"Or boy, but it's a girl. And you need to get your butt in that seat, drive very carefully into town, and go home for the day."

Ann sighed. "Yeah, I probably should. At least get back into town." Luz ducked her head briefly as Ann gently lifted the dog's body into the back of her truck. She peeled off the gloves she wore and tossed them into the bed, too, rubbing her hands for warmth.

Finally she swung into the truck, not yet encumbered by her slight baby bump or bulky jacket. "You sure are bossy this morning!"

"It's from the subbing, Ann. My teacher self took over my body, but I'll be fine in a few hours. And no," she added, as Ann opened her mouth, "I do not want to go back full time."

"Okay," Ann said with a shrug. "But I was going to ask how spending the night with Aaron was." She turned the key in the ignition, winked, and rolled the window up.

Great. Ann never knew anything—she stayed too busy. Which meant every single person in Rose Creek did know, and someone mentioned it to her.

Luz headed back to the house, again thinking of Esmeralda. She would know. She would make sure Aaron knew that she knew.

Would Aaron be upset to find his name linked with hers when he clearly wasn't ready to move on from his love for his late wife?

Chapter Seventeen

The cold held on for two more days, the temperature only rising into the forties, but at least not freezing at night, since the clouds never cleared.

Luz took out some sweaters she hadn't worn since Atlanta and did some online shopping—books about how to start shelters, baby clothes in gender-neutral colors, a few romance novels. None of the spicy titles, though—she didn't want to be reminded how quickly and hotly passion could flare.

She hadn't heard from Aaron again, and wondered if she'd scared him off. First she'd thrown herself into his arms and then smashed a plate on the backs of his ankles. She tossed aside a sheaf of printouts on regulations and wondered if she'd lost the research skills that made college a breeze.

All that seemed clear was that the state regulated how animals should be euthanized. She'd be damned if she'd run a kill shelter. So maybe she'd better research legal ways to raise money for a non-profit entity. Or how to get rich legally, quickly, and permanently.

Smiling, she got up and stretched, and the phone rang.

Well! Finally! Aaron's number glowed on the screen.

She swiped the phone and said hello.

There was momentary silence, and then Chloe's voice came on. "Luz? Hi. It's me."

She sounded so unsure and hesitant. "Hey, girl! I'm so glad to talk to you," Luz assured her, honestly.

"Really? You're not mad at me or anything?"

"Absolutely not! Why would I be?"

Chloe warmed up then. "Dad says tomorrow the sun will come out, and we can go see you after school! Is Rumbles okay? Does she miss me?"

The words tumbled out, and Luz closed her eyes for a moment, cherishing the excitement and the closeness.

"Rumbles is fine, and she misses you. Right, Rumbles?"

Luz held the phone away from her ear, and then spoke again. "Sorry, she's eating the leftover ice cream and can't talk."

"She's not in the house!" She held a slight pause. "Is she?"

Luz laughed. "No, and it's too cold for ice cream."

"Dad wants to speak to you," Chloe announced. "Bye."

"Hey, Luz." Aaron's voice, tinged with amusement, echoed in her ear. "Chloe has missed you."

"Ditto. So you're bringing her over tomorrow?"

"If you'll have us."

"Sure."

"Luz, I talked to Mrs. Baker—she's feeling great. They're not sure what made her dizzy, but she's fine now."

"Okay. Ummm, good. I'm glad." Luz wasn't sure why he was mentioning Mrs. Baker, so she threw a lot of words back, hoping to give him what he wanted to hear.

"Would you have dinner with me Friday? I mean, a real dinner, somewhere noisy."

"The diner's noisy on Friday—"

"No. Follow the conversation, Luz," he chided, teasing. "Mrs. Baker can babysit Chloe—she says she's missed her. We can go have an adult dinner."

"Oh."

"Somewhere just noisy enough where we can finish the discussion we started the other night."

She remembered. The interrupted chat about Lily. She shuddered. What could she say, really? Lily's own mother, accidentally or deliberately, had let the child take a pill that almost killed her—a pill like Luz's own migraine medicine. And had accused Luz of drugging her at school because she knew Brian was cheating on her once again.

"Aaron—"

"We've never really had a chance to talk, Luz. Don't you think we should? I mean real, not will-we-be-interrupted kind of stuff?"

The man knew how to intrigue a woman. He probably didn't mean the kind of will-we-be-interrupted stuff she would like to explore. But nothing would happen if she didn't give it a chance.

"Sure, Aaron," she agreed slowly. "See you tomorrow, then."

He didn't try to keep her on the line, just said goodnight and hung up.

But a tiny flicker of hope raced through her. She didn't think Esmeralda was a threat anymore. Hope grew stronger, felt more like lust. She didn't have to fight that fight. Now she only had to compete against memories. Maybe—just maybe—she could confront those and win.

•••

Chloe and Rumbles clearly thought they belonged to each other. Their greeting lasted well beyond any time Chloe might have to ride. Darkness still came early, and Luz wished fervently for daylight savings to kick in and provide more time to get things done outside without artificial lights.

Ann's addition was finished, and ready for use, and Chloe inspected it with great care before dusk fell.

"It's so cool!" she decided. "But I don't want Dr. Ann to have sick horses here. Or ponies. Couldn't she just keep horses here for kids who don't have any?"

She glared when her father laughed.

"Why not?" she demanded. "At school, they gave a kid a bike. Why doesn't anyone give kids horses?"

"The world would be better," Luz agreed. "But for now, I bet your dad wants you home thinking about school, not another horse to take care of."

"Absolutely," Aaron agreed. "Chloe will see you Saturday. And I—I'll see you tomorrow."

Chloe's argument evaporated. "Daaad—"

He took a visible breath and nodded at Luz. "We'll talk in the car, baby."

They drove off, and as childish as it was, Luz crossed her fingers and watched until the SUV disappeared, hoping Chloe wouldn't make her dad have second thoughts about an adults-only evening.

She made a thorough check of the area near her fence, walking from the mailbox almost to the end of the fence line. Thankfully, there hadn't been another dog discarded—but the last one lingered like a nightmare, and she almost dreaded mornings coming.

But tomorrow…she couldn't quit smiling. Telling Aaron about Lily suddenly felt liberating, explaining her love for the little girl. He'd understand why she'd said she wasn't ready for a daughter yet. She took a few steps and stopped. Was she?

She could love Chloe like a daughter; she already loved— liked—her a lot. But was it enough to take a chance on losing again? She shook the thoughts away and headed around the house to the barn to check the animals a last time.

The horses were mostly dozing, and Rumbles was munching hay like the little glutton she was. Candy huffed when Luz didn't offer anything else and the guinea hens stirred in annoyance over being disturbed. The cats weren't around, but they seldom were out in the open after dark.

On the way back through the barn, she stopped by the little office, opening the door and flipping on the light just to be sure she hadn't left anything lying around. She'd gotten bad about that recently.

A small ivory book lay on the desk. Chloe must have forgotten a diary or something, although she hadn't seen her bring anything in.

She smiled as she went over to retrieve it. Kind of hard to watch Chloe constantly when her dad had shown up looking incredibly sexy in a torso-hugging long-sleeved sweater.

She picked the book up. It was more a journal than a diary, and not ivory—the cover had been white years ago. With fingers that didn't cooperate, she slipped off a strap holding it closed and glanced at the first page.

Her mother's neat, tiny handwriting jumped out at her.

Her heart hammered. She had never seen this book anywhere, even when she'd undertaken the difficult task of disposing of her mother's belongings after her death. It hadn't been here before—so someone had put it on the desk, knowing she'd see it.

She shuddered. While she and Aaron had been watching Chloe and ogling each other somebody had slipped in and left her mother's journal, then disappeared.

The only person she could imagine coming and going so silently was Ross Thurmond. But why did he have her mother's journal? And why had he returned it in secrecy?

Chapter Eighteen

Bright sunshine and warm temperatures had returned. No dead dogs left to taunt her for some sick reason she couldn't decipher. And the promise of a romantic night with Aaron along San Antonio's beautiful Riverwalk, made it impossible for Luz to stop smiling.

Aaron hadn't characterized the date as romantic—he'd only talked about talking. Her smile broadened. Just sitting across from a table, watching his green eyes dance and the dimples come and go…romantic.

The kitten with no name scooted in front of her, and she stumbled, trying not to land on it.

"You're a menace," she muttered, and then grinned. "An evil menace! Bet Chloe will like your new name, Menace."

The kitten changed course again, darting over her feet, running for her life from unseen danger.

Even though she almost tripped again, Luz laughed and patted herself on the back. At last the kitten had a name. Menace wasn't abandoned any longer.

She glanced at her watch. Aaron told her he'd pick her up around five, so that he could spend a couple of hours with Chloe before leaving her with Mrs. Baker.

She'd agreed, and offered with a laugh to pick him up in her truck. He refused, citing the fact that the SUV was newer, had GPS so they wouldn't get lost, and was sexier.

She'd teased him about that claim, but only briefly. Let him keep thinking that way.

Luz spent the rest of the morning walking around her barn, yard, and the small acreage her parents had owned, wondering how best to use it. She should put in a garden and grow vegetables, and maybe she should research kennel design. She didn't think she'd have much call to house large animals, although she'd heard horrible stories of abandoned livestock.

Her phone buzzed, and she fished it out of her pocket. Ann's office number, which surprised her.

"Hello?"

"Luz? This is Teri." The young woman's voice sounded frantic, and Luz's breath stuck in her throat for a minute.

"Is Ann okay, Teri? The baby—"

"Ann's not here. She had a doctor's appointment."

"Okay, then?"

"He called. That sick man called—Hermie called!"

"Calm down. What did he say?"

"That the doctor should go watch him kill his horse." The receptionist's voice ended in a choking sound, like a sob, but then she seemed to regain some composure. "He told me to call the doctor, that he'd wait, but Ann will be so upset—"

"Don't call her. She probably has her phone off if she's with the doctor anyway. Look, just call the sheriff."

"I did. A semi hit a van on I-35. He and the deputies went to help until the state troopers get there."

Damn.

"Look, Teri—tell the dispatcher to send someone out as soon as possible. I'll drive over there and see if I can talk some sense into him."

"You shouldn't—"

"I have to. I'll call when I get there. If I can't do anything, I'll leave."

"But—"

"I have to go, Teri. It'll take me fifteen or twenty minutes to get there as is."

She hung up the phone and went for her keys. For a brief second, she thought of her mother's pistol. But she was going to trespass on someone's property. And she wasn't sure she could shoot someone even if she had to. Grabbing the keys and checking to be sure she had her phone, she raced out the door, flung herself into the truck, and headed toward the ramshackle farm a couple of miles away.

• • •

Aaron paused outside the Country Critters Veterinary Clinic, peering in the window with a smile. He thought for a moment of stopping in and saying hello to Ann and her assistant, just to kill time. He glanced around, though. Ann's truck wasn't anywhere in sight. He waved at Teri, behind her desk, but to his surprise, she motioned him in with desperate hand gestures. "Teri? Everything okay?"

"No! Mr. Estes, I'm scared for Luz! And for the doctor, when she finds out—"

The fear in her voice slammed him in the chest. "What's wrong?"

"That sicko called—that Hermie Clark! He wanted the doctor to go to his place—said he was going to kill his horse—"

Ann had witnessed that once before. He remembered the sickness in Luz's face when she told him. The baby—

"How long ago did Ann leave?"

Teri shook her head. "No! Not Ann! She's at the doctor in San Antonio. Luz said she was going to go stop him!"

No. He couldn't see another woman he knew dead. He couldn't—

He gulped in air. "Tell me how to get there."

He listened to Teri's brief, hurried directions. Between those and the GPS he should be able to find Luz.

"Don't tell Ann if she calls you," he shouted over his shoulder. "But call the police or something."

He didn't hear Teri's answer because he was already throwing himself into the SUV.

•••

The place was easier to find in the truck than on a horse, but then again she'd been in Rose Creek a little longer now. She swerved into a faint path worn through a dry pasture. Ahead of her she saw the decrepit farmhouse, one side perilously near collapse. To the right, the barn, equally in disrepair, with a tiny corral made of patched boards and poles that defied gravity to remain standing.

She threw the truck into the park and jumped out, her heart racing.

A little sorrel mare raced around the tiny enclosure, her panic clear. Even from the truck, she could see large welts from a whip cutting into the horse's hide.

Luz shoved the truck into park and bolted out, shouting as she went. "Mr. Clark! Hermie! Hermie Clark!"

She climbed up on the fence, feeling it sag. No one was in the ring. Maybe she could scramble over the top and open the gate before Clark made his appearance.

But she was too late—the gate was on the opposite side, near the barn. And Hermie Clark came out, holding a bullwhip in his right hand and dragging a chain saw in his left.

Calm. Be calm. Teri will keep calling the sheriff. Someone will come…

Hermie entered the ramshackle pen, carefully closing the gate. He put the saw down, sent a chilling smile her way, and latched the gate.

"You're not the doctor," he said, speaking loudly enough to be sure that she could hear. He walked into the center of the ring; the mare changed direction and raced into the fence, then turned and circled in sheer terror.

"Shoulda left her tied up—she was scared. Couldn't fight back much—hardly moved when I cut her." He spit tobacco in a stream on the ground, wiped his mouth with a beefy, dirty hand. "She screamed pretty good when I stuck her with the knife." And he laughed.

Tears stung Luz's eyes, and her fingers dug into the old wood of the fence. She wondered if she could kick it down fast enough to let the mare out. She moved, shaking the slats, trying to gauge how well they'd hold up. This side was probably the strongest part of the fence, dammit!

"Mr. Clark, I'm Luz Wilkinson. Please don't do this."

He walked a few paces closer, effectively separating her from the panicked mare that stopped briefly, leaning against the fence on the barn side, sides heaving, her neck lathered and sweat darkening her flanks.

The eyes he turned on her again shone with craziness. "Wanted Dr. Ann to come like she did last time. Heard she's gonna have a baby—ain't that something?"

Luz shivered. Could this deranged man be a threat to Ann? The horse whinnied and started, and Clark swiveled toward her.

Luz clambered over the fence, hoping she could keep out of the whip's reach and clear of the mare when Clark attacked her again.

She tried to keep her voice steady, to not show the fear or loathing she felt. "Mr. Clark, I was there last time, remember? I'd just come to town. My horse threw me."

He turned back to her, and his thick lips pulled back in a smirk. "Oh. Yeah. I remember." He nodded. "You helped Doc Ann back to her truck."

He remembered them? They'd helped each other, Ann and she, holding each other up. Luz had stopped to throw up before they got back to the truck.

Not this time.

"Why, Hermie?" She tried to soften her voice. She'd had in-services on dealing with confrontational teens, but not on trying to get through to someone this sick.

Across the ring, the mare had paused again, sides heaving. She watched them nervously, her ears flicking back and forth, ready to bolt again.

If she could just keep Hermie focused on her instead of the mare…she sidled a few steps along the fence, ready to go back over if she had to, thinking maybe she could inch closer, then race over and throw the gate open.

"Need me some meat," he leered, his eyes sweeping over her, his insinuation clear. And insulting.

She didn't know if he'd reacted to Ann the same way; she'd gotten there too late that day.

Again she was thankful her friend hadn't come—her practice was stressful enough without a madman's crazy taunts. But she really wished the sheriff or a deputy would come.

She moved again and Hermie Clark chortled. "You think I don't see you tryin' to get to the gate? Bitch!"

He swirled suddenly and lashed out. The mare shied from the whip and lunged away, racing helplessly in circles again.

Luz could hear her own gasps of breath, and feel the acid rise in her throat. She wouldn't lose it. She fought down the bile, the urge to puke, the sharp fear.

She was being stupid, and she knew it. She couldn't walk away, and she knew that, too. For a faint moment, she wished she were home, counting the hours until dinner with Aaron. She almost snorted out loud. Dinner with Aaron was a luxury she couldn't think about right now.

"I'll buy her," Luz offered. "Name your price. You can buy food."

"Shoulda left her tied up," he repeated in a flat, emotionless voice. "Easier to hurt 'em like that."

"God, you're sick." She couldn't bite the words back, but he laughed.

"Maybe I am, maybe I'm not. You're trespassin', though—the law says you can kill trespassers to defend your property."

"I'm not here to take anything."

The whip cracked again, in front of the mare, who threw herself around and thundered straight at Luz. The horse was too near the fence to climb it, so Luz took a few steps toward the center of the pen—bringing her close to Hermie.

He laughed again, and she felt goose bumps break out on her arms.

The sudden sound of an approaching car startled them both.

"We got company," Clark muttered, even before he turned to look.

Luz took her eyes off his and twisted to see—not the flashing lights she'd hoped for. Her eyes widened as the door of the SUV flew open and Aaron leaped out.

"Oh, look—it's the man you been ballin'!"

"Aaron—stay back!" Luz implored as he climbed the fence. Three people and a horse in the tiny enclosure might make escape even more difficult. Aaron had never handled a panicked horse. She doubted he'd ever dealt with a man holding a whip and with a chainsaw at his feet, either.

She remembered her father working with chainsaws—unwieldy and unpredictable. Maybe he meant more to threaten than use. The memory of the other horse rose in her mind. He'd used the saw on her.

At least she'd handled horses…

The loud crack of the whip and Aaron's cry of warning registered too late. The leather cut into Luz's shoulder like a knife, knocking her to her knees.

"How'd that feel, girlie?" Clark asked, his eyes glittering.

"Touch her again and you're dead," Aaron said coldly, jumping off the top rail into the enclosure.

"You think, city boy?" The man spat at Aaron's feet. He snapped the whip again, but this time in the air, inches away from Luz.

He turned his head toward Aaron. "You just come closer and see what I do to her," he snarled.

Aaron stopped, his body tense, indecision in his eyes.

Luz rose slowly, and then flung herself at the whip, kicking Clark's ankle in an attempt to trip him. He just cursed at her and shoved her back so hard that her legs buckled and she wound up on her knees. She thrust herself back as he lifted the whip and grabbed his wrist, willing him to not hit the mare again, but the man was all muscle and fury, and he shook loose and sent her reeling backwards. She caught a boot heel in the sod and fell again, her injured arm under her.

Desperation showed in the mare's eyes as she suddenly left the fence, crossed the ring, and launched herself in the air.

Luz could see she wouldn't clear the fence, though, and watched helplessly as the mare and fence crashed to the ground.

Hermie lifted the whip again, but Aaron lunged forward, catching Hermie's wrist and twisting it, then smashing his fist into the man's nose. Hermie howled in pain and collapsed on the ground, blood streaming down over his lips and chin, and Aaron grabbed the whip and the chainsaw.

The mare thrashed around, drawing their attention. "Let's get out," Aaron suggested, and then said, "Do I hear sirens?"

The sheriff's car turned into the drive just as they scrambled out through the opening in the fence the mare had made. Luz's heart sank a little as she saw Ann's truck right behind.

Behind them, the mare moaned, and Luz watched as she managed somehow to gain her footing, a piece of the fence sticking out from one shoulder. The sorrel took a tentative step, then stopped, clearly too hurt to move any longer.

Luz wanted to walk over to comfort her, but her legs turned liquid and she sagged to the ground, shaking. Immediately Aaron was on his knees by her side, an arm around one shoulder, his other hand brushing grit from her face, cupping her chin, and turning her head gently.

"Are you all right? Did he only hit you once?" The concern in his voice soothed and steadied her. Briefly, she reached out and ran her own hand over his cheek.

"I'm fine," she murmured. "Thanks, Aaron."

"Do we need an ambulance?" the sheriff pressed, leaning over them. "Told 'em to stay at the wreck just in case—"

"Luz needs—she's bleeding," Aaron told the officers as he clambered up and helped her to her feet. "That psycho hit her—"

"I'm fine." Luz looked at her shoulder. Blood stained the strap of her tank top, but it was already drying; she couldn't have been hurt badly.

"So what happened?"

Luz ignored the sheriff. "Help her, Ann," she begged. "Please."

"You and I need to have a little talk about stupidity," the vet muttered, already walking towards the mare, talking gently.

In the ring, Hermie Clark staggered to his feet, retching, and then wiped his mouth with his forearm.

"These here are trespassers, Sheriff!" he shouted, limping toward the fence, the eyes still too bright, hate twisting his face. "They got no business here! They busted my fence! You gotta arrest them! They're trespassin'!"

"Shut up, Clark!" The sheriff glanced at Luz's shoulder as another car pulled up and the deputy hurried over.

"Book him. Animal cruelty. Read him his rights."

"Nothing's really going to happen, is it?" Luz demanded. "This would have been his third—"

"We'll look into it," the sheriff said, "but usually things like this don't draw much time."

He walked over to where Ann was still examining the mare, standing back a little when the horse threw her head up nervously.

"Don't guess she much likes men right now," he observed. "Don't know what the hell drives people to torture critters—it's like those poor dogs that have been showing up."

"Did you find another one?" Luz asked, thinking that if he had, then she wasn't being targeted after all.

The sheriff pushed his hat back and shifted his weight a little.

"No, ma'am—just the ones you and the doc called us about. But it's just a crime. Doc, how is she?"

"Not good. She'd been starved—look at her. Guess he fed her just enough so that she could try to get away from him." Her lips tightened, and anger burned in her cheeks.

"Ann, calm down." Luz edged close, talking to the mare, working up to her head. She hadn't been wearing a halter, and the vet had fashioned one out of the lead she always carried with her. Careful not to slip the loop off the horse's nose, Luz placed a hand on the mare's head and stroked her gently.

"I'm perfectly calm," Ann spat. "Why did you tell Teri not to let me know? What kind of stupid idiot comes rushing out alone—" She stopped. "God, getting pregnant turned me into Ram," she muttered. "I'm acting just like he did!"

"Because he loves you, and what Luz did is crazy!" Aaron retorted, and the mare rolled her eyes.

Two heads snapped in his direction. "Sssssht!"

"Sorry," he apologized, and moved back a couple of steps.

"Doc, what's gonna happen? Legally she's still his, at least 'til we can get some charges filed and such."

Ann looked at Luz. "She probably should be put down," she said gently. "She's malnourished, she's all cut up—I don't know if she'll ever get over being afraid."

"Try?"

"Luz—"

"We can put her in one of the stalls." Luz ran a hand down the neck, coated with gritty residue from the sweat and the fall. "Look, I know it's hard on you, but I'll feed and watch her."

"If she's not better in a couple of days, she shouldn't suffer anymore, Luz."

"I absolutely agree."

"You did pretty well for a city boy, Aaron," Ann said, smiling a little. "Think you can do one more thing?"

"Such as?"

She pursed her lips, still debating, before asking, "Can you pull a trailer?"

He snorted. "Took a camping trailer across the Rockies. I think so."

Luz raised an eyebrow. "I didn't know that."

He grinned wryly. "You don't know a lot. Every time we plan on talking, something crazy interrupts us."

Luz laughed, but she knew it was true. Chloe, Ross, Esme— and now a madman.

"I'll drive Luz into the doctor," Aaron went on. "Where's this trailer you need?"

"You're hurt?" Ann glared at Luz.

"Not really. He hit me with the whip, but only once. And I'm not bleeding anymore."

"Damn. I need you here, but you should see a doctor, Luz. Let me see—maybe you need stitches."

Luz shook her head, stepping away from the mare. "No! I am not taking off my clothes here in the middle of nowhere so a veterinarian can use a horse needle to sew me up!"

The sheriff looked uncomfortable. He mumbled that he'd talk to them later and headed back to the safety of his car.

"Luz, are you coming or not?"

"Aaron, I'll pop into Dr. Villa's office when I finish."

"Look, if you don't mind, Aaron, just go get my horse trailer—it's parked behind the office. Take my truck." She fished keys out and handed them to him.

"Be right back."

"Good. The sooner the better." She held her cell phone up. "Unlike you, however, I'll tell Teri you're coming."

He waved dismissively and jogged off.

"You know, Luz—"

"Not now, Ann," Luz interrupted curtly. "I don't want to hear anything about Aaron Estes!"

"You're going to tell me you aren't glad he showed up?"

"No." Luz wouldn't go that far. "I'm grateful he showed up. He helped save the horse's life—and who knows, if I'd fallen or something…" She took a deep breath. "I'm glad Aaron came," she repeated. "But right now all I want is to close my eyes and pretend today never happened."

Ann shrugged. "Fine with me." She bent over her bag, extracting a needle and a vial of Ketamine. "Just don't fall asleep before the meds kick in. Hold her!"

Luz tightened her grip, but the horse and she just stood head to head, too weary and heartsick to move.

• • •

By the time Aaron returned, the mare had been patched up. She stood quietly, still groggy, but seemingly unalarmed when Aaron walked up, remembering only at the last minute to slow his steps and speak softly.

"How are you, Luz?" he asked, ignoring Ann and the mare altogether.

"Ann's the one you should worry about." Luz sighed. She indicated a neatly stitched gash on the horse's leg. "She bent over that for hours."

"We haven't been here for hours," Ann retorted. She stretched and rubbed her belly absently. "I'm fine, and Aaron asked about *you*. Let's see if we can load—" She stopped, suddenly alarmed. "Chloe—"

Luz flinched. Why hadn't she remembered Chloe? She didn't have a watch. She couldn't tell how long they'd been here, either—everything seemed blurry.

"I called Mrs. Carter and Ms. Baker. They agreed that Ms. Baker could take her home. Chloe knew she was staying with Mrs. Baker tonight anyway, so she shouldn't worry." He smiled slightly. "They're making triple chocolate brownies, whatever those are."

Just the thought of his daughter chased all the weariness, the worry, from Aaron's face. Love gleamed from the green eyes, and even the faintness of the smile didn't disguise how Chloe was always with him.

The way Lily had once dominated her every thought, been her sunshine...

Luz stumbled a little. The bright sunshine disappeared, and she heard someone call her name from far off, a faint sound of alarm. Then nothing at all was left.

• • •

She came to as Aaron was buckling her into the SUV, and struggled momentarily against the restraint, disoriented. "What— Aaron, the mare, Clark—"

"The sheriff arrested him, remember? Calm down!" He peered at her closely, and then laid a hand gently against her cheek.

"You fainted, I guess. Shocked the hell out of Ann and me. Are you okay now?

She nodded, but didn't answer, realizing suddenly that her mouth was dry and her shoulder hurt.

He shut the door carefully and hurried around to climb in, turning on the air conditioner.

She slumped against the seat, letting her head loll against the cushiony upholstery.

"What did Ann say?"

"That's she glad this isn't a scene from a *novela*, because anytime a woman faints in a *novela* she's pregnant. Or dying," he said dryly.

"Well, one of the two isn't true in my case," she mumbled, then realized what she'd said and jerked upright.

He shot a reassuring smile her way, but looked worried. "We're going straight to Dr. Villa's office," he said. "Ann was worried about shock."

"And the mare?"

"She said she'd settle her in and make sure everything was okay. She said she might call Ross Thurmond to watch over things until you got home." His voice turned grim. "I told her not to bother, that I'd stay there tonight to help you."

They pulled into the clinic's parking lot, and Aaron checked his watch again. "We need to hurry. The doctor might want tests or something and then we'll have to go into San Antonio."

We were supposed to be there two hours from now, anyway. Can't I catch a break?

They walked into the empty doctor's office, and the receptionist stuck her head out the window. "Go right back," she told Luz. "Dr. Villa and Betty are waiting."

"You all knew I was coming?"

The receptionist arched her eyebrows, and then winked at Aaron. "This—"

"—is Rose Creek," they all finished together.

Behind her, she heard the receptionist ask Aaron if he was sure he didn't need help, and giggling at something he said. She hoped Aaron rushing to her rescue hadn't made him even more interesting to everyone—the receptionist had a husband and three kids!

"You look awful," Betty told her, holding a chart. "And you haven't come in for…"

"Two years," Luz answered curtly. "Because I was fine. I am fine!"

Betty pushed open an examining room. "Fine people don't faint," she scolded. "We heard what happened—that psychopath should be locked up before he hurts people. Well, worse than he hurt you."

Luz gave up. She followed the nurse's orders and changed into the gown Betty left, wobbling a little on the chair, realizing she felt drained. Across the room, she stared at a painting of an old cabin with a horse tied outside it.

Dr. Villa came in quickly, a petite woman with graying hair. Luz thought of the battle Dr. Villa had waged caring for her parents as their health slipped away and had to fight back tears. Again.

"The shoulder's not too bad," the doctor assured her in quick order, then dabbed it with a liquid. "Might sting," she cautioned, seconds too late. "Doesn't hurt that bad, though," Dr. Villa complained as Luz hissed and jerked away violently. "I have two-year-olds come in who don't behave like such babies!"

"It's been a bad day," Luz protested in her own defense. She hesitated, but decided to ask. "Doctor should I feel so—so nervous? So afraid that something else worse is going to happen?"

"Well, you saw that first horse Hermie Clark butchered. You knew he would have killed the other one, too, right? And you put yourself in a ridiculous situation trying to save it." Dr. Villa's frown showed her displeasure. "No animal is worth killing yourself over, young lady!"

Luz snorted, thinking of the doctor's popular toy poodle. "Not even your silly little Tabú?"

"I would not jump into a corral to save my dog if I thought I'd be hurt, no." She softened her tone, though. "Luz, you don't look like you've been sleeping well, and your blood pressure went way up with everything that happened. I'm giving you a mild sedative."

"No! I will not take—"

"You will. Look, I know the whole story about that little girl, Luz. The one they accused you of drugging. Your mom would talk about how unfair they were treating you over in Atlanta. Remember we had to deal with your insomnia and anxiety when you first moved back here. You've taken this same prescription. It's one pill, for one night, and I want you to take it."

"I have animals to feed. An injured horse…I can't."

The doctor handed her a prescription form. "You need to pick this up before the pharmacy closes. I'll walk you out."

"Doctor, that picture on your wall…where did it come from? Who painted it?"

Dr. Villa looked startled by the question, and stopped to peer at Luz again. When she apparently felt satisfied that Luz wasn't delusional, she answered. "Ross Thurmond. Not my cup of tea— the other rooms have fields of wildflowers—but he gave it to me." The stern features relaxed into a small smile. "He told me my dog and I were his best friends."

The information seemed enormously important, but her head pounded dully, and her legs still trembled under her, so Luz just filed it away to think about some other time.

Aaron stood up as they came out, and Luz looked at the window.

"I gave the co-pay," he said. "The receptionist needed to close the register."

"She needs to get to the pharmacy and home," Dr. Villa said, her tone authoritative. "She's not driving, right?"

"No, I am."

"Off with you," the doctor ordered. "I'll lock the door as you leave."

Aaron took her arm. Luz wanted to draw away; she didn't want him treating her like a girlfriend. Or a wife.

The thought brought her up short, but he gently slipped his arm around her shoulders and urged her through the door.

Behind her, the bolt clicked softly.

"My truck—"

"Was picked up already." He helped her back into the SUV. "The deputy offered and got someone to follow him home. Just lean back and rest, Luz. You're pale."

She didn't want to risk falling asleep, but holding her head up took too much effort. She made herself comfortable.

She woke up when Aaron stopped by the front porch and reached over to shake her gently. "We're home."

She didn't open her eyes to look for a few precious seconds. She just sat there, eyelids pressed closed, letting the word reverberate in her heart. *Home?*

"Do you need help getting out?" he prodded, but now he was on her side, holding the door open.

His words evaporated with their reality—they were just two messed-up people who couldn't even manage a dinner date. Sighing, she slipped from the vehicle and followed him in.

• • •

She hadn't really noticed Aaron's disheveled state before, but the fogginess that had descended over her for much of the afternoon seemed to be clearing. He had blood on his shirt and one pants leg, a cut on his hand, and a bruise on one cheek.

He'd gotten them all rushing to her rescue.

She frowned. She hadn't asked him to. But he'd been a lot more willing and a lot less judgmental than she might have expected.

174

He raised an eyebrow. "What?"

"You're all bloody. And dirty."

"Not my usual look, I admit." He glanced down at his shirt. "Not my blood, though."

"I'm glad. I just wish it hadn't happened at all."

"Yeah." He shoved his hand at his hair and stretched. "Seems we had a dinner date, but—"

Luz shook her head. "I couldn't. I need to shower and change. And wash my clothes." She looked down at her shirt, spotted with blood, too. Most of the blood on the shirt was hers—or the mare's. A momentary flash of the previous horse, mortally wounded, made her suck in a deep breath. "I'm not up to dinner. If you're hungry—"

"Not hungry, but I need to clean up too." He sighed. "Guess I'll head home."

Home? Luz didn't want him to leave. If he left, he would pick Chloe up and go to their home. Selfishly, she wasn't ready to let go of him yet, even after the ordeal they'd gone through. Or was it because of it?

"You could shower here—nobody'd have to see you getting home like that."

"Usually don't see anyone—the neighbors make themselves scarce."

"True." Luz grinned wryly. "But you heard news of what happened already got out. I have a feeling folks might drop by to see you with all kinds of excuses."

"Gotta love small towns," he returned with more amusement than annoyance, she thought. "So…I can shower here. But what would I wear?"

"I can throw your clothes in the washer, and they'd be clean and dry in an hour or so."

"But until then?"

Nothing? "Let me look around—if worse comes to worse, you could wrap yourself in a towel or a sheet for an hour, couldn't you?"

He considered that, and then nodded. "Sure. Sheets are functional. I'll go after you."

"No. You go first, so your stuff will be ready. Let me go find you something."

A few seconds later, she returned, smiling.

"You're set. Just drop your clothes outside the door."

"This has been a weird day," he noted.

Luz heard the water running moments later, and a bare arm extended out the door, dropping a handful of clothing before disappearing. She'd dreamed of an arm once, wrapped around her, comforting her—just an arm in a yellow sweater. Nothing sexy about it.

Luz snorted. *You know you've been alone too long when a man's bare arm turns you on.* She went to get her own clothes off and everything into the washer.

She wouldn't mind Aaron wandering around buck-naked. Not a bit. But would he mind?

Unbidden, the thought came to her that *his* marriage had not ended in divorce. And that Stella still owned his heart.

Chapter Nineteen

Aaron wanted to help her feed the animals. In a towel and his underwear.

At least, Luz assumed he had underwear under the bath sheet, because he hadn't included anything to be washed. Leaving the question of briefs or boxers, and raising the specter of "going commando."

"I'm fine," she repeated. "You can't run around like that outside."

"It's not that cold, it's getting dark, and I shouldn't leave everything to you." He sniffed. "You already cooked."

"A boxed hamburger meal isn't cooking, it's just fast."

"Wouldn't you rather wait until your clothes finish?" She looked at the clock above the counter. "Another fifteen or twenty minutes?"

"You've been staring out the window toward Ann's place every five minutes. If we go now, we can actually sit down and eat." He grinned. "We'll only be missing the Riverwalk and a romantic setting."

"You're stubborn."

"One of my flaws—I don't change my mind often." His smile faded. "On the other hand, Luz—I want to see the mare. Poor thing."

His words touched her. Not so long ago, he'd been perfectly happy staying outside the barn while she and Chloe visited horses or tacked up Rumbles.

"There's hope for you yet," she decided.

He raised an eyebrow. "Hope? For me?"

"Horse people are by and large good people. Mom said never to trust someone who claimed to be a people person—to always go for the one who walked up to the family pet first, or admired an old horse grazing out in the middle of nowhere."

He chuckled. "Bet your mom favored you."

She smiled, remembering the mother who had never met either human or animal she didn't like. "Maybe. But I've heard it usually works the other way."

"One thing surprises me, though…"

"Yes?"

"You don't like Esmeralda. She's a horse person."

"True—and guilty as charged. Sort of."

"Sort of?"

"I don't love her. I don't like that when she first came to town, she went after a married man. When Ann and Ram were having problems, she tried to drive them even farther apart. But I'm sure she has qualities."

"Like?" he challenged, his eyes twinkling and the dimples engraving his cheeks.

Luz thought. "Ummm. Well, children. She helps troubled children."

She saw the grimness in Aaron's face before he spoke, and kicked herself. "By lying to their fathers and snatching them away from the woman he chose to take care of them?"

Bingo. She didn't voice the small triumphant exclamation, though, just said gently, "Other children. Rose Creek is small—I know she has helped several families here."

He turned his head for a moment, and then nodded. "She probably has. I decided not to file a complaint with anyone over her doing that to Chloe because it was at least as much my fault as hers."

He sounded sincere, taking most of the blame for what was an unconscionable act, an atrocity professionally. This man who doted on his daughter, worried incessantly about her…

Unbidden, she thought of Brian. How he'd been indifferent to the pain he inflicted when he told her he had a newborn daughter just two days after the wedding, indifferent to Lily's suffering when her real mother took her away. Seeing him so unexpectedly had been such a shock. He must have left, or she would have heard, even with all the horror she'd faced in the last hours. And she didn't know why he'd come, but she was glad in a way that he had. The coldness she'd felt when he turned up suddenly at school, calling her name, made her remember every little lie she'd pieced together when he'd let Lily's mom attack her. And now she knew what she wanted in a man. Yes, she wanted Aaron. And he was worth fighting for. Even if she didn't know how one fought a dead lover's memory.

Unable to speak, she went to the stove, ran the spoon through the pasta again, and double-checked that the stove was off.

"So—can we go? Or do we stand and stare out the window, wondering?" To prove his point, he pressed the curtain aside and flattened his face against the glass.

When he leaned over, the towel hiked up, exposing strong thighs. Too bad she had given him the bath sheet. A shorter towel…she sucked in a breath just as the buzzer blasted out the open laundry room door.

Aaron turned around and heaved an exaggerated sigh.

"Guess you're going to make me get dressed, then?"

She didn't want to. But she nodded reluctantly. "What if the pastor and his wife drive by while we're near Ann's place? They'll see you. Or—" She grinned. "What if the towel falls off altogether when we're feeding Candy, and he bites? Or—"

"Okay, just can it!" He glared at her in mock anger. "Bet your mom was much nicer than you!"

"Much!" Luz called as he headed off to reclaim his clothes.

• • •

"She must be starving," Aaron said a few minutes later, watching as Luz crooned to the mare and used a flashlight to look her over.

"Well, Ann said not to feed her tonight—that if she's still groggy, she might choke." She reached in through the narrow slats of the stall to stroke an uninjured bit of the horse's neck. Aaron stood beside her, looking in, his face concerned.

"She can't be comfortable in this mousetrap."

"The stall helps her stay on her feet. Horses—"

"Need to stay on their feet for their systems to work. I've heard that's one reason horses with broken legs are usually put down. But—"

"Ann had to give her a fairly large dose of sedative—she was in a lot of pain. See how sleepy she looks? She's still dopey."

He reached through the opening in the stall too, his arm not fitting as easily as hers had. When he petted the mare, his arm brushed hers, and tiny shivers of fire darted over her bare skin. She hoped he didn't notice that she licked lips that were suddenly dry and edged a little further away—a much better response than turning to him and locking her arms around his neck. The pastor and his wife actually did drive by on the way to their farm further outside Rose Creek almost every evening.

Gossip would happen anyway. She wouldn't mind if he knew about Lily. And, she reminded herself, if she knew how he would feel about her trying to take Stella's place in his life.

• • •

The cheesy hamburger-macaroni skillet dinner might not have been gourmet, but they ate every last bit of it. Aaron insisted they use the paper plates he'd found, pointing out that they'd had a hard day, and wouldn't have had to do dishes if they'd gone into San Antonio.

Aaron called during the meal to check in on Chloe, and promised he'd bring her to ride. He passed her the phone when Chloe insisted on talking to Luz, as well.

Luz threw the plates out and rinsed the silverware while Aaron walked over to the front door and turned the knob. From the kitchen, she could see him bend over to look at something.

"The lock!" They said it together, but she laughed and he didn't.

"You know, I probably could fix it myself," he said. "I don't know why I've waited."

"Probably because you kept telling me I should do it," Luz said. "I'm getting better, but I'm not a carpenter yet."

"Thing is, there have been those dogs thrown along your fence." He caught her hands. "Luz, I know this is a friendly little town, but—"

"Times change. Things happen. I know."

He squeezed her hands gently. "It bothers me, you being here alone, without even Princess. Thurmond—"

"I haven't told you!" Luz pulled her hands away. "Aaron, you know something? I think we misunderstood everything with him."

Aaron caught one of her hands again and led her to the sofa. "Why don't we sit?" He gave her a mirthless grin. "We can sit here and look at his painting of horses' butts."

"Patience. My mother called the painting Patience," she reminded him. "Did you know he does jobs around Chloe's school?"

He turned on the couch, facing her instead of the painting. "No. Don't much care, either. I don't like him, Luz. Don't trust him." He paused. "You're going to hate this, but something about him makes me feel as creeped-out as I felt with that Clark bastard. Maybe more, because everyone knew Clark was sick. I think Thurmond's sick, but that he hides it."

She turned away from the picture, pulling her legs off the floor and tucking them under her. "He apologized to me after school," she explained. "Told me he didn't mean to keep interrupting us, that he was just used to the old Rose Creek—everyone just walks in when they visit, and that my mom and dad were used to it."

Aaron shook his head slowly. "Know what I think, Luz?" he asked, his tone gentle. "I think you're one of these love-everyone softies who couldn't think badly of the devil himself. Ross Thurmond walked in on us at odd times, don't you think?"

"Yes, but—"

"Even if he always did that, you're not your mom. We'd told him we were together, even if it wasn't true. There's no reason for him just to show up like that."

"Ann sends him sometimes. *She* trusts him!"

"Okay."

Aaron's tone indicated he didn't agree, but didn't want to argue. Annoyed that he hadn't changed his mind, she added, "Dr. Villa has one of his paintings. Said he gave it to her and her poodle—quit smirking."

Aaron pretended to wipe his smile away.

She laughed, but added her final note. "Did you know he had my mom's journal?"

Aaron straightened and tensed noticeably. "And that doesn't bother you?"

"Well, it's strange—although technically, I just figure he had it somehow and thought I should get it back. It turned up on the desk in the barn. I don't know how that could have been anyone else."

Aaron stood up, stretching, his face unreadable. "Did you read it?"

"No! I mean, it's private. And I've been busy."

"True. But why would a man keep a woman's journal when the woman was somebody else's wife?"

"My mom didn't cheat on my dad," Luz gritted.

"I didn't mean to imply that." He shrugged and smothered a yawn. "Sorry—long day saving damsels in distress."

"Like I asked you to," Luz muttered, but didn't volunteer that she was tired, too. Or had wondered more than once about Ross Thurmond's apparent fascination with her mom.

She stood, too, unsure what to say.

Aaron looked around the room. "San Antonio would have been easier," he said. "They kick you out at closing time."

Her breath caught somewhere in her throat. Did he want to stay? Or was he telling her goodbye?

The clock ticked loudly in the kitchen, reminding her how quiet the house was at night. How lonely.

"I'm not kicking you out, Aaron," she murmured. "Stay?"

He crossed over to her, again catching her hands. She wasn't sure if he looked surprised or apprehensive.

"Luz, I—" He dropped her hands and caught her face instead, cradling her, his thumbs moving gently against her cheeks. "I can't promise anything." He closed his eyes briefly. "I don't want to hurt you, but—I don't even know if I can stay in Rose Creek. Chloe—"

She bit back a sigh of relief when the name he whispered was his daughter's, not his dead wife's. She could love Chloe. And she could hold on to Aaron.

"Don't," she said softly. "Don't talk. I don't want talk, or promises. I just want you to stay, Aaron." She stopped short of pleading, vaguely remembering she had a rule against begging a man for anything ever again.

Aaron's lips turned up at the corners slightly. "Getting kicked out's grossly overrated. Come here." He eased her across the slight distance between them, his eyes dark and soft, fingers still burning her cheeks.

She trailed her hands up his arms, feeling the muscle and warmth, his presence. Need flared hotter, and she locked her hands beside his head and reached up to press her lips against his.

He accepted the invitation, his lips warm and hungry, one hand slipping from her cheek to cradle her head, the other sliding down her back in a teasing caress.

She leaned in to him, reveling in the feel of his body, the slight tremor along his hard length. Being wanted back—that had been even longer ago than wanting someone.

He trailed kisses up her neck to whisper against her ear, "Let's get out of here."

She drew back a little, startled, her fingers digging into his arms. "As in where?"

His laughter rumbled against her neck and he scooped her up. "As to the only room in this house with a door that locks!"

"Oh." She let a tiny escape of relief escape, and then turned a little to nestle against his chest, rubbing her lips across the thin fabric of his shirt. "That's okay then!"

A step inside the room, he slid her down the length of his body, a caress in itself. She murmured incoherently and would have slipped his hands behind his neck, but he caught them, placed a kiss in each palm, and turned around, making a show of locking the door.

Then he turned back to her, flashing his dimples and waggling his eyebrows. "Think we might get the front door fixed tomorrow?"

She drew a shaky breath. "With the right motivation."

He laughed and swept her up again.

"Well, then, let's see what it takes."

• • •

She couldn't believe getting a lock fixed would need so much motivation. She stirred, too lazy and satisfied to actually move yet, the feel of Aaron beside her—inside her—still almost impossible to believe. She couldn't remember being so free, feeling so wanted—not even in the earliest hours of her marriage. Not ever.

She smiled and turned to face Aaron—but his side of the bed was empty. For a moment she waited, listening, hoping he'd merely gone to the bathroom, but the sheets were cold.

Stella. The thought slammed her in the chest as she slipped out of bed, the coolness of the night air raising goose bumps all over her body. She wrapped her robe loosely around her, for comfort more than coverage. Or maybe he just regretted their wildness, that he'd tasted her, enticed her, given her everything she needed, and now he was beating himself up for betraying his dead wife.

She found him in the kitchen, in his briefs, elbows propped on the sink, staring out a window into darkness. She fought back one brief moment of self-pity. She'd gloried in the way he made her feel, responded with all the cooped up passion and need of so much time alone. Yet apparently her joy would be sacrificed to his guilt.

How petty can I be? The woman he loved died saving others. She employed the same mental trick she always did, forcing herself to see from the other side. Had Brian not been cheating, manipulative scum—if he'd been a first responder, and hadn't come home— would she be able to let go so easily?

Silently she padded across the floor and wrapped her arms around his waist, laying her cheek against his back, trying to be comforting, not seductive, understanding, not borderline angry.

"I'm sorry," she whispered.

She felt him tense, and then he pushed off the sink and straightened. She let her arms slip from his waist, and he turned.

"Why are you sorry?" He tilted her face up, peering at her. "Did I get too carried away or…?"

She reached a hand up and caressed his cheek. "You can't let her go, can you?" she prodded gently. "Stella."

"Damn Stella!" Aaron's fist exploded against the sink, rattling the handful of dishes in the rack. He opened the faucet and splashed water on his face, letting it run down onto his chest.

Then he gulped air and reached out, drawing her close, but not holding her.

"No, you know what? I did come here because of Stella—but it's not what you think. Not why. Can we sit?"

She nodded, and he led her to the couch, settling her in the corner she usually sat in, but not sitting himself.

"So?"

"Have you read anything recent about Alabaster?"

She lifted her eyebrows, surprised, before remembering he'd thought she would snoop. "No."

"But you heard about the little boy who died. A teacher and another student were hurt. I think I told you Chloe was the student Stella saved."

"Yes." Aaron's face twisted in pain. She shook her head and held out her hand. "Aaron, I didn't mean to drag anything out. Come sit. Don't talk."

"You should know. If we're going to be together…" He came to the couch then, dropping to his knees and clasping her hands. "I'm an ass sometimes," he said. "I know that. I don't mean to be, I'm just not—who I was." He squeezed her hands.

"I can understand that," she assured him, pressing the back of one his hands to her cheek. "You wouldn't know the woman I was in Atlanta. And Brian only cheated—he wasn't taken away from me by some madman. But Aaron, it's okay. I can understand you not being over a woman like Stella—"

He snorted and freed her hands, but she clung to the one she held. "A woman like Stella? A woman who cheated every time I left town? A woman who led a local BDSM club?"

He heard her gasp and laughed bitterly.

"Yeah. The shooter? Someone who had a falling out with her."

He stood and walked toward the door, spun on his heel, and came back to practically throw himself on the far side of the couch.

"The cops tried to protect her at first. The media played up the hero thing—but someone started whispering. Alabaster's huge compared to Rose Creek, but it's just a small, southern town too, really. Someone saw that Chloe was her daughter—human emotion angle at first. 'Mother saves own daughter from school shooter.'"

"But then people started remembering that they'd seen her out. She'd ask for day shifts or take leave when I was out of town to meet with her friends. I knew we were having problems, but I just thought she hated how often I traveled. Yeah, right." Bitterness laced his words. "Wanted me gone more often, more likely. Then some pictures got out—and dumbass that I was, I'd never even had a clue. My hero wife!"

Tears rolled down Luz's cheeks. She didn't even try to stop them. How much hurt did anyone deserve? She'd thought losing his wife had been as bad as it could get, but his pain and anger cut like a knife.

"Those last visits I made? Investigators, trying to be sure I truly didn't know what Stella was into. Guess most husbands would have, right?" He shrugged. "We had Chloe, money—I thought we had everything."

"You loved her," Luz whispered.

He stared at her for a long moment. "Not by the time she died," he said eventually. "As hard as I thought I had tried, I'd just grown…empty…where she was concerned." He stood again, and massaged the back of his neck. "She asked for a divorce the night before she died. But even then I thought—I kept thinking—that if I just got my act together, I could fix everything. I told my company I needed to quit traveling. I told Stella I'd do anything— anything—for her. Because I wanted Chloe to have a real family. But Stella laughed and said there was nothing else to be said."

"Was she always so…I don't know what the word is."

"Wild? Free? Those were the ones she used a lot." He stared at the painting on the wall, but she knew he didn't see it.

"She was, I guess. In college—that's where we met—I didn't mind. We'd do whatever she wanted, go where she said, and try anything she wanted in bed. She took me to meet her folks once and picked up two hitchhikers on the way. They slipped off with some of her folks' stuff. Things like that should have been a warning, but I'd never met anyone like her. I never wanted to go back to the monotony of my life."

"But you changed your mind?"

"When she told me her parents told her never to go back. She took criminal justice classes, got her degree, got pregnant—I thought we should settle down."

"Did she want Chloe?"

He smiled. "Yeah. We were in complete agreement on wanting our baby girl." The smile slipped again, though. "And then—the rest. And I wound up knowing my wife was responsible for the death of a child, and the injury of others." His voice dropped to a whisper. "And that I did nothing to stop her."

"No!" Luz jumped up, fists clenching, furious. "How can you blame yourself—"

"I didn't see. I should have been able to. She told me often enough I'd lost my edge." He looked up at the ceiling for a moment, and then slowly stood to face Luz. "She told me I bored her. That I wasn't man enough to satisfy her."

The words she wanted to say lodged in her throat. Words meant nothing anyway. She reached out, caught his hand, and urged him close.

"Come back to bed," she whispered. "We don't need any more sadness tonight."

"But it's what's true," he muttered. "Truth—"

"Can wait. Tonight, it can."

He started to argue, but she pressed a gentle kiss against his mouth and shook her head.

"The bedroom door locks. We'll lock the door, and nothing else will get in." She tugged his hand gently, glancing at him. "Not even the truth."

He pressed his eyes shut, and when he opened them, managed a smile. "I'm all yours."

She doubted that was true, either, but for the rest of the night, she knew that would be enough.

Chapter Twenty

By the time Luz managed to drag herself away from Aaron and back to the reality of mouths to feed and chores to do, Ann was already checking on the mare. Luz couldn't quit smiling. Thinking of Aaron grumbling about not being able to touch the stove because she didn't trust his cooking made her smile. The cool air that closed in around her, still more dark than light, made her smile. Ann's raised eyebrows and the absence of a sarcastic greeting almost made her laugh.

"So, how is she?" Luz prompted, when the vet refused to speak first.

"Much better," Ann replied professionally, then grinned. "As you seem to be."

"Yeah, I'm fine." Luz's nonchalance dissolved in laughter. "Fine, fine, fine."

"Hmm."

"Somehow I thought I'd earned more than that," Luz said, reaching in to pet the mare. Ann had given her hay and water, though, and the mare ignored Ann and Luz in favor of her food. "I'm delighted. Just—"

"Don't you dare tell me you're worried! You practically pushed me into his arms a few weeks ago when he drove into town."

"I'm worried," Ann continued, as if Luz hadn't spoken. "He may not even stay, Luz."

"I survived a monster like Brian who gave me a baby two days after our wedding and spent the next four years screwing anything in a skirt, including Lily's mother. I survived having my little girl rushed to the hospital and almost dying, and Brian helping end my career! There is nothing—nothing—I can't survive now."

"Not even Aaron leaving?" Ann asked gently.

"Especially not that. No man has the power to destroy me, Ann. Not anymore."

"Yeah, you told me that." She sighed, and glanced a final time at the mare. "Just remember that if it ever comes up again." She picked up her bag, kissed Luz's cheek, and left.

. . .

Her mom and dad had instilled old time values in her. She knew there was heaven and hell—she just really hoped she wasn't being blasphemous to decide she'd gotten to heaven a little early.

"You know," Aaron told her one morning, propped up on her pillows and cuddling her against his chest, "some people don't spend their mornings like this."

She ran a hand over his chest, and then further down, smiling lazily when he stiffened and fished her hand out.

"Behave! I'm serious! Because after most people send their children to school, they actually get dressed and do stuff."

"Most people probably get dressed *before* they send their kids to school. I don't want to behave or be serious—and we do stuff," she protested, kissing the taut skin of his stomach.

"We should get jobs. You run a shelter. I'll manage it and look for some freelance stuff. We have to set a good example."

She kissed his chest.

"We do. You go home every night."

"And it's hard. But I'm serious."

She scooted up and kissed him and he buried his hands in her hair, kissing her back.

Then he held her away.

"Teach me to ride, Luz."

"Okay." She leaned over and kissed his shoulder. "I can do that."

"I'm serious."

She grinned and pushed his hands away so that she could kiss him again. "So am I. We can start anytime you want."

• • •

A few days later, Luz rode along the shoulder of the road. Occasionally, she looked back to see if Aaron was there. He was, and if the long ride made him uncomfortable, he didn't show it, just gave her one of his teasing smiles.

"You put me on Cherokee here out of pure meanness," he called, and tried to push the old chestnut gelding into a faster trot. Figured you'd bring me out here and lose me by just trotting off into the sunset and laughing at us for not keeping up!"

She smiled. The chestnut was slow, but he was steady. Aaron didn't need a fall—he was doing so well. She was riding one of the horses her mother had taken in for some bargain basement price—a flashy pinto that tended to shy a lot, but wasn't too difficult to stay on. Her mother had accumulated six horses—people who couldn't take care of them any longer would practically give them away rather than allow them to be put down or sold to strangers. The smile slipped as she wondered again about what connection her mother and Ross had shared.

"Feeling guilty?" Aaron asked, finally drawing closer to her.

"No, just nostalgic. Remembering my mom."

"I've heard a lot about her since I moved to Rose Creek. Wish I could have known your folks." He smiled at her. "They'd have liked me."

They would have. They'd even tried to like Brian, for her sake.

Shadows of the past suddenly chilled her. "We should go back."

He leaned over and kissed her cheek, and the little pinto danced away.

"Cut it out!" She frowned at him, pretending to be irritated. "I don't even make out in cars!"

"I wouldn't know." He grinned. "Every time I get you in a car you're unconscious or covered in dirt and blood from saving the world."

He straightened in his saddle and looked around, suddenly recognizing where they were. "I didn't think we'd ridden so long—isn't this Clark's place?"

She nodded grimly. "Yeah. And I really hadn't thought about it, but if you kept on down this road and took the cut-off with a cattle guard—you'd find Ross Thurmond's place."

He reined his horse around. "Thanks, but no thanks. No need to find him."

"Nope, none at all," she agreed. "Wanna race?"

He laughed. "I'd throw something at you, but I don't have anything handy. This horse couldn't outrun his shadow."

• • •

Chloe didn't have school on Valentine's Day. She shared the news with a great deal of jubilation while helping Luz decorate sugar cookies to take to school.

"We have the party tomorrow, but it's really Friday," she complained. "They shouldn't change holidays, right?"

"Well, we can complain about the party," her father offered, swiping a cookie and getting swatted by Luz and Chloe at the same time. "Maybe we can make the school cancel any party that isn't on the actual holiday."

"No, it's okay." Chloe poured red sprinkles on a heart and frowned at the window. The weather had turned blustery, and she hadn't been allowed to ride. "But this weather sucks."

"Chloe!"

"What?" She turned innocent eyes on her dad. "What did I say?"

"Don't sweat the small stuff," Luz suggested with a grin. "The good news is your daughter has a party tomorrow and then she'll be home on Friday, Saturday, and Sunday!"

"True," Aaron agreed. "And she'll probably be here all three days riding in freezing rain."

"Luz—"

"Yes, Chloe?"

Chloe licked her lips, apparently worried about something.

"Do you still miss Princess?" she asked softly. "Do you remember her?"

Luz set the pan of finished cookies down and went around the table to hug Chloe. "Yes, I do miss her. And I won't ever forget her."

"You didn't have her very long."

"No." She searched for the right words, sensing Chloe wasn't just wondering about Princess. "Love doesn't take very long, if it's real."

Across the table, Aaron's eyes were unreadable.

Chloe nodded. "I guess." She moved some of the sprinkles around, finally choosing a bottle of blue. "Do you think she's still alive?" she asked so softly that her words could hardly be heard.

"I hope she is," Luz answered truthfully. "I tell myself that she is."

"Even if you never see her?"

"Even if."

Chloe sighed, and picked up a cookie. "Can I eat this blue one? It's broken."

The cookie looked fine, but Chloe's face still looked troubled, and Aaron's face had settled into the old lines of hurt.

"Sure, we have plenty." Luz gathered a couple of cookies together, put them on a plate, and handed them to Chloe. "Go take a cookie break," she suggested. I need to bake this batch before we decorate any more."

Chloe nodded and left without comment.

"You're good with kids," Aaron murmured.

"I don't feel good with her—or you." She rounded the table and hugged him. "I feel that you all deserve to be free of the pain."

"We're better."

She rested her forehead against his arm for a moment. "I hope so. Aaron, don't you think we should talk to Chloe about us?

"She knows, sort of. I mean, I told her that you and I were dating, and that I'm pretty much always here until she gets out of school." He shot her a teasing grin. "I don't give her a lot of details about all of our hard work, though."

She returned his smile, but straightened abruptly, as an idea occurred. "Spring break is only a few weeks away! You know what you should do?"

"I'm afraid to ask," he grumbled, pressing a kiss on her forehead as if she were as childish as Chloe.

"Take Chloe to see the wildflowers! Drive north and through the Hill Country…"

He blanched. "Never mention spring flowers—wildflowers— to me. Never!"

"But—"

He shot a glance at the door, and then looked down at her. "I'm sorry. I overreacted. But the last thing I remember from that day was blood on the daffodils. I—I can't—I'll be back."

He stalked out of the room, and she heard him talking softly to Chloe in the living room.

Feeling their pain in her soul, she went back to baking cookies.

• • •

Luz turned her idea over in her head again. She loved the idea, but would she be forcing Aaron's hand?

He came in from the living room, and looked at the trays of cookies.

"Those things are good," he hinted, and she waved. "I need twenty-four, plus some for the teachers and staff. As long as you don't go crazy, dig in." She looked at the door to the living room.

"Where's Chloe?"

"She drifted off."

"Oh." She frowned. "Is she okay?"

"Just tired. Someone had her baking cookies all afternoon." He cocked his head as a hard rattling sound began.

"Sleet?"

"Or hail. Either way, it's really blasting us."

He grinned. "So…how do you feel about a sleepover?"

"Does Chloe need a blanket or pillow?"

"You think I don't remember where they were when we needed them?"

The memory of the bath sheet he'd worn while he was waiting for his jeans made her smile.

He laughed. "You were hoping it would fall off, weren't you?"

She chuckled, too. "Desperately." She gave in to temptation and picked up one of the cookies. "Aaron, I had an idea, but…"

"About?"

"A Valentine present for Chloe."

"Figured I'd go into San Antonio tomorrow while she's at school," he said, finishing another cookie and resolutely moving away from the table. "I hope she'll be able to go tomorrow and not miss her party. Why?"

"Would you like Rumbles to be her present from both of us?" She held her breath after she asked, still afraid he'd think her offer was somehow too much, too binding.

"Wow!" he said softly. "That would sure beat a stuffed bear. But—"

"No strings. No promises," Luz added. "If you ever leave, you'd be free to take her."

"A pony, though? You've put so much time and money into your Mom's horses."

"It really wouldn't be different than it is now. She'd come ride, but she could call Rumbles hers."

He walked over and kissed her. "You know, leaving sounds harder all the time." He kissed her again before retreating to lean against the counter. "You look worried. About the leaving part, or the sleepover?"

"Both," she admitted, and he chuckled.

"Smart girl!"

•••

Aaron had given her flowers for Valentine's Day. Luz smiled as she fingered one of the roses mixed in with spring flowers. There were no daffodils, no yellow flowers at all, but the fact that he'd given her flowers must mean he was able to deal better with his memories of that awful day. The irises in the arrangement were almost the color of the bluebonnets that would soon take over fields, yielding eventually to paintbrush, changing the Texas landscape from vibrant blue to flaming red. Maybe by the height of the wildflower season, he'd be willing to take Chloe to see all the spectacular color.

The bouquet was holding up spectacularly. It had been almost two weeks, and not a seriously wilted flower in the bunch. She wondered if the flowers would start to fade now that the weather had finally climbed out of the sixties, unseasonably cool for this part of Texas going into March.

Residents in Rose Creek were fond of going around mumbling, "*Febrero loco y marzo otro poco*," whether or not they spoke Spanish. The saying was, loosely, "February's crazy and March is crazier."

She knew it was true—she'd seen the drastic changes within a single day for much of her life.

Now the only change seemed to be the emptiness in the house. In spite of the bright sunshine pouring in, Aaron and Chloe had gone into San Antonio yesterday and wouldn't be back until Friday. After deciding definitively that he'd never allow Esmeralda to counsel his daughter again, Aaron had unexpectedly gotten an appointment with a new counselor he thought might help Chloe.

Luz glanced at the clock. How could it only be ten? She'd done everything she needed to do. The animals were tended to, she'd eaten breakfast, agreed to have a family come out on Saturday to let their children ride the ponies—where was Aaron when she needed him?

She smiled. Okay, maybe "wanted" was more accurate, but this day might never end.

She pushed up off the couch and decided to go weed her nondescript garden, but the sudden sound of a car rushing up her drive took her by surprise.

She saw Ross's old truck jerk to a stop, and when he slid out of his truck, seemingly in a hurry, she stepped out on the porch.

"Ross, is something wrong?" She caught her breath. "Ann's okay, isn't she?"

"Not comin' from her place at all," Ross said, pulling his hat off. "Sorry I came rushin' over, but I don't have your number, and well—I thought you'd wanna know."

"Know what?"

"You still missing that pit bull? The one that didn't cotton to me?"

"Princess? Yes! Have you seen her?"

"Well, it's the darnedest thing—dog that looks like her just curled up in the cow's stall in my barn. I only saw her once or twice before, but I'm pretty sure it's her, 'cause she won't let me nor the cow get near her."

"Let me call Ann."

"Well, you can, but yesterday when I went by to pick up some feed for old Mr. Jarvis, the doc said she had an appointment today. Thought maybe you'd just want to go see if it was her and if you could just get her to leave with you."

"Sure. Let me get me my stuff, and we'll go." She grabbed her purse and checked her pocket for her cell phone, then hurried down the stairs after Ross, who was already climbing into his pickup.

Hope surged through her as she tossed her purse and the cell phone on the passenger seat and turned her truck on, screeching out after Ross. Princess alive? Chloe would be just as happy as she was. Heck, Aaron might pretend otherwise, but he'd be delighted as well.

The distance to the farm seemed longer than when she and Aaron had ridden it together. She pulled her truck past his parking place near the barn, thinking that if she needed to carry the dog, the distance would be that much shorter.

She vaulted out of the truck and hurried into the barn after Ross, a little surprised that although old, this building was better maintained than Clark's. In fact, some of the wood appeared new, and she was surprised to see a couple of stalls that had mesh over the slats on the top half of the stall doors.

"There in the back, Miss Luz. You go on first—I don't wanna get bit again!"

She slowed as she reached the stall, wrinkling her nose as the smells hit her. There were barn smells, but also…dog feces? She peered in, and the stubby head lifted slightly. The stump of a tail thudded, and Princess whined.

"Oh, Princess!" Luz held her hand out as she approached, but the dog lay there, not standing, and Luz went to her knees, fearful the dog might be injured or sick.

Behind her, the stall door shut and she heard the wood-on-wood sound of a bolt being pushed closed.

Princess raised her head and growled.

"Shut up, you no good bitch!" Ross yelled at the door, and hit it with a fist.

Princess dropped her head, cowering.

And everything became crystal clear.

"Why do you have Princess?" Luz demanded. She walked over to the door, rattling it. "Ross, this is insane. Let me take the dog and go home!"

"You're softer'n your momma," he said absently. "At least she toughened up in the end. But you—you go runnin' off to save some nag. Or a worthless dog—any critter, huh?"

He leered through the mesh at her. "But who's gonna save you, pretty li'l Miss Luz? That worthless man of yours?" He laughed, the sound loud in the barn.

Luz fought to stay calm. "Ross, this is crazy. You know everyone in town. They know you. You don't want any trouble. What are you going to do with me? Why did you do this?"

He pressed his hands against the mesh, looking in at her, thinking. She noticed that the mesh only gave slightly and discarded the idea she could get through that.

"What am I gonna do with you?" He paused for a moment, and then snorted, his tone insulting. "Or what am I gonna do to you, that's more the question. What do you think I'd want a woman like you for?" He dragged his eyes over her from head to toe. "Can't buy a woman in Rose Creek," he muttered. "Everyone always watching and no one putting out anyway. Having my own woman would be better."

He moved a few steps away, and she watched him circle around in the aisle. He went to the other stall door and opened the meshed top portion.

A huge black-and-white pit bull lunged forward, dragging a chain, barking and snarling in a deadly rage as he tried to clamber over the partition.

"This here's Marco," he told her, grinning maliciously. "He's the reigning champ. He'll probably get your stupid dog tomorrow night, just to get him goin' for the main match."

"Ross—you?" Luz looked over her shoulder at Princess, quivering, her eyes pleading for help. "My mother liked you! She trusted you. How could she have not known?"

"Now hold on, Missy. Couple of things. Your ma didn't always like me. Oh, she was a damn good actress. Hid how she felt about me to keep your pa safe from himself—and from me, too, maybe." He paused and spat into the straw, then cleaned his mouth with the back of his dirty hand. "And I don't fight these dogs; I just help the guy who runs the fights. He's new to town, only been doin' it for a couple or three months."

"But why would you help?"

"Back, Marco! Get back!" He pushed the top of the stall closed, literally beating the dog back with it. "That bastard gets out, we'll all be dead," he muttered. Then he walked back over to lean on her door again as if nothing were wrong.

"You asked about your ma. Almost forgot."

He gave her another smile, one that made her cringe inwardly. He was as crazy as Hermie Clark—maybe worse, because no one could come racing to her rescue. The stall looked solid enough to hold a fighting dog and certainly solid enough to keep her here.

"Now, your ma and I, we had an arrangement, a real *personal* arrangement," he murmured. "Suited me more than her, but she was smart enough to know she didn't have no other choice. You might wanna think about that. She took back her word, of course, after your pa died. But when she was trying to save him…" He laughed and hit her door with his fist again.

"Right stupid of you to leave your purse and your phone in your truck. Ain't nobody going to know where you are 'til after… whatever we decide." He leaned on the mesh again, his fingers sticking through. For a second she considered trying to injure him somehow, smash his fingers, but she didn't see anything around. Didn't think it would help, either, probably just piss him off.

"You think real careful, Miss Luz," he advised. "We can get along, or we can't. Tomorrow we'll have company." He paused. "You wouldn't like what they'd do to you. I wouldn't either. But I'm not a stupid man. If you and I ain't agreed on what you *will* do for me, then I reckon that the dogs won't be the only thing for sale tomorrow. And if you're gonna be up for sale it might as well be to me and not some guy who comes to watch things die at a dog fight."

He rattled the mesh, leering through it. "Gotta go, got stuff to do. But you think real hard about what's going on. I can make it easy or hard, but tomorrow night…" He shrugged. "Then, the boss says what I do."

"Don't go!" She came to the door and lifted her own hands against the mesh, trying to appeal to the Ross she knew, not the madman threatening her with death. "Ross, this is crazy. People know us both; they'll look for me. They'll want to help you if you're in trouble—this is Rose Creek, for heaven's sake!"

She thought his expression softened for a moment, but then he smirked. "Rose Creek. Never had a dime or a minute for me, did they? Oh, sure, busy work to hand money to me, but an invitation to dinner or some kid's birthday, or a woman sayin' yes to a date?" He took off his cap, fanning his face and running a dirty hand through the short, gray hair. "Don't matter. Only woman I ever wanted was your ma, and she never wanted me back." He plopped the cap back on his head and winked. "Course, that didn't stop what had to happen from happenin', but she shouldn't never have married your pa."

Without another word, he started off.

She couldn't let him go, had to get him open to the door. "Wait! I—I need to go to the bathroom. At least just let me out for a few minutes."

He didn't look back, but she heard him snigger. "Then just squat, honey. Ain't no cameras in the stall." He turned then, waving at the ceiling of the barn. "Don't know how they work, but those cameras see everything that happens out here. And the boss has folks who watch 'em. 'Magine that—gettin' paid to sit on your ass and watch an empty barn all day." He puffed out his chest a little. "That's why I'm expectin' a call about why a woman ran into a stall. I'll have to tell him you came to save your dog. I couldn't let him see me draggin' you in. And I need a good reason for when I take you to my other place. So don't even think about tryin' to get out somehow."

Whistling, he left the barn. Minutes later she heard a truck turn on. His? Hers?

Tires crunched on gravel, and she was alone. She dropped to her knees, and Princess limped to her, emaciated again, nosing her for comfort. Given the dog's physical condition and fear of Ross, she suspected he'd had her since she ran away. "Too bad you can't talk, girl," she sighed. "I could use some help right about now." She spent a few minutes petting the dog while she studied the stall, looking for any weakness or opening. She couldn't find one. Finally, with a last word to soothe Princess, she stood up and went to the door, looking for any bit of mesh she might be able to pry loose.

• • •

Aaron bit back a curse as a car shooting onto Loop 410 W almost bounced off his car. Chloe had her earphones on and her eyes glued to the screen of a handheld game, oblivious to the traffic and tired of the sites he dutifully pointed out.

She made him smile. Always. *Kind of like Luz.* He frowned, but more at the traffic than at the realization that he missed her. He had driven in cities much worse than San Antonio, but here he was, feeling stressed and irritable. One morning without Luz, and he was a wreck. He should think about that.

Beside him a horn blared, and he jerked back to total focus on the lanes of speeding vehicles all around him. He'd have to think about Luz later. Signs for their exit rushed at him, and he turned on his signal and started working his way over to the turn lane.

Hours later, he watched Chloe sleep, almost lost in the vastness of the hotel bed, a little annoyed that neither of them had spoken to Luz. Not that she was at his beck and call, but it wasn't like her to have ignored the three calls, either.

Chloe stirred a little, and he stood up, ready to let her know he was there if any of today's events brought back her nightmares. After the shooting, she hadn't dealt well with crowds, with strangers closing her in, and this was a busy city full of bustle and noise. They'd both jumped when a bus backfired near them, and she'd hardly eaten any supper.

But she just mumbled something incoherent and turned over, clutching the hotel pillow to her like one of her stuffed animals.

He kicked off his shoes and headed over to the couch to watch the evening news. Since Rose Creek didn't have a station, he and Luz usually watched this San Antonio channel. As he settled into a comfortable spot, he wished again Luz could have made the trip with them. And that she'd answered the phone, dammit! Why hadn't she?

They hadn't fought. Could something have happened to her? What could happen to her in Rose Creek?

And then he thought of Stella and Alabaster and his forehead beaded with cold sweat.

He started to dial Ann's number, but cleared the number and tossed his phone to the far side of the couch.

Luz had misplaced the phone and not noticed yet, or it had run out of battery. He wouldn't risk disturbing Ann if she and Ram had one of their rare early nights. The woman was pregnant, for heaven's sake. Luz was fine.

And he would not let memories of Stella make him an emotional cripple. He wouldn't.

• • •

Luz didn't know the time, how long Ross had been gone, or even if he'd come back, although she supposed he would. Pain throbbed in her hands, and she glanced down. She'd given manicured nails up when she left Atlanta—long nails got in the way of moving hay and bossing half ton horses around. Nevertheless, the flesh around two of her nails was seeping blood from the scratches and cuts she'd gotten trying to pry one strand of mesh loose. Once or twice she'd thought the steel moved, but then she realized she was getting nowhere. Then she'd spent untold time going around the stall, pushing and prodding the planking—all new, all solid.

She finally slumped down in the cleanest part of the stall, where the dog hadn't soiled the straw. Humiliation and anger throbbed through her along with the pain from her hands. She'd had to do exactly what Ross had said, relieving herself, while half expecting to find him leering in at her.

She thought of all the women leads in popular series and films who would simply kick the door down, and wished life were that easy. You could be strong, "feisty," and independent, but if the damn walls were solid enough, you weren't going to get out on your own.

Princess nudged her, and she stroked the battered head absently. Maybe, if Ross did open the door, Princess would feel protective enough of her to attack. She didn't want the dog hurt, but it was coming down to doing something, or…

She brushed the specter of death away, and thought of Aaron and Chloe. They'd be back tomorrow. Had they tried to call her? Would they wonder why she hadn't answered?

She doubted it. Aaron had seen her leave her cell phone lying around, knew she didn't always keep it charged. And he and Chloe had planned to go for dinner and visit the San Antonio Zoo since Chloe's appointments had taken up all of today. They wouldn't head back until tomorrow evening, Aaron had said.

Tomorrow would be too late, if Ross could be believed.

And the beast she could hear clanking his chain and growling occasionally certainly wasn't here to be a birthday surprise for some child. She'd never seen a larger, more vicious-looking dog, and the scars on his body spoke of any number of fights.

She pushed Princess away and stood up again. Time to do something. She just didn't have a clue what might work.

Ross came back as darkness was falling. She heard him come through the door, and there was a shuffling as if he were dragging something along. He turned on a light switch somewhere. Across the way, the pit bull began to whine and pull on his chain. Feeding time? And how could anyone feed that thing?

She wasn't wrong; Ross came down the corridor carrying a large bowl of food and a bucket of water. She watched without comment as he paused outside the dog's stall and knelt down, fiddling with latches she hadn't noticed on the bottom of the door. He raised a portion of the door, and a black snout thrust out, teeth bared, snuffling and growling as the dog inside tried to get to his food bowl.

Ross pushed the food in, then went to a corner and pulled out a small, three-pronged garden rake. He got down again, and fished around in the stall until he pulled out another bowl, which he filled with water. Then he carefully latched the hooks again and got up, a little more stiffly this time, and brushed at his pant's legs.

For a moment, she thought he was leaving without speaking to her, and couldn't decide whether or not to call out. Maybe her own stall had one of those feeding slots. Maybe—

But then he was back, and she saw what he was half-dragging, half-carrying was a canvas, easily the size of the painting in her living room, its back facing her. She felt prickles of fear scurry up her arms. Somehow she knew whatever was on the front of the canvas would hurt her.

Ross took his time. She supposed it was his form of torture. Not physical, but he was a master at inflicting mental anguish. He propped the painting against the opposite stall, slanting it so that if the dog— Marco? —lunged against the door, the painting wouldn't fall and reveal itself ahead of time.

He left again, and came back with a stool and a fast food bag. The scents coming out were normally something she'd avoid, but her stomach rumbled and clenched. Her lips were parched, but he lifted the drink cup up and toasted her, as if he planned on drinking it himself while she watched.

"Oh, hi," he said then, as if he'd forgotten she were there. He laughed, slapping his knee as if he thought nothing was funnier. "Just kiddin'." He stood up and walked over to the door. Princess rumbled low in her throat.

"Princess, no!" Luz hissed, not wanting the dog to give Ross pause if he decided to open the door.

"Oh, don't worry about her. Worthless as they come." He bent the straw a little and poked it through one of the diamond-shaped spaces.

"Drink up. It's water, not soda. They say that's better for you."

Luz took a long sip before responding. Then she stepped back from the door. "Ross, couldn't you hand it in—it's hard to drink."

"I'm thinkin'." He sat back down on the edge of the stool. "Guess you're feelin' a mite lonely. Lover boy not gonna be sneakin' into your bed the minute he sends his little one off to school?"

She lifted her chin. "Aaron is none of your business, and neither is Chloe. Let me go home, Ross."

"Sure, sure. And I guess you won't call the police or nothin', huh?"

He laughed when she couldn't force the lie out. "Maybe you're as tough as your ma after all—she always had trouble lyin', too." He pulled the burger out of his bag, letting the bag fall to the floor and opening the wrapper. The hot meat smell filled the stall. He pinched off a small portion with his filthy fingers and pushed it into the stall.

"Here you go."

Luz took it, but pretended to let it fall, and Princess immediately snapped it up.

"When was the last time you fed my dog, Ross? I can't believe you have Ann thinking you're some kind of animal expert."

"Oh, I know animals. The two-legged kind as well as the four-legged kind. I got no call to mistreat Ann's animals."

"None of this makes sense."

"See all that new wood holding you in?" He chuckled. "Call it panelin' if you want to. You think the little bit Ann and the others gave me would fix up this place? Dogs is like any other animal— here to be used."

Luz leaned her forehead against the mesh. "Let me out, Ross. Just let us out. I'll take my truck and go home." She kept her tone soft, just short of pleading, but he was unmoved.

"Want some more burger?"

"Not if you're tearing off little bits and sticking them through, Ross. I can't—they'll fall." She'd been hiding her hands, trying to keep him from seeing how futile her attempts to escape had been, but tried a different tactic.

She lifted both hands, gripping the mesh, forcing herself not to recoil at how bloody and grimy her hands were after just hours of captivity. "Please," she said simply.

He noticed immediately. "Been tryin' to dig out?" He snorted. "Stupid. If dogs can't get out, ain't no way you're gonna."

"I can't stand being locked up." She pushed her fingers further through the mesh, scraping them and biting back a moan over the pain that seared through her hands. "Just let me out for a few minutes."

He seemed to actually consider it. Hope speared through Luz, and she wished that Princess hadn't retreated several feet away. If he opened the door, she'd have to get through and try to get away. Unless Princess came with her, she'd have to run first then try to bring help. Briefly her eyes flicked to the closed door across the corridor, and she moistened her dry lips. *Please Princess, help me out here.*

"You gonna run for it if I open the door?" Ross challenged, settling his hands on the wooden latch.

Her heart hammered. Should she deny it? Beg? Not say anything at all?

She pulled her fingers back. "No. Just a few minutes, Ross."

And he laughed. A twisted laugh that made Princess whine from her corner and killed all Luz's momentary hope.

"I'm not stupid, woman," he snarled, hitting the mesh with his fist.

She silently cursed herself for pushing. Maybe silence would have been better. But it was too late.

"I'm gonna tell you now how things are gonna be. And you're gonna tell me yes or no. 'Cause tomorrow afternoon, when the boss comes—you're only safe if you're where I put you. Never seen anybody half as bad."

"What is it you want?"

"Gotta show you somethin'." He walked over to the canvas, picked it up, and backed across the stall, keeping her from seeing the other side. Then, slowly, he turned.

Luz gasped and staggered back, almost falling, staring in shocked disbelief at the nude portrait of her own mother.

"What…why do you have that? Who painted it? How—" She lunged at the door, shaking the mesh. "Let me out!"

"Your momma never cottoned to me." He ran a hand lovingly over the painting. "She wouldn't have sat for me if she had her way. 'Course, she was young here."

His words snaked through her senses.

"Your pa worked hard, but that oil business…" He made a snorting sound. "Leavin' your mom all the time to go off to those oil rigs, even when you were a tiny thing."

"Mom would never have posed for that—never!"

Again the derisive snort. "You think? You didn't even know your ma, did you, runnin' off to Georgia the month you graduated, livin' there until they kicked you out."

Luz stiffened, wanting to protest, but what would it matter? He'd talk until he tired of listening to himself. She sank down to the stall floor and crossed her legs under her, tired, too.

"See, she didn't want to sit for me. But one afternoon, I'd come over to help do some heavy stuff. Your pa called me clear from Louisiana and asked me to go by."

"Your ma offered me a beer while I was working, and I had my own little stash in the truck. I got to talking to your mom, and, well, she was lonely."

"You raped her," Luz gritted through clenched teeth.

"You know when a woman wants you and when she don't." Ross seemed intent on torturing her. "She said she didn't but she wanted me, all right." He snatched the cup off the stool and hurled it against the stall door. "Then, after, she was gonna go to the cops, but she chickened out. She knew if I didn't get her, your pa would!"

"My father would never have hurt her. He loved her." She raised her head to glare up at him. "He would have killed you."

"Yeah, he would have." Ross chuckled. "And everyone in Rose Creek woulda said your ma screwed around on your pa. See, in a little town like Rose Creek, things are different than in cities. Folks don't much like a woman who sleeps with someone other than her own man. They think she might go after theirs next, you know? If folks had shunned her, where would your ma and her little girl have been, huh? Your ma knew, too. She knew she'd get your pa or me killed if anyone found out anything. Wasn't a man more jealous in Texas than your pa, and she knew he'd try to kill me if he found out. Knew 'bout some little traps I kept set around my place. Didn't want your pa to wind up killin' me or being killed. She made me promise not to tell him."

He put the painting down beside the door, this time on her side. He continued to press close against the mesh. "So, Luz, you might wanna think. Your ma was real nice to me. Sat for this picture so I wouldn't tell anyone. And I kept my word. Never touched her again. Guess she didn't want you to think bad of her, either. Or maybe she knew I'd do just what I said if she told anyone, even you. I'd have taken this painting right down to the middle of Rose Creek and made sure everyone knew she sat for me." A long pause and she heard the wood move slightly outside. "She learned to hide her hatred of me real well. People thought we were the best of friends. Guess in the end she was smart enough to know it didn't matter anymore. Water under the bridge, and no one ever saw her like I did." He turned to run a hand over the nude figure in the painting, before turning his malevolent stare on Luz.

"Now it's all up to you, Luz. That bastard you're sleepin' with— he don't deserve you. You and your ma sure do have bad taste in men."

He spoke in a strangely singsong way, as if trying to reason with her—or with himself. Suddenly she heard the bolt slide back. Adrenaline surged through her. She uncrossed her feet, trying to be careful. When she saw the door move slightly outward, she jumped up and forward. Startled by her move, Princess, too, lunged forward—and the door slammed back, the bolt sliding immediately into place.

And Ross burst out laughing like the mad man he was.

"Well, now we know!" he chortled. "Make up your mind by tomorrow morning," he leered, "'cause you're out of time. You can be my woman for a time, just mine—or the boss will take you for whatever he wants. For himself or the highest bid or the crowd. You might not think so now, Luz, but I'm a lot better for you than he is." Whistling, he retrieved the portrait and retreated, turning off the lights in the corridor as he left.

Defeated and tortured, Luz sank back down, and Princess lay down next to her. She wrapped her arms around Princess's head and let thoughts of Aaron and Chloe fill her head and heart.

•••

Something was wrong. Aaron tossed his cell on the bed, shoved his hands in his pockets, and walked over to the window. He pulled the curtain back and stared down at the bustle of people below.

Chloe still slept, turned away from the light he let in, her hand thrown across her face.

Almost nine. Luz would have answered her phone. She had no reason to ignore his call. If she'd lost her phone, she would have found it by now. Probably.

And there was the feeling in his gut: the one similar to when his aunt died. Beads of perspiration popped out on his forehead in spite of the coolness in the room.

He'd felt this way when he woke up the day Stella died, too.

Stop it! Enough being a basket case. Enough constant fear and worry. Enough.

He retrieved his phone and punched in Ann's number.

She answered on the third ring.

"Hey, Aaron. What's up? How's Luz?"

"You haven't talked to her today? Or late yesterday? I'm in San Antonio."

"That's right, she told me you were going. No, I didn't get out there yesterday, and to be honest, I'm in San Antonio too. Doctor again, darn it!"

"Oh." He hesitated. "Are you okay?"

"Sure. Is everything okay with Luz? Should I call her?"

"No, don't worry. She must just have been busy." He glanced again at Chloe. "We're heading on home anyway."

"Okay. Oh, gotta go!" Her phone went dead.

He walked over and pulled Chloe's blanket off. She mumbled something and pulled it back up.

"Up and at 'em, young lady! Time to go."

Chloe sat up, rubbing her eyes. "I thought we were going to stay."

"I changed my mind." He kissed her forehead. "Let's go see your pony. And Luz."

She jumped out of bed and hugged him. "Let's go!" She thrust her feet into shoes and reached for the pillow she'd brought along on the trip.

He laughed. "I think you can change first." He waved at the bathroom. "Go ahead. I'll be here when you're ready."

• • •

Luz woke up when the dog across from her began growling and moving around in agitation. She scrambled up, startling Princess, who stood pressed close to her legs, growling the low rumble that she saved for Ross Thurmond.

"Well, mornin', Luz!" The handyman looked into the stall and wrinkled his nose. "Phew! Not exactly fancy quarters, is it?"

Luz kept her face impassive and tried to control her anger. She needed to be ready to make a move if he gave her any opening.

"You thought any about our little deal?" he leered.

The anger came out in spite of her efforts. "I slept in a stall with a dog in our own pee and crap."

"But it don't need to be like that anymore," he wheedled. "You can live like a queen." Something sick lit his eyes. "I can paint you, like I did your ma. Just like that."

His cell phone went off then, and when he checked the number, he flinched visibly.

He turned and walked away several paces, but she could tell from the snatches of conversation he was upset.

She saw him shove his phone back in his pocket and heard his loud, "Shit!"

Then he walked back and forth in the corridor several times, twisting his cap and kicking at the straw and dirt, his face visibly contorted with rage.

Finally he came back and perched on the stool, and just sat staring at her, putting his hat on only to immediately jerk it off again.

"Fuck him!" he muttered, and spit into the dirt at his feet. Then he slipped off the stool. "Got a little problem," he said through the mesh.

Did he think she was so stupid she hadn't figured that out?

When he didn't volunteer any information, she prodded him. "What problem?" A mirthless smile touched her lips. "Sheriff coming over?"

"No, why would the sheriff come? The sheriff and me are buddies, Luz. Patched his roof last month for a quarter what the pros wanted." He fell quiet for a moment, looking worried. "No, the boss, that's the problem. Stan—he's the one that runs things—he just said he ain't comin' 'til tomorrow. Gotta feed that monster another day." He paused again and walked up and down, but in a shorter path. He seemed to be thinking out loud. "And something ain't right, either." He stopped and stared blindly at her. "Maybe he plans on tellin' someone—lettin' them find me with his dog."

Then he shook his head. "Nah, I'm just bein' an old ninny-man. No one knows 'bout him or me. He's paid me every penny he ever said he would, too." The leering smile returned. "I got lots of money now, Luz. Have to hide it so people won't know. But lots."

Then he frowned. "But I don't like him jerkin' me around, either." He gestured at the pit bull's door. "Old Marco there would as soon eat you for breakfast as dog chow. I ain't gonna feed him this morning, just in case you try to leave." He laughed. "I got somethin' I gotta do. That'll fix things. I'm gonna send old Stan a message I'm waitin', just in case he's gonna try to do anything."

Luz watched him disappear.

Her throat burned and her lips were dry and rough. She felt weak from lack of food and water. Slowly she lowered herself back to the hay on the floor of the stall. What had her mother endured at Ross Thurmond's hands? She wished she'd read the journal. She hadn't taken the time, and now it was too late—maybe forever too late. She took a deep breath and tried to relax, tried not to think. If she could find a way out, she'd need her strength.

•••

The trip to Rose Creek never seemed longer. The breakfast they'd eaten quickly in the hotel lobby had only taken a few minutes, and the traffic was no heavier than usual. Still, time seemed to crawl as he drove.

Several miles away, Chloe suddenly called out and pointed out her window. "Look, Dad! Is that smoke? What's burning?"

Fearfully, he tried to pin the plume of smoke in relation to Luz's home. Too far over, he was fairly sure. The way smoke could play tricks, probably not even near Rose Creek. But he changed plans abruptly.

He would take Chloe to school. Just in case.

He slowed for the exit ramp and turned in toward town.

"Aren't we going to go to Luz's house?" Chloe protested immediately.

"No. I think school first, and then I might come pick you up early."

They arrived at the school a few minutes later, and he gaped in astonishment at all the trucks and cars. Students spilled out of the building in an orderly way, climbing into parents' vehicles and being taken away.

He couldn't breathe for a minute, thought that any minute he'd see the carnage of Alabaster, the crush of emergency vehicles. He gulped air, and acrid smoke bit into the back of his throat.

Mrs. Carter hurried up, and her expression was reassuring. She didn't appear particularly concerned about whatever was going on.

"Mr. Estes! We didn't think Chloe would be here today, so we didn't send you the bulletin."

"Bulletin?"

"We need to dismiss the children—just a precaution. There's a bad brush fire out on the property beyond Ross Thurmond's place, and when the wind whips up the way it does this time of year—well, it's just better if the kids are at home so their parents can keep them safe if the fire turns some crazy way. Sometimes acres and acres are affected."

Damn. He couldn't keep Chloe until he checked in on Luz.

"Excuse me, I need to speak to Mrs. Gonzalez." The principal left him standing there with Chloe and went to explain the situation to another parent.

He'd try Mrs. Baker. He'd have to waste precious time, but—

"Hello, Aaron. Chloe." Emeralda Salinas came over, smiling at them. He'd dressed her down for the incident with Chloe, but she was here.

"Esme, could you watch Chloe for me? For maybe an hour or so?"

"Sure," the counselor said without hesitation. "If Chloe doesn't mind."

Chloe didn't look happy, but she didn't argue. Thankfully.

He didn't have time.

"What's up, Aaron?" she asked, reaching out to corral Chloe's hand.

He didn't want to answer, but supposed he should. She answered for him, though.

"You're probably dropping in on Luz," she said. "The fire's not out that way, Aaron." She paused. "Chloe, can you ask Ms. Baker to give you my purse? See, she's over there by the door and she said she'd keep it for me."

"Okay," Chloe agreed and raced off.

"Esme?"

"I didn't want to scare Chloe."

"What?" Aaron looked over at his daughter; she was already on her way back, stopping to say something to one of her classmates.

"It's weird. A pilot looking over the fire found two trucks out in the middle of the pasture where it started and is burning the worst."

"Trucks?"

"One is Luz's. The other is Ross Thurmond's."

"What? How?"

"No one knows, and the firefighters are trying to cut their way in. The only guess I've heard is that one of them drove over there to check on property or an animal." She shrugged, puzzled. "Hopefully they'll be okay."

Her voice held no real assurance.

"I've gotta go." He hugged Chloe and kissed her. "Listen to Ms. Salinas," he ordered. "I'll be right back."

He climbed into the SUV and maneuvered out carefully, mindful of all the children and parents and unwilling to scare Chloe. As he drove, he turned over what Esmeralda said. Why would Luz have been out in the middle of nowhere? Since yesterday?

No. Maybe her truck had been stolen. Or she'd believed someone's hard luck story and loaned it out. He'd go by her house, and she'd be there or at the barn. He'd be able to breathe again.

But even as he slowed and signaled a turn, he knew.

She wasn't home. She wasn't dead in her truck. Ross had her.

Ross, you bastard. What have you done to Luz?

• • •

Luz woke to the overwhelming stench of something burning. She staggered to her feet, disoriented, and looked around; there was no sign of fire, but the smoke smell made her gag. When had she dozed off? And what was burning? Brush? That was a common hazard around here and Rose Creek was suffering through a draught. Brush could be sparked by passing motorists or—or someone intent on hiding a crime.

She went to the door, pushing against it, finding it as solid as it had always been. Behind her, Princess growled.

"We gotta get outta here," Ross said, materializing out of the smoke and heat. "Listen, you come with me or you stay and burn."

"Princess…"

"Oh, no! You ain't bringin' that poor excuse of a dog."

Luz didn't argue. Maybe the fire wasn't as close as he said. She'd get away from him and come back for Princess.

The idea of the chained dog burning sickened her, but she couldn't think about that.

Beside her, Princess stilled. Ross moved closer and Luz drew her head back.

"Gas? Ross, I smell gas fumes. What have you done?" Realization hit, and she clamped her lips closed. A blur of movement made her blink, but she bit back her gasp of shock. And joy.

Ross had been so absorbed in her he hadn't noticed Aaron, coming up behind him quickly and quietly. He whirled just as Aaron got there, cursing and lashing out with his fists, but Aaron sidestepped, grabbed one of his arms, and twisted it violently.

Ross cried and crumpled to his knees, and Aaron jerked the bolt back.

The pit bull's chain rattled and clanged, and the sounds of him trying to come through the wall were terrifying.

"Get out, Luz! Run to the SUV and get in. The door's open!"

"Princess!" The dog staggered out of the stall, almost unable to walk. Luz had carried her before and she bent down to scoop her up, only to collapse in the corridor.

Aaron flung Ross into the newly vacated stall and rammed the bolt shut, jerking the door to test it.

"For God's sake, Luz, are you okay? We've got to get out!" He helped her up and steadied her for a minute.

"Clumsiness and lack of food," she murmured reassuringly.

He clutched her close in a brief, fervent hug, then scooped her up and headed toward the entrance at a trot.

"Princess, carry Princess," Luz pleaded. "I can walk on my own."

He sighed, but set her down, and went back to pick the dog up.

"Look!" Luz pointed at the tree line on the far edge of Ross's property. Sparks glowed in the tops of the dry, stunted trees, and a sudden spire of flame shot upwards. "We can't leave Ross, Aaron."

"I was going to call someone."

"What if they don't get here in time? He can't die. Not here."

"What does that mean?" Aaron settled the dog in the middle of the SUV. "Water and food in the front," he called. "Be ready to go."

"Don't let him let that dog loose—he'll kill you!" Luz shouted after him. She slid halfway out of the truck, then forced herself back in. In her state, she'd be a liability. A bottle of water stuck out of a bag, and she drank half the bottle, never taking her eyes off the barn.

Relief swamped her when Aaron rushed out, dragging Ross after him. One of Ross's arms hung crookedly, and he stumbled after Aaron without protest. Aaron threw open the cargo door and shoved Ross in on top of the luggage. Furiously he jerked his belt off and bound the man's hands behind him, ignoring the yelps of pain and the profanity. He slammed the door shut, came around and got in.

"We're watching you, Thurmond!" he warned, and wheeled around, heading for the highway. They pulled off the drive as a fire engine barreled in, then took the road back toward town.

"Where's Chloe?" Luz asked, her voice already stronger.

"The school evacuated the students. I asked Esme to keep her."

"Esmeralda?" Luz echoed, surprised, knowing how upset Aaron had been with the counselor.

"Look, she wouldn't have been my first choice, but I needed to find you. And she isn't a monster, really."

"True." Princess whined a little, and Luz twisted around in her seat enough to pour a little water in her hand, which Princess lapped at thirstily. To Aaron's credit, he said nothing about the water that slipped to the carpet. Nor to mention that she hadn't bathed in over a day, and the glances he kept slanting her way seemed relieved, not disgusted. Tiny little bubbles of happiness floated through her.

When she finished giving as much of the water as she could to the dog, she turned back to Aaron, who grinned ruefully and jerked his head in the direction of the console. "Hand sanitizer if you nee—want it."

She smiled back, fished out the hand sanitizer, and slathered it on her hands and halfway up her arms, relishing the cleansing burn. "So, how did you find me?"

He slowed as he came into Rose Creek, and looked at an intersection before continuing through it.

"They found your truck out in a field with Ross's, burning. They figure he started the fire. They don't know he took you, but I figure that's why." He stopped and pulled into a parking space in front of the sheriff's office. "I knew something was wrong last night when we couldn't get you on the phone. This morning…I don't know. We came home early because I wanted to be sure I wasn't having one of my usual panic attacks. When I heard they found your truck and his, out in the middle of nowhere, I just knew he had you."

Luz shivered as she opened her door. "He planned on taking me somewhere else. I'm glad you came." She slid another glance his way. "He raped my mom," she whispered. "And made her sit for a picture, but she never told anyone."

He reached across the seat and squeezed her hand gently. "Don't think about it now. We'll talk about it when you've had some time to deal with what just happened."

"Let's give Ross to the sheriff."

The sheriff wasn't in, but the deputy manning the office took down Luz's information, shaking his head repeatedly.

"Why, Ross? Everyone in this town respected you."

Ross responded curtly to the questions the deputy asked about personal information, but refused to answer anything else.

"Ross, why the carcasses? Why did you torture me that way?" Luz asked, as the deputy made to lead him away in handcuffs.

"You Wilkinson women keep choosing useless pieces of crap for your men," Ross hissed, and spat at Aaron's feet. "I wanted you to be good and scared before I went for you."

The deputy took him away with a jerk.

"Aaron," Luz said.

"Sssh." Aaron folded her into his arms and hugged her close.

She returned his hug, but pushed out of his arms. "I know you left the car running, but Princess…"

He squeezed her hand. "Let's go home."

Chapter Twenty-one

Being without transportation was the pits. Luz glanced at her watch. Aaron had promised to come pick her up and take her car shopping. She smiled. Maybe being without transportation wasn't the end of the world, after all. Aaron came earlier and he and Chloe stayed later, just in case Luz should need something unexpectedly. At least, that was his excuse. And she didn't mind. Still, two weeks without wheels was long enough. Sooner or later she'd need her own car.

Atlanta seemed so far away now. Something told her that Aaron would stay in Rose Creek. Because of her. She hugged that thought close, realizing that Brian's betrayal had robbed her of confidence and optimism, along with everything else. Being able to find hope and excitement again felt incredibly good. Brian hadn't been seen since he'd turned up at the school. Probably miffed because she'd blocked his number, he'd decided to force her hand by trying to corner her. She drew a deep breath. How had she fallen for such a manipulator, a man who thought others existed for his use?

She looked out at the fence. A plywood sign hung there, its back a plain white rectangle, but the front proclaimed her parents' place—hers now, she reminded herself—Second Chance Animal Shelter.

Chloe, Ann, Aaron, and she had debated the name, but Aaron had been insistent. The animals here had been given second chances.

He had drawn her close and whispered, "We have a second chance, too. The name fits."

So where was he?

Almost on cue, she heard tires on gravel. She picked up her purse and pulled the curtain aside to verify that it was Aaron.

Surprisingly, though, he seemed to have come with most of Rose Creek. Ann's truck pulled up next to the SUV, followed by the Bakers, Mrs. Carter, and a host of other vehicles she didn't know on sight. *What on earth?* She dropped her purse and went out to greet everyone, a little worried.

Aaron bounded up the steps, gave her a kiss in front of all the onlookers, who broke into cheers, and led her down the steps.

"Luz, we have something for you," Ann said. "To help with the shelter and everything, now that you got all the paperwork filed and it'll be official pretty soon."

"We're real glad you got out of that mess with Ross," someone added. "Imagine, livin' here all our lives and never really knowin' the man!"

A double cab pickup turned in and followed the drive up to the crowd. Luz's eyes widened as Ann's husband popped out one side and Chloe out the other. She ran up to Luz and hugged her.

"Ta da!" she trilled, like a game show hostess, waving at the silvery new truck.

Luz slanted a puzzled look at Aaron. "Ta da?" she echoed.

Aaron draped an arm around her shoulder. "Everyone in Rose Creek is upset about what happened to your truck, and excited about the shelter. They decided to replace your truck."

"And no arguing," Ann warned, "because Mr. Temple gave us a huge discount, and Ram welded hooks all over the back to hold kennels and railings and anything else you need—even painted them to match!"

"Come see it, Luz!" the sheriff ordered, and half a dozen of her friends urged her forward, handing her the keys and talking all at once. Even the folks she didn't know as well crowded around with good wishes and comments about the situation with Ross.

"Good end to that dog fight ring!" one of the local ranchers declared. "Beasts. Glad ol' Stan didn't get away. If Ross hadn't talked just in time, he might have made his run for it."

"Too bad the fire didn't just take out all the Thurmond place. He'll be gone too long to need it."

Luz edged away from the truck, trying not to be noticed, but not wanting to hear anything else. The volunteer firefighters, with help from some of the closer communities, had managed to save the barn and part of Ross's house. The fighting pit, hidden in an old chicken coop remodeled on the inside, had burned to the ground. The sheriff had confirmed Ross set the fire to confuse anyone looking for Luz, while sending a veiled threat to Stan and his buddies. Luz thought the fire had been stupid, but it had hidden some of the key evidence, and Ross was clearly deranged anyway.

Her mother's picture, singed and grimy, had survived. She didn't know how she felt about that. She still hadn't forced herself to open the journal. She knew she had to, for her own peace of mind, though. Why had Ross returned it? To make her continue suffering? Every time she thought of the picture, stashed away now in the barn, she wondered what kind of hell her mother had suffered over the years. Had Ross really wielded power over her, or was his domination all in his own mind? Relentlessly she pushed the worry away once again.

"Too bad that whole barn didn't burn," someone else said.

Luz thought of the pit bull. Ultimately, he'd been spared the agony of the fire, but he'd been put down by a vet who came in from San Antonio. Ann had been unwilling to risk her baby by trying to tackle the long-tortured beast.

"We're celebrating, not mourning," Aaron whispered, returning to her side. "Smile—look, the reporter from the *Rose Creek Monthly* wants a picture." He stepped away, while everyone assembled around the truck, calling her to join them.

The photographer took pictures and cell phones flashed away.

The commotion seemed surreal. She'd attended functions in Atlanta with more people, more cameras flashing, more pomp and circumstance. None of them made her feel as humbled and loved as this celebration. But the clamor around her didn't quite drown the persistent worry. Why wouldn't her mother have told someone about Ross? Could she really have feared these good people would condemn her for something not her fault?

"Time to go," someone said, and people started to dribble away.

A person or two sidled toward the back of the crowd and Luz held up a hand quickly. "Wait! Just a minute, please."

Attention turned back to her, and she swallowed hard. "There's no way I can thank you for this," she said, waving at the truck. "I'll consider it—and the shelter—something that belongs to Rose Creek more than me."

Disavowals and "you're welcomes" swirled around her, and she saw Mrs. Baker dab at her eyes.

"I came back from Atlanta feeling nothing would ever be right again," she added. "Y'all have made it right, and nothing could mean more." Tears started to trickle down her cheeks as she finished her thoughts. "More than the shelter, though, more than welcoming me home—you were lifelong friends to my mom and dad. I'm proud to live in Rose Creek and honored to know all of you."

Thunderous applause greeted her words and many of the visitors waited for a chance to hug her before leaving. Through the farewells, Aaron stood nearby, grinning at her when she looked his way and returning handshakes and hugs himself.

A woman came over, her daughter holding her hand and smiling at Chloe.

"Mr. Estes, I'm Reyna's mother, Erica Barnes," she introduced herself. "Reyna and Chloe are classmates."

"Yes! Chloe talks about your daughter all the time," Aaron said. "What can I do for you?"

"Reyna asked a couple of the girls in her class to a sleepover tonight—pizza, popcorn, and a couple of movies. For her birthday. We wondered if Chloe could come?"

Luz held her breath, knowing how hard simple questions like that were for Aaron. His face tautened, and to her, his smile looked forced. But he looked at Chloe.

"What do you think, Chloe?"

"Could I?"

"You won't be nervous?"

"Of course not," Chloe scoffed. "You know nothing scares me!"

"Yeah," he agreed, sighing. "I do know that." He nodded at Reyna's mother. "Thanks."

Luz watched as Erica gave him the information on place and time, then she stood with him as they drove away.

"I'm going to go check on Princess," Chloe announced. "I haven't seen her today!"

Suddenly, everyone was gone. Luz smiled. "You did good," she noted. "Hardly flinched when Chloe got the invitation."

"Quit pushing it," Aaron muttered, but without real irritation. He drew her to him. "You never got it—I'm not this quaking blob of petrified jelly."

She stood on tiptoes and silenced him with a quick kiss. "I know. You just worry about Chloe, and that's only right." She stepped away, smiling. "Still, you did good."

...

Aaron dropped Chloe off at her party, leaving an overabundance of stuffed toys, pillows, and clothing.

"It's hard, isn't it?" Reyna's mother said, smiling sympathetically. "We lost my husband three years ago. Sometimes it seems like yesterday, and it's always to do with protecting my little girl.--I try every day to shield her from any more pain, because she's already been hurt so much. The simple words were like a knife, stabbing into him, because he understood so well. And they were a salve, soothing the ragged wound, because he could hope again, for Chloe and for himself.

He said goodbye to girls who were eager to go have fun, and walked away still feeling better. If he wouldn't have Chloe, at least he and Luz could make good use of the night. Not that the days weren't fine. He smiled. He'd teased Luz that if they eventually married, their song would have to be "Afternoon Delight." She'd just laughed and hadn't dismissed the idea of marriage or said it was too soon.

Was it too soon? He loved Luz. He'd realized that when he knew she was in danger. She'd given him laughter back, and hope. But he remembered that she'd said she'd never marry if there were a child in the picture. That she'd accused him of interviewing her to be Chloe's mother. He understood her fears, just as she'd understood his. She'd had no way to keep Lily from being snatched away. You could lose a birth child—your child—to tragedy, but if the child was alive and yours, you could always seek legal protection. You could fight for a child. Luz hadn't had the right to fight for little Lily. But she loved Chloe; he could see it. Maybe tonight he could make it clear to her that he wanted *her*.

He swung by his house to grab some clothing and turn on a light or two. Probably not necessary in Rose Creek, but old habits were truly hard to root out. Then he high-tailed it back toward Second Chance.

Luz met him at the front door with a smile and a no-holds-barred kiss that knocked everything in his head right out. His hands slid down her back teasingly before clasping her bottom to lift her against him.

After a moment, though, she pulled away.

"The stove's on and don't even joke about anything burning yet," she warned. "We've had enough heat for a while."

She cast a glance at the steaks sizzling in the pan and smiled. "I could put candles on the table and we could pretend we're finally having our romantic dinner," she suggested. He pulled her away from the stove and back into his arms.

"We've had our share of romantic food," he protested, pressing a kiss on the corner of her lips.

"Spilling cereal in bed? We could probably do better." She turned back to the stove. "Go do something useful. Or see what's on TV. We are going to appreciate this meal I slaved over for twenty minutes."

He laughed and retreated.

She set the table, resisting the urge to look for candles and wary of flowers. Romantic trappings were a nice touch, but they had each other. She couldn't think of anything more romantic than that. When everything was ready, she went to the living room and pulled him off the couch, kissing the corner of his mouth but sidestepping him as he reached out to draw her against him.

"Dinner," she insisted firmly, and he sighed plaintively. "And don't wolf your food down, either!"

They ate in silence for a few minutes before he looked up thoughtfully. "Would it screw up the mood if we talk?"

"When you put it that way, it might."

"I hope it won't. But your speech got me thinking."

"Did I say something wrong?"

"No. But you mentioned Atlanta. Luz, I know about the divorce—how bitter it was, and how he let that woman steal Lily away. You told me you thought that the stress helped lead to your father's death. Those are hard knocks. But you must have had friends. A career. Yet you came back here. Why did you leave Atlanta? Or maybe my real question is, would you ever want to go back?"

She shook her head. "No. I left a bunch of people I *thought* were friends. Because when push came to shove, they weren't." She finished a bite of her food then pushed the plate away. "Teaching is more political than people know, sometimes. I was new and excited. They named me the grade head in my second year." She shot him a rueful smile. "I thought all those more senior teachers congratulating me meant it."

"They didn't?"

"Not all of them. I suppose I stepped on toes."

"You?" He couldn't imagine Luz stepping on anyone's toes. "And you left it all because of some false accusation. I really don't know how anyone could accuse you of hurting someone."

"What brought out this curiosity?" She got up and removed their plates. "Don't get up," she warned, as he started to. "I even have desert."

"You did all that in twenty minutes?"

She went to the refrigerator, opened it, and pulled out a bowl of grapes.

"Yeah," she answered, grinning. She sat back down, plucked one off the stem, and fed it to him.

"You mentioned Atlanta, and that's tied to who you were before. I just wondered." He took another grape. "I know that if things hadn't worked out the way they did, I'd still be in Alabaster," he added, shrugging. "Guess I just wondered how you felt about Atlanta before everything happened."

"I liked the city just fine. Loved my job. I could have my career back, but I don't want it anymore, okay?"

"When Esmeralda called me, while I was back in Alabaster, she mentioned that Brian had gone to the school. Then you mentioned Atlanta, and it made me wonder. I just want to know how things are, Luz. To be sure he'll never be part of our lives."

"I should have left him the week after our wedding," Luz retorted. She reached across the table and placed her hand on his. "We need to let go, Aaron. Our doubts will kill anything else we can have."

"Why didn't you leave him, though?" He flipped his hand, catching hers and squeezing it gently. "You were married as long as I was, pretty much."

"Lily. She was a week and a half old when Brian brought her home—two days after our wedding."

"And you stayed with the creep even after he surprised you that way?"

Luz shoved her chair back, tucking her arms against her stomach. "I listened to lies, okay?" she snapped. "Lily's mom had a drug problem. She'd been arrested. Brian told me he'd never see her again. That he had sole custody of Lily." She paced the length of the kitchen and came back, propping herself on the edge of the kitchen table, almost shaking with emotion.

"Do you remember the first time you held Chloe?" she demanded. "Do you remember the way she felt in your arms?"

"Yes."

She pushed off the table and shrugged. "Then you know why I couldn't leave him. Nothing that ever happened was Lily's fault."

"Luz, maybe I shouldn't have asked."

She went to him and wrapped her arms around his shoulders, stopping him as he started to get up. "I'm glad you did," she whispered, kissing his cheek. "I want you to know about Lily. Sometimes it still hurts to talk about her, though."

He leaned his head back and turned his face into her neck, rubbing his lips over her neck until she shivered. Then he turned the chair a little, careful to avoid her feet, and clasped her hands.

"You got such a bum deal, though," he pointed out. "There was never any proof, right? Just that the child had taken migraine medicine? How could they just have removed you so quickly?"

"A lot of times, if there are complaints against teachers, we're removed immediately from the classroom. You'd want that if you thought Chloe was in danger from a teacher."

"Yes, but…"

She sighed in his ear and let him go, going around to sit down next to him again. "I could deal with the suspicion. Although it hurt, I knew they'd find out the truth. But my principal never spoke out in my defense—not once. That really destroyed me."

He reached over and pulled her into his lap, wrapping his arms around her and hugging her tightly. "On the offhand chance I ever meet Chambers, I get to smash his face," he muttered.

She smiled against his neck. "Having someone defend me is nice. You're a few years too late, but thanks. And it wasn't Brian's fault that the administration didn't back me up. He didn't take sides—not even his wife's side. He and his parents worried more about themselves than what happened to Lily."

"So you had to fight everyone alone?"

"Nah. My dad came over to fight my enemies. He told anyone who listened that the Chambers—Brian and his parents—were railroading me because they didn't stand up for me. As powerful as the Chambers are in Georgia, a word or two from them in my favor would have ended everything so much faster. Dad insulted a lot of people on my behalf."

"Good for him!" Aaron whispered and sensed her smile die.

"Yeah, but you know what happened. He hadn't been well." Her fingers traced his face. "He died the month after I was cleared of any wrongdoing."

He clasped her closer, rocking her gently. "You can't blame him for trying to help you. He wouldn't want you to feel guilty."

"I know." She slid to the floor and pulled him to his feet, clasping his hands. "You probably wanted to add that you'd do the same for Chloe, right?"

He fidgeted uncomfortably. "Luz—"

"Aaron, it's okay. It's what I'd want the father of my children to say...to mean. Brian never acted in Lily's best interest. Ever."

He squeezed her hands and bent over to kiss her. "We're both good at putting kids first, aren't we?"

Luz took a deep breath. "Would you like something to drink?"

"We could have the drink Ann wanted to smash over the truck." Aaron grinned. "She's probably still mad you wouldn't let her christen it properly."

She laughed. "Or mad she can't drink wine." She pushed him toward the living room. "Go get the entertainment set up. But I have to warn you, I don't drink very often. I'm not responsible for anything I do tonight."

He grinned. "I'm counting on that." Then he laughed. "We've never spent an actual night together. We've spent all our time hiding from the sunlight. We may just roll over and fall asleep."

Luz shrugged. "If that's all my city boy's up to," she teased. Then she caught his face in her hands. "I hope you know I'm kidding, Aaron. You can feed guinea hens and muck stalls with the best of them." Then, remembering, she turned serious. "You saved my life, finding me. I don't know that I'd have gotten away from Ross without you."

He looked uncomfortable with the praise, and she straightened and stepped away, wiping a tear away with her fingers. "I'm getting all mushy. I'm going to check my e-mail and see if I have anything I need to take care of. Then we'll call it a night."

"Go ahead." He stood and reached for his plate. "You cooked. I'll rinse these off and come drag you away from your computer if you forget we're spending our first night together. Ever."

Most of the new e-mails were spam, but she had a letter from a nearby feed dealer inviting her to pick up donated feed and set up an account for the shelter to purchase at discounted prices.

I can do this, she thought. Hearing Aaron come into the living room, she corrected herself. *No, we can do this.*

She discarded a couple of e-mails without doing more than glancing at the source, and then her gaze and fingers froze. Aaron, standing nearby checking his messages on his phone, must have noticed.

"Something wrong, Luz?"

She swallowed. "I have an e-mail from Brian." She reached for the touch pad. "I'll delete…"

"Why would he try to contact you again?"

"I don't know. But there's no need to find out."

He caught her hand, leaning over. "There's an attachment," he noted, then read the subject line. "Atlanta video."

"Maybe you should open the e-mail," he suggested finally. "Later you might want to remember more of what you had back there."

"I don't think so."

"I'll leave the room," he offered. "You decide."

He turned, but she grasped his arm. "Pull up a chair. Please. I want you here." She managed a grin, though she felt shaky, nervous about what Brian wanted to do to her at this late date.

The message was short. *Luz, you wouldn't take my calls or talk to me when I went to visit, but I want you to have something to remember Atlanta by. Something good. Take care. See you later.*

She waited until Aaron sat down, then opened the file and hit the full screen button.

They watched the video in silence. Luz barely recognized the woman on the screen. She was so in control, so bubbly, so clearly adored by all of the kids clustering around her, calling her name, asking for help.

"That was one of my best classes," Luz whispered eventually. "I'd forgotten how much fun and how bright they were." She didn't say so, but she was thankful that it was also the year before she'd had Lily in her class.

She'd drunk too much wine and tea, and got up to go the bathroom, glad that Brian really had sent such a harmless video. Maybe he had a single decent bone in his body after all.

She rejoined Aaron on the couch just as the ceremony naming her as a "Rising Teacher of the Year" ended.

"Pretty spectacular!" he crooned, kissing her. "What's next, Most Beautiful Teacher?"

There was a brief empty space, and she returned his kiss. "No, maybe just the school Christmas Party or something. I know Brian went to that." She grimaced. "Probably kissing up to run for the school board or something."

But when pictures flashed on the screen, she gasped. The picture of Luz holding a tiny baby in pink blankets filled the screen. The camera caught her smile, the tears glistening in her eyes, the wonder as she held Lily.

And more footage followed quickly, edited to make the greatest impact: Lily sitting by herself, walking...

"Do you want me to stop it?" Aaron asked, but his voice sounded far away.

Wordlessly Luz shook her head, and watched the story of her little girl going from infant to kindergarten graduate in a few short minutes. She herself appeared in most of the video, holding Lily's hand, kissing her, reading to her, singing to her. And then the screen went blank.

"Luz..."

"Don't say anything. It's not your fault."

"I should never have urged you open it!" Aaron stood up and helped her to her feet.

"Someday I'll be glad I have it," Luz said tonelessly. "Let's call it a night."

• • •

They walked to the bedroom together, and even though they were alone, Aaron locked the door.

When Luz walked to the bathroom to change, he knew how deeply the video had affected her. He stripped down to his briefs and waited for her on the bed. She lay down beside him, but not touching him.

"Aaron, could you just hold me?" she asked, and he folded into her arms, holding her close, hoping he could help her find comfort in the loss of her child, knowing that her loss was real and soul deep.

•••

Sometime in the early hours of the night, Luz woke. Aaron's arms still sheltered her, and she felt cherished and protected, able to bear the sadness of reliving those days and years with the little girl who could never be hers again. She snuggled closer, burrowing her face into his bare chest. She doubted he'd planned on this kind of a night when he'd let Chloe go.

She smiled against him. Maybe there were a few hours left to make up for lost time. She let her hand run the length of his body from his chest down, and felt him stir as she teased and touched.

He moved suddenly, sitting up and reaching out to catch her and slide her up his body until his lips found hers.

"Ssssh," he whispered, when she started to say something. "Just kiss me."

Words didn't seem that important anyway. She shivered in pleasure as his hand ran down her back, caressing bare flesh and concentrated on pushing the past away and seizing the moment.

•••

"You're only doing this because you don't think our breakfasts are romantic enough," Luz complained as he pulled her chair out from the table. She smiled as Pam hurried over to clear their table.

"It was nice to see you all so early," the waitress said cheerfully. "Y'all have a good day now."

"Well, I don't know that I'd call this romantic, but neither of us had to eat the other's burned biscuits or spilled milk," Aaron pointed out.

He paid and ushered her out on the sidewalk. "I'll have to pick Chloe up around noon. Mrs. Barnes said they talked all night."

"Spring break's almost here," Luz observed. "I still think—"

Aaron stopped and touched a finger to her lips. "Don't nag," he said gently. "I'm better, but I'm not going to look for wildflowers on purpose."

She shrugged. "Actually, I was going to say you should take her to visit her grandparents—make her meet them whether they want to or not. She deserves to know them. Besides, they'd have to love her!"

He sighed. "You'd think." Then he smiled again. "The morning's turned out pretty well, hasn't it?"

"Beautifully," she agreed, and stood up on tiptoes to kiss him.

They walked a few more steps toward the SUV when suddenly Brian came out of the bakery door, a white bag in his hand.

"Well, hello!" he called.

Luz went white and sagged against Aaron. Never had she expected him to return; she'd thought she'd never see him again once she'd refused to speak to him when he'd shown up before.

"Mama! Mama Luz!" a childish voice shrieked suddenly, freezing them in their steps. "Mama!"

Lily hurled herself at Luz, wrapping her thin arms around her waist. "Don't go! Mama!"

Aaron's face went white and he took a step back. From a few steps away, Brian smirked.

"Lily, I can't…Lily!" Tears welled in her eyes, and she tried to take a step back, but the child clung to her, clutching her desperately.

"I love you," the girl sobbed. "Mama, don't go."

"Lily, baby, you know I can't. Brian, help her!" Tears streamed down Luz's face. She tried to pry the child's fingers away gently, but still Lily clung to her, her body shaking.

Finally, Brian moved up.

"Lily, come with me," he ordered, unfastening the child's fingers. "She loves you, Luz," he said cruelly. "You're really the only mother she's ever known." He swept the girl up into his arms and carried her away, still crying.

"Mama!" Lily screamed again as her father buckled her into the car seat. "Mama Luz!"

The tortured voice ringing in her ears, Luz ran.

• • •

Luz saw the SUV turn into her driveway hours later and braced herself. Aaron would be angry—she'd refused to let him pick her up when he'd come after her, hadn't let him calm her or comfort her.

She'd walked home, and the distance and heat of the day were like salve applied to her wounds.

Surely Aaron would understand. The shock of seeing Lily again, the little girl's pain had been more than she could bear.

Chloe hadn't come? Sudden dread pricked at her. Chloe had been coming to ride; in fact, they'd talked about inviting Reyna, too.

She opened the door before he got there, and he stepped into the room slowly, his expression unreadable.

"Aaron, where's Chloe?" She wrapped her arms around his waist. "We can't hog the whole day to ourselves."

He gently unwound her arms and lifted her hands, kissing each one, and then moving away.

"Luz, we can't do this."

She stared at him. "Aaron, what are you talking about? If you're angry about this morning—how can you be mad at me? Do you have any idea how unbearable, how much what happened hurt? I needed time."

"Exactly," he agreed softly. "And I'm not angry. But I came to say goodbye."

Luz stared in disbelief.

"I've talked to Chloe's teacher and principal. I'm taking this week before spring break and next week to decide some things. But Luz, you need me to step out of your life."

"No!"

"Lily and you need each other." He circled in his hands, trying to explain. "She's your little girl, Luz. And I don't think you'll ever be able to go on without her."

Anger simmered, driving away the dread. "I've done without her for four years, dammit, Aaron! What kind of woman do you think I am? That I'd go back to Brian when he used me, cheated on me, took Lily away once? Do you think I'd hurt her by trying again?"

"I think you need time. To be sure."

"That's crazy! Look, Aaron, you never promised me anything, but don't you dare insult me pretending this is about Lily. Is it that you think I won't love Chloe enough, couldn't put her first?"

"Luz, as bad it was with Stella, even if I'd known for sure about the cheating, and the bondage, and—whatever—I would have stayed in that marriage if I'd had a choice. For Chloe, because I never had a family. I wanted…I want…her to have a family." He reached out a hand, but she swatted it away.

"I don't believe this."

"Something made Brian think he could get you back if you saw Lily again," Aaron said. "Lily tore your heart out. Will you really be able to forget that scene? I don't think I can. What if the bastard doesn't leave right away? What if he stays here and you see Lily at every turn?

"Luz, I'm doing this for you, whether you believe me or not. I want you to have time to change your mind if you want Lily back in your life."

"Just get out, Aaron." The words whispered out, but then she straightened and wiped stray tears from her cheeks. She walked to the door and opened it. "Go."

After a minute, he did. On the top step he turned. "I couldn't bring Chloe to say goodbye," he said. "I—none of us needed that. And Luz—" He stopped, and even from that distance she heard his sigh. "Never mind," he said, and she closed the door.

Chapter Twenty-two

When your world collapses, the best thing to do is plod on through the rubble. Luz snorted at her own dark thoughts, but there didn't seem to be much point in denying to herself that Aaron's departure had thrown her back into darkness.

She went through the days as she had after coming back to Rose Creek, doing what needed to be done, without much passion, but at least with commitment to the animals. The mare she, Aaron, and Ann had saved no longer needed medical attention, Luz had two mixed breed puppies she was seeking homes for, and the rest of her motley crew all remained unchanged.

Only Aaron and Chloe were missing.

"I should really name the mare," Luz confided to Ann, when she came over to visit. "If Chloe were here, I would have asked her."

"You miss her, too, don't you?"

"Yeah." Luz sighed. "I do."

"You know, they might be back. There's still tomorrow and the weekend before school starts again."

"You say it like I care."

"Because you do," Ann said quietly. "And if he comes through that door—"

"He won't. I changed the stupid lock he fixed."

"Luz."

"Drop it, Ann." She softened her tone. "Please?"

Ann shrugged. "Tell you what. If you haven't found a home for Lady, I'll buy her for Andrea when she's old enough."

"Who's Lady?"

"The mare." Ann patted her belly. "And you've met Andrea, or at least seen her sonograms. Don't you like the name 'Lady'?"

Luz smiled. "We'll see. She's a really good size for kids, isn't she?"

Ann took a sip of her orange juice and sighed. "I hate orange juice. My mom drank everything—even wine—and I came out okay!"

They were silent for a moment, lost in their respective thoughts. Then Ann straightened and stretched. "Did you finish the journal?"

"Yes. I won't say I feel better, but I suppose I understand why she didn't want anyone to know anything, either. She shouldn't have felt guilty, Ann. She hired a man my dad didn't trust to help her, but she always thought the best of everyone. Then she blamed herself for being friendly to him and offering him beer that time. Thought maybe the folks in town wouldn't believe that had been all there was, especially if they ever saw the painting."

"Worst thing anyone can do is stay quiet, though," Ann said thoughtfully. "Bet if she could ever have imagined that he'd kidnap you…"

"Let's not talk about that," Luz interrupted. "I'm putting the past behind me now. All of it."

"Know what you should do, Luz?"

"What?"

"Go up to the Hill Country and see the bluebonnets before they're gone. March is half over and the weather's already warm."

"I can't get away. Besides, you used to go with me. And before that, I'd always take Mom. I missed that ritual when I was in Atlanta."

"Exactly. Start a new ritual. Get your head clear. Hey, I heard Esme's moving up there this summer."

"Yeah, I heard. I'm surprised, but maybe she'll find what she wants somewhere else. I didn't, but she might."

"Go see the wildflowers," Ann said again. "Ram and I will stay overnight."

Luz raised her eyebrows. "Hope there aren't any problems with your mother-in-law?"

"No, she just fusses over us too much. Ram and I could use a romantic night alone."

"A romantic night?"

"Don't look so shocked. Pregnant people can enjoy sex."

"That's not why I'm worried," Luz retorted, smiling a little. "For some reason, romantic nights at my place are just doomed."

She thought for a few minutes while Ann forced down the rest of her juice. "Maybe I will," she said eventually. "The last time Mom and I went, Mom came back so happy and at peace. I want that."

"Go find it, then." Ann straightened, and checked her cell phone. "Time for me to get busy. This weekend?"

"What's the rush?"

"Really?" Ann asked. "Do you know how quickly the bluebonnets fade?"

"Not that quickly, but if the two of you need my place that badly, come on down. I'll get a hotel overnight on Saturday and be a bum again for a whole day."

"And I'll call Ram and tell him we're gonna have a weekend away!" Ann grinned. She pocketed the phone and went out the door whistling.

• • •

The bluebonnets were spectacular. There were scattered bluebonnets even around Rose Creek, but as she headed north, the fields became blue sheets of color, tossed out on a landscape green from spring rains.

Luz drove without a real destination in mind, not too worried about finding a room. Spring break might be in full swing, but college and high school kids would be out on beaches, not reveling in the perfect beauty of a field of wildflowers.

She turned off I-35 in Hondo, getting away from the frenzied rush of traffic and taking quieter roads. She pulled in eventually to a tiny rest stop looking out over a field full of flowers that crept out from under the pasture fence and carpeted the drainage ditch and the bank sloping away from the parking area.

She smiled as she wandered over and sat down at one of the two concrete tables. She and Ann and she and her mother had always stopped here, absorbing the special aura of peace and beauty the landscape offered. The fact that few other motorists found it as special was a bonus.

Afternoon sun massaged her shoulders; here in the Hill Country, the temperature was cooler than in Rose Creek, but still warm enough to lull into her a state of mindless contentment.

Tires crunched on the gravel behind her and she stirred reluctantly, glancing over her shoulder to be sure the newcomers didn't look like trouble.

When she saw the green SUV, her heart thudded painfully. *Damn you, Ann.*

She started for her truck, but Aaron cut her off.

"Hello, Luz."

"I can't believe Ann set me up. Let me by, Aaron."

He reached out and caught her wrist. "In a minute. Just let me say something."

Luz looked around. "Where's Chloe?"

"Never mind Chloe, this isn't about her. It's about us."

Luz shook her head and pulled her wrist free. "There is no 'us,' Aaron. There was just you deciding what I could or couldn't do with my life."

He looked out across the bluebonnets for a long moment, and then turned back to her.

"Maybe you're right. I didn't think so—I really believed what I said, Luz. That you needed time to see if you'd be okay without Lily after seeing her again. And if not—I thought I was giving her back to you. By letting go."

He walked a few steps away, into the flowers. "I never thought I'd be able to do this," he said.

"Do what?"

"Walk in all these glorious wildflowers." He walked back up the slight slope, and tilted her chin up to gaze into her eyes. "You did this, Luz. You helped me laugh, and you helped me let go. There are things we can never let go. But you helped me be okay with having more."

"More?"

"More than fear that I could lose Chloe. More than just the love I have for her." He let her chin go, catching her hand instead and raising it to his lips, pressing a gentle kiss to her palm.

"Maybe when I told you I wanted you to have time, it *was* fear, I don't know. I couldn't stand to have Chloe lose a second mother. Maybe I was just seeing her pain in Lily—and my pain in you."

Luz looked up at the clear sky, then back at him. "That day that you left, I felt like I lost a daughter for the second time," she said softly. "Losing Brian didn't hurt, but losing you…" She closed her eyes, shutting out the memories. Shutting out the hopeful light in Aaron's eyes.

"Trust me to stay, Luz." His words whispered out to her, and his eyes pleaded. "Trust us to be right together. To give our love for each other its rightful place."

When she opened her eyes, he was still there. And his eyes still spoke truth to her fear. "All right," she conceded, stepping closer to him. "We can do that. We can put our love first so we can build an unbreakable family."

She actually heard his sigh of relief. He reached out and tilted her face up, worry still clear in his face. "I practiced what I'd say on the drive up," he murmured. "None of the words came out the way I wanted. But as long as they're right…"

"You're wrong about one thing, though," she murmured, wrapping her arms around him. "This *is* about Chloe, too. Do you trust me to love her?"

He closed his eyes for a brief second, then leaned forward and kissed her forehead. "I trust you with everything that matters to me—her life and mine." He urged her close and lowered his lips to hers, kissing her with sweet passion. With total trust. Then he pulled away just a little. "That's my final offer," he whispered. "Take it or leave it."

"Oh, I'll take it," she whispered back, and pulled him close again.

About the Author

Leslie P. García grew up here and there, spending much of her childhood in rural Georgia, and virtually all her adult life in deep south Texas. Married and surrounded by children and grandchildren, much of her writing touches on family. A passion for animals, a twenty-year teaching career, and the strange twists and turns that life can take have provided more stories than time to write.

Wildflower Redemption is the first in the Texas Heart and Soul Series. Watch for Esmeralda Salinas's story in the future.

Leslie loves to hear from readers, and can be reached at all the electronic haunts:

E-mail: lesliegarcia2000-author@yahoo.com

Facebook: *www.facebook.com/LeslieP.Garcia*

Please drop by *Return to Rio* for updates, guest posts by exciting authors, and other miscellaneous content!

More from This Author
(From *Unattainable* by Leslie P. García)

Jovani Treviño slipped from the pickup, his boots thudding dully on the dry soil as he looked around carefully but not with particular unease. A crescent moon climbed up over the far side of the interstate, but here darkness allowed considerable isolation. Cars speeding by on the freeway wouldn't notice him, and if they did, hopefully they'd avert their eyes, assuming someone needed to take a leak.

Only moments passed before a second, dark vehicle pulled in behind him. The driver switched off the headlights but left the parking lights on. Jovi reached into the cab and pulled the lever to open the hood then moved to the front of the truck. Seconds later the newcomer joined him, extending his hand briefly.

"Jovi."

"Hey, Rick." Almost immediately, both turned their attention to the engine.

"So—you gonna apply for the job at *Nueva Brisa?*" the newcomer asked.

"Tomorrow," Jovi agreed, turning at a slight rustle in the weeds that framed the roadside clearing, then relaxing when he realized the noise couldn't have come from anything large.

"Still jumping at shadows?" Rick shook his head. "We leave the job, but the edge never leaves."

"You don't let anyone leave," Jovi retorted, slapping a mosquito seconds too late, and rubbing his arm. "Tell me why I said yes again."

"Cause you're one of the good guys, we pay well, and you get to be close to your mom while she gets back on her feet. It's win-win, Jovi."

"Cut the bull, friend. I left DEA because no one wins—the work's important, but the war's unwinnable, Rick."

Rick Ortega shrugged his thin shoulders. "Maybe."

"And this one smells."

"Why?" He nudged Jovi with an elbow. "Cause we're looking at some honey the locals call untouchable?"

"Unattainable." Jovi motioned Ortega back and slammed the hood. "Your reasons for looking at this woman are shaky at best, and if I'm investigating her, I damn sure won't be thinking about her looks."

"Touchier than ever," the DEA agent muttered.

"And in a week or two, when my plane lands in Florida—I'm done, Rick. No more arm-twisting, no favors. I'm serious."

"Look, I know you mostly came until your mom beats her pneumonia—not so much to help us. But you're perfect, Jovi— the border's home to you, but you've been gone long enough you're an outsider now."

"Hell, I was always an outsider. Everywhere."

"Whining isn't your style, *amigo*," Ortega chided. "You know how things are. No trust left—our side or theirs. The cartels are winning. For Christ's sake, they're slaughtering innocents on the streets a mile from here." He jerked his head toward the tree-framed skyline. Behind those trees, the Rio Grande whispered its newly violent song to the night. "Check her out, that's all. She worked for a major importer, but quit suddenly. Her father left her some money, but—" He shook his head. "Something's not right, buddy."

Jovi glanced at him. "Because her father left money?"

"No. Because insurance aside, her father shouldn't have had money to leave. The ranch is a joke—big property value, but no livestock except horses. On paper, he sold horses—horses we're not real sure existed. Horses! No market for horses right now, going on back even before his death. The man went through a bitter divorce from the wife, yet got big bucks from the ex father-in-law, Lionel De Cordova."

"De Cordova? Man!" The name surprised him. "But for all his sins, I never heard he trafficked."

"We know some of the younger cousins do. Nobody's tagged him, true. But the foreman you're replacing? Arrested in Sinaloa several weeks ago. Arranging to drive a load to El Paso."

"So she has to know?"

Ortega shrugged. "Hard to say. The man's a Mexican national, and the story wasn't broadcast here. We only found out through our sources. But if he worked out of her barn … "

"She either knows or she's stupid?" he suggested.

Again, Ortega made a slight gesture of denial. "She'd been in New York and Houston more than home until recently. She worked for an import firm with headquarters in Houston and branches all over Mexico, as well as in several border towns. The horses were more or less at the mercy of the foreman and the two grooms."

"Sketchy at best," Jovi pointed out again. "This is my last call, though," he repeated, walking to the driver's side and pulling the door open. "This job's too hard on the soul, Rick. Too much lying and too many half-truths—and to save what?"

Ortega paused by the open door as his friend climbed back in. "Did I tell you that little four-year old girl—Lisa, remember her? She turned seven yesterday. They put her photo on one of those news lead-ins."

"Damn you," Jovi snarled, thinking of the child he, Ortega, and others had found cowering in the corner of a crack house after a deal turned particularly violent. And her brothers, 5 and 8, lying broken on the floor in their own blood. His last official case—the last case he'd tried to stomach.

"Sometimes we win," Rick insisted, and slapped his arm. "*Suerte*," he ended, walking away.

Luck. Jovi shook his head, turned on the truck, and poked the radio button. He wouldn't need luck if he kept his mind on work and on the stable full of thoroughbreds waiting for him in Florida. As he eased back onto the access road, blessed darkness and George Strait's melodious voice surrounded him.

In the mood for more Crimson Romance?
Check out *Take Me Out* by Leslie P. García and others at
CrimsonRomance.com.